# The Famous Flower
## of Serving Men

# The *The* Famous Flower of Serving Men

*Deborah Grabien*

THOMAS DUNNE BOOKS / ST. MARTIN'S MINOTAUR ⚜ NEW YORK

THOMAS DUNNE BOOKS.
An Imprint of St. Martin's Press.

THE FAMOUS FLOWER OF SERVING MEN. Copyright © 2004 by Deborah Grabien.
All rights reserved. Printed in the United States of America. No part of this book
may be used or reproduced in any manner whatsoever without written permission
except in the case of brief quotations embodied in critical articles or reviews. For
information, address St. Martin's Press, 175 Fifth Avenue, New York, N.Y. 10010.

www.minotaurbooks.com

Library of Congress Cataloging-in-Publication Data

Grabien, Deborah.
        The famous flower of serving men / Deborah Grabien.—1st ed.
            p. cm.
        ISBN 0-312-33387-0
        EAN 978-0312-33387-4
            1. Women theatrical producers and directors—Fiction. 2. Inheri-
tance and succession—Fiction. 3. Historic buildings—Fiction. 4. London
(England)—Fiction. 5. Folk musicians—Fiction. 6. Theaters—Fiction.
I. Title.

PS3557.R1145F36 2004
813'.54—dc22

                                                            2004046799

First Edition: November 2004

10 9 8 7 6 5 4 3 2 1

# Acknowledgments

Some thanks and acknowledgments are due, not only for this novel but for all the stories in this series.

For editing and specific source materials: everyone at Pari-Salon4665; all my beloved anarachs, with special thanks to Betsy Hanes Perry (period costume), Juliana Egley (theatre expertise), Jeremy Epstein (maps), and Beverly Leoczko (for measuring the fright factor); Marta Randall, fresh wise eyes; Carlo Caldana and Jennifer Langoski for slapping my French grammar into shape; and the musicians of the U.K. folk world, especially Martin Carthy, the best guitarist alive.

For non-stop handholding, the deepest possible editing, moral support, and for taking time away from her own writing to perform the above-listed tender mercies, Marlene Shannon-Stringer.

Thanks to Ann Adelman for a superb job of copyediting.

The Woodside Priory, Benedictine Order, for details I needed.

Jennifer Jackson, agent extraordinaire.

And above all, to the best editor that ever walked on the surface of the earth, Ruth Cavin, for the things that made these the best books I could offer my readers.

*Dedicated to Nic. Hello, sweetie!*

A note about the historical events and personalities portrayed in this book:

Some are real. There was certainly a Peasants' Rebellion, for example; the peasants did in fact burn certain sections of London; and the name de Belleville was, in fact, given to the legitimised bastards of the de Valois family. These are a few of the things in this work that are historical fact.

Some things, however, are not. And being the author, I'm not going to say which is which. I'm just going to sit back and let my readers see if they can sort out fact from fiction.

So, if you're grinding through databases or reference books and you catch a glimpse of an impossibly smug person in the corner, watching you plough through the fourteenth century and listening to you swear as you do so, pay no attention. It's only me, knowing I will have done my job.

# Prologue

On a raw January night in 1979, a homeless man and a small dog wandered into a nameless alley off Bouverie Street in the City, and prepared to set up sleeping quarters.

It was brutally cold. Europe was seeing one of its worst winter seasons in half a century, and Londoners were currently miserable, dealing with iced-over streets and an incessant windy downpour of sleet that needled the skin and made safe walking an impossibility. Few people willingly came outdoors in this weather, but the homeless man, a beggar of many years' standing, had no choice in the matter.

He surveyed his chosen refuge with a practised eye. The north side of the alley offered the most shelter; there were two doors in the long wall of whatever this building was, one that looked like a loading dock, with old-fashioned pocket doors, and one just a normal door, a few feet away. The loading dock had a bit of an overhang, cutting back on the wind and the sleet. The dog sat at his feet, patient and obedient, shivering.

The homeless man piled his bits of carboard and tattered cloth atop a sheet of plastic he'd found behind a warehouse, near London Bridge. The plastic would keep the damp out. He curled up, whistled for the dog, made room for the little terrier to curl up beside him, and pulled an old battered sleeping bag around them both. The dog, grateful but used to this ritual, snuggled close.

"Bloody Margaret Thatcher." The man spoke aloud, also a nightly ritual. His eyes were almost shut. The dog listened, or perhaps not. "Things get worse when you put the Tories in. We could rot here, think they'd care? Not bloody likely . . ."

This time, the dog answered him. The man opened one eye. What in hell . . . ?

Against his side, warm under the pile, the dog had gone rigid. His master had a sudden clear vision of the animal, legs planted, short coat bristling, teeth bared, glaring at something twisted and ugly and wrong.

Someone was whispering. The man lay very still, listening, both eyes wide and staring at a faded filthy pattern of red and black plaid that was the lining of the sleeping bag. Someone was there. Someone had come. Someone was whispering. Why couldn't he understand a word of it? And why was he afraid to look outside the safety of his blanket?

The dog began to whine. It was loud, much too loud, muffled by the warmth of the man and the pile of cloth and the stifling reek of a sudden, inexplicable fear that the man could neither articulate nor control. He lay, listening to a dark alien rasp that sounded like the hissing of an adder. He had never been so frightened in his life.

The whines became a howl. There was a scrabbling, a kick, and then the terrier bolted, exploding out into the alley, howling and barking as it went.

"Oi! Come back here!" The man was on his feet, his fear of whatever was whispering unseen in the darkness momentarily swallowed by the greater terror of losing his only companion. He peered into the sleety night. Something was wrong with his eyes. There were street lamps out on Bouverie Place, but he could see nothing but odd shapes. Was that mist blocking his vision, winter mist, come up from the River Thames . . . ?

He smelled it suddenly, smoke, a pungent reek of burning that was tainted with something darker. In his mind, as clear as his mental picture of the dog bristling and growling, he saw people in wooden houses, the houses burning, the people trapped and screaming, no way out, no way down, and only death waiting.

He began to cough, to choke, his eyes watering. Someone whispered, counterpointing the screams of those trapped. Out on Bouverie Street, the dog whimpered.

With shaking, uncoordinated hands, the homeless man retrieved his belongings. It was hard to move, his feet felt leaden and slow, and he had never been so afraid. But all he possessed was there. Without this pile, he'd be half-frozen to death before the break of day. He couldn't simply abandon it.

He dragged the pile clear of the alley, listening to the noises become part of the shadows and fade out behind him. The dog ran to him and sat, pressing up against his legs.

They moved away, the man muttering under his breath. He wasn't aware of his own speech, and would have been very surprised indeed had he realised he was praying.

# One

*My mother did me deadly spite*
*For she sent thieves in the dark of the night*
*Put my servants all to flight;*
*They robbed my bower, they slew my knight.*

Penelope Wintercraft-Hawkes, fumbling for her latchkey, heard the shrilling of her telephone from the other side of her front door and swore under her breath.

The weather, a bitterly cold day in early December, was not conducive to standing about out of doors. Under a weeping grey sky, London bore the look of a medieval woodcut into which centuries of grime had settled. The streets, the cars, the faces of the people, all seemed blurred and indistinct; even the pigeons, hunched in tight miserable groups against the season, looked dark and sooty. With the early winter night coming on quickly, the city seemed almost theatrically grim.

"Damn!" Penny heard a faint click and a distant beep, as her answering machine switched into record mode. Ah well, no point in worrying about it. She'd missed the call, whoever it was. Hopefully, it wasn't that producer in America, calling to give her the details for the Oregon Shakespeare Festival next season. That would be an expensive call to return.

By the time she finally located her key, the caller had long since rung off. Penny let herself into her flat, pulled off her boots, and hung her wet coat up to dry. Then she headed for the kitchen to sort out her dinner and check her messages.

Penny's flat consisted of three good-sized rooms, plus bath and loo, in the untrendy yet comfortable North London neighbour-hood of Muswell Hill. It was on the ground floor, the bottommost of three, and also boasted access to a small, charming garden. Penny paid an extra monthly fee to garage her vintage Jaguar, and would willingly have paid twice again as much. She doted on her car.

Around the time Charles Dickens was rolling the name "Edwin Drood" around in his mind, and deciding it would do nicely, the house had been the comfortable home of a large family belonging to the upper middle classes, who had made their money in trade. Like the others in its row of eight, it had long ago been converted to flats, to accommodate both London's ever-growing housing crunch and the owner's grudging awareness that few people could find the kind of money realistically required as rent on a ten-room house. People with that kind of money to spare for London housing either spent exorbitant amounts of rent on small, ugly apartments with spectacular views of the Thames, or bought *chichi* little mews houses in Hampstead or Belgravia.

Penny stowed milk, butter, and a nice wedge of sharp double Gloucester cheese in the small fridge, mentally giving thanks for the takeout counters in Harrod's Food Hall. She'd got a wonderful thick soup for supper, all beans and lentils and savoury bits of spicy ham, exactly right for a cold raw night. All she needed now was the seeded roll she'd bought, and a small pan in which to heat the soup, and her evening would be set.

The after-dinner agenda was pleasing to contemplate: curling up with a good mystery novel and a glass of wine. For once, she had nothing work-related to sort out; her theatrical troupe, the Tam-burlaine Players, was on hiatus until the new year. On the personal front, her longtime lover, Ringan Laine, was in Yorkshire, combining his two fields of interest: playing a series of solo shows at local folk clubs at night, while restoring a sixteenth-century church for the lo-cal Preservation Society during the day. He wasn't due back in the south for a few days yet. Penny had no commitments. She was free to relax.

As she stirred soup and sipped wine, the intermittent blink of her answering machine's message indicator caught her eye. For a moment, relaxed and looking forward to an evening of indolence, Penny considered letting it wait. That impulse lasted only as long as it took for her professional common sense to assert itself. Penny sighed, turned the flame on the cooker down to a flickering simmer, grabbed a pen and the notebook she used for messages, and ran back the tape.

There were two messages. The first, which must have come in moments after she left the flat that morning, was indeed from the Shakespeare Festival in America. With rare percipience, the booking agent had left Penny not only his return number but his e-mail address as well. Enormously cheered by this display of consideration, Penny saved the message, with all its details, and pressed the "play next" option. As she listened, her brow furrowed, first in bewilderment and then in disbelief.

"Yes, hello, good afternoon. I'm trying to reach Penelope Wintercraft-Hawkes. My name is John-William Gunther, and I'm the solicitor handling the estate of your recently deceased aunt, Mary Theresa Isabel Heatherington. I'm calling because, under the terms of your late aunt's last will and testament, you've been left a piece of property in the City—E.C.4. If you would ring me at your earliest convenience, I'd like to wind this up and give you the necessary documents to sign, and information for the transfer of title, once probate is complete. . . . "

Penny hit the "pause" button and sat staring at the wall, her mouth slightly ajar. Aunt Mary? Who in the world was Aunt Mary? Why had she never even heard of such a person?

Mentally, she ran down the list of aunts: Her father had one sister, called Helena. He also had one brother, Penny's uncle Hugh, who'd been cheerfully and openly homosexual his entire life; certainly no aunts there, Mary or otherwise. Her mother's family? It had to be her mother's side; of course, Mum's own mother had been married twice, and wasn't the first chap, who'd died young, been called Heatherington?

Still, Penny couldn't immediately place anyone called Mary. She ran down the distaff list in her head: Two sisters, Veronica and Jacqueline, both happily married for decades. One elderly and rarely seen brother about twenty years older than his half-sisters, Stephen; child of the first marriage, married to—

"Oh, for heaven's sake." The solicitor, apparently uncomfortable with the French tongue, had Anglicised the name: the ancient aunt by marriage, Marie-Thérèse, was quintessentially French. *My word*, Penny thought, *she must have been near ninety*; she'd been a good ten years older than her husband, and Uncle Stephen, that strange reclusive man, had been a full generation senior to his half-siblings. Penny made a mental note to send a condolence card, thought about her Uncle Stephen for a few moments, and mentally cancelled the note. He was very much not a cards-and-flowers sort.

But that bit about having left Penny property—was this Gunther person joking? That the situation as stated might, in fact, be true simply didn't seem possible. Penny had never actually met Marie-Thérèse; she had seen her on one occasion only, and that had been nearly eleven years earlier. Penny, just beginning her career, had been performing and producing her first shows at the Edinburgh Festival. She had made an unusual and as yet to be repeated decision, and stepped away from her chosen field, Jacobean and Elizabethan period drama. She had opted instead to indulge in three intense performances of French high tragedy from the earliest days of the Académie Française: Corneille's *Le Cid,* Racine's *Phèdre,* and *Andromache.*

Marie-Thérèse had attended all three of those shows. She had caught Penny's eye during the curtain call, and had lifted one magisterial finger in a tiny salute. She had then departed with no further contact, other than a ridiculously embellished visiting card with her name etched into it, left without explanation at the backstage door.

She had been the very essence of a transplanted French *grande dame,* Penny remembered; aloof, mysterious, contained. She had also looked spectacularly eccentric, the predominating strangeness being a towering nest of silvery hair, studded with plastic bird ornaments. That, at least, was impossible to forget. In fact, the entire audience had noticed.

At no other time could Penny recall having so much as seen her aunt by marriage. They had never spoken, there had been no cards at Christmas, no solicitous birthday phone calls inquiring after each other's health, no point of contact at all. So why would she leave Penny so much as a fond farewell, much less hard property? What on earth was going on?

Penny rewound the tape for a single beat, hit "play," and listened to the rest of the message.

" . . . once probate is complete. So, if you would be kind enough to call during business hours at my office . . . "

"Damn!" So much for her quiet, uncommitted evening with a classic whodunit and a slowly diminishing bottle of Pinot. Nothing a mystery author could write was likely to take her mind away from the phone call that, now, must wait until tomorrow.

The soup, forgotten on the burner, suddenly bubbled up in the pan and threatened to overflow. Penny hastily turned the cooker off, tipped the soup into a mug, picked up a spoon, and sat down. Her brain was racing.

On an impulse, she pushed her food to one side, picked up the phone, and dialled her parents' home, Whistler's Croft.

"Hampshire two six nine seven. Hello?"

"Mum? Oh, good, you're just the person I needed. It's Pen."

"Yes, darling, I know. Unmistakable voice. How are you? Is all well? How's dear Ringan?"

"Well, in reverse order, Ringan's freezing his bits and pieces off in the far north until Friday, all seems to be fine in general, and as for me, I'm highly bewildered, which is why I'm letting my soup go cold."

"Eat your soup," Sophy Wintercraft-Hawkes said placidly. "We can talk while you're eating; if I remember correctly, I trained you to be able to do two things at once, provided they were simple tasks. And if your weather in London is anything like ours, hot soup is absolutely essential. It's quite cold and wet here. Now, do tell me, why are you bewildered, dear?"

Between mouthfuls of soup and roll, Penny explained the phone call from the solicitor. Her mother, who had the rare gift of being really able to listen, offered no interruptions.

" . . . and I only saw the woman once in my life." Penny set the empty cup down and stifled an unladylike burp. "So I really don't understand, Mum. Why on earth would she leave me damn-all? How likely is it that she'd have property, as in real estate because that's certainly what this solicitor bloke, Gunther, made it sound like, here in London, and in the City, no less? As I remember, they lived in Scotland, up at the back of beyond, near Inverness— you know, all purple mountains and sheep and gorse and fish and whatnot. And lastly—all right, this really should have come first, I suppose—am I thinking of the right person, and is she actually dead?"

"Well—let's be methodical about this, shall we?" Sophy sounded rather amused. "In the first place, yes, that would be Marie-Thérèse, Stephen's wife. A very peculiar woman, I always thought, but really I suppose it was only that she was so awfully, well, French. They really can be odder than most, can't they? And secondly, yes, she is quite certainly your late aunt. She died about a month ago, most disreputably, in fact."

Penny blinked. "Disreputably? Wasn't she rising ninety? I mean, I would have assumed . . . " Her voice trailed away.

"When it comes to anything concerning my half-brother Stephen," Sophy said crisply, "your best course is to assume the oddest circumstance you can possibly imagine, and then add baking soda, and perhaps a dash of nutmeg. Yes, she was ninety; it was actually her ninetieth birthday. She died because she fell down some stairs and broke her neck."

"Oh. Well—why is that odd? Or disreputable? Sad, yes, I can see that, but why disreputable?"

"Because, dear, it was nearly midnight at the time, and the stairs in question led down into what I believe is called a Goth rave-up club, in Glasgow. Apparently, she was celebrating her birthday by sharing a flask of single-malt whiskey with some of the local talent."

Penny gasped, swallowed wrong, and promptly choked. A few minutes later, tears of joy streaming down her face and the taste of Harrod's Savoury Lentil Bean Soup forever ruined in her sense memory, she managed to regain some control of herself.

"Are you all right, Penny? You sounded rather in need of medical attention for a minute or two." Sophy was trying not to laugh, as well; her daughter could hear it in her voice, kept genteelly below the surface.

"Fine. I'm fine." She wiped tears of laughter away. "Well, good on Aunt Marie-Thérèse, anyway. If I'm checking out on my nineti-eth birthday, I'd say getting snockered on Lagavullin in a mosh pit with someone named MacTavish would be a lovely way to go, al-though I'd rather actually be dancing at the time, or if Ringan's still around—no, I don't want to shock you. But—that property, Mum. He said the City. Would she have had that kind of lolly to spend? Even if she'd owned something here since the Second World War—no, really, too much. This is not a city in which property can be had on the cheap."

"As to that, I honestly don't know." Penny heard the soft chink of porcelain as her mother poured her customary evening cup of de-caffeinated Earl Grey. The sound brought childhood back to Penny; for a wistful moment, she thought she could smell the tea, a vagrant imaginary perfume, wafting through the phone line. "But anything's possible, I suppose. I only met the woman twice, and exchanged commonplace civilities in the French tongue, and do you know, she's left me something as well—a ruby tiara, according to the letter I got. I've no idea where she got such a thing, or why she'd leave it to me, but I'm supposed to hear back from her solicitor about it when pro-bate's wrapped. And yes, same chap. Name of Gunther."

"A ruby tiara? Are you joking?"

"I am not. So you see, dear, as to your question—well, she must have had some money, outside of Stephen's. He has about as much as we do, and while I won't pretend we've ever been even near middle-class, we don't run to London real estate or ruby tiaras to leave to virtual strangers on a whim."

"No, we don't, do we?" Penny shook her head, as if the physical gesture might clear her mind. The mystery had got muddier rather than clearer. "All right, Mum, I'll call and let you know after I've met with this Gunther bloke. Give Daddy my love, and I'll talk to you soon."

"Ms. Wintercraft-Hawkes? This is a pleasure. Please, have a seat, do."

John-William Gunther, Solicitor, had a one-room office in a small block just east of St. Paul's. He had taken Penny's call at one minute past nine that morning, had cheerfully said that any time that worked for her would suit him, and here he was a bare hour later, a small round man a few years younger than Penny herself. He had lopsided dimples, a mass of unruly curls that looked completely untamed, and the shrewdest pair of bright blue eyes Penny had ever seen. She was taken off her balance, and therefore cautious, from the moment he answered his bell and admitted her; he was not what she had been expecting, and nothing in her mind could link this pink young man of barely thirty to a wildly eccentric and very antique Frenchwoman.

"Can I offer you some coffee?" He had an interesting voice, a nice tenor with a kind of clipped twang underlying his enunciation. "I got completely addicted to the idea of decent coffee when I lived in America, and I'm afraid I simply can't go back to tea now, no matter how hard I try."

"Actually, some coffee would be lovely, providing it's the same stuff you're drinking." The aroma of proper coffee—a very good dark grind, judging by the scent—had found Penny and hooked her nicely. It smelled wonderful. "Where in America did you live? I know both coasts relatively well, but not much of the enormous in-between bits."

"Boston. I was in Harvard Law School, two years of it. My mother's an American lawyer, gave up practising awhile back. She insisted." He plugged in an electric kettle and loaded a *café pressé* with dark rich ground beans. "I'm glad she did, too. I might never have learned about decent coffee, much less soft-shelled crab cakes and proper baked beans, if I'd done all four years of university in Edinburgh."

"Harvard and Edinburgh? That's quite a pairing. You don't sound Scots to me, at all. And trust me, I should know." Penny relaxed a bit. So, that clipped backbite in his voice was merely a bit of

Boston peeping out. Besides, it was hard to distrust anyone who offered coffee that smelled as enticing as this. "Is that where you met my aunt? In Edinburgh?"

He grinned, and try as she might, Penny couldn't help grinning back; Gunther's smile was lopsided, loopy, and completely endearing. It was perfectly spontaneous, and the net result was to give him the look of a very friendly and uncomplicated small boy.

"Ah," he said cheerfully, "cross-examination! No, I'm no sort of Scots, I just went to school there for a bit. And yes, indeed, I met your aunt in Edinburgh, and in the weirdest way imaginable. Nothing to do with the law. It was a very strange thing, still a mystery in my life. She approached me at a reading of some very bad French poetry in a coffeehouse, and handed me a business card and a personal cheque. Said she needed a good obedient solicitor— that was her word, obedient. Nothing arduous, just someone to take instructions and file them away until needed, and perhaps to occasionally handle some property transference business, and here was a retainer, was it enough? I was so startled, I just sat and blinked up at her like seven sorts of fool. She had a talent for surprise; that cheque was for five thousand pounds. I was in the planning stages of opening an office in London, and that got me over the hump."

"My word. And here I was, wondering if she had any money!" Penny stared at him. "You say she'd never seen you before? Surely, she must have known something about you?"

"If she did, she never let on. And I can't imagine how she could have known me, because believe me, I certainly didn't know her. She wasn't the sort of person one forgets easily, either. The hair alone would have stuck in my mind, what with all those plastic birds she had nesting there." He was silent for a moment, pouring Penny's coffee. "You know," he continued thoughtfully, "it was damned lucky for both of us that I actually *was* a solicitor. I don't think Madame Heatherington was the kind of woman to take no for an answer."

"Well, I don't know. I didn't know her at all." Penny spoke slowly. "But I'm beginning to wish I did."

"The thing is, to this day, I haven't a clue how she knew my profession. A bit of a witch, I think. Mind-reading, or whatnot. Every once in a while, I'd get instructions by post or phone, generally about property, and carry them out. I never actually came face to face with your aunt again. I know, it's a peculiar story, isn't it?"

Penny sipped her coffee, which was strong, black, and very good. She felt, obscurely, as if she ought to be choosing every word of this meeting with extreme care; the circumstances were surreal enough to bring out Penny's need for control. Both the chance to exert herself and the desire to do so were rapidly fading, however. Mr. John-William Gunther was so transparently friendly and honest that mistrusting him had begun to seem ill-mannered. She wondered fleetingly whether this trait was a help or a hindrance to him, considering his profession.

"Very peculiar," she said. "This is wonderful coffee, Mr. Gunther, and I'm quite enjoying myself in general. But shall we get down to business? To tell you the truth, your phone call gave me a sleepless night, because my brain simply wouldn't shut down. I never actually met my aunt Marie-Thérèse; I saw her eleven years ago, when she sat in the front row for three Edinburgh performances of French dramatists, in which I was playing. Are you sure she's left me property? And what sort of property?"

"Oh, yes, quite sure. She's left you a theatre. And please, do feel free to call me John-William." Gunther pushed a thick brown manila envelope across the desk to Penny. "These are the original documents, by the way. I've made copies for my own records, of everything except whatever is in the small sealed envelope which you'll find inside. She's left you a derelict theatre—derelict in the sense that it will need some major restoration if it's to be used for its original purpose, or so I understand. Even without any restoration, of course, the property is still very valuable—after all, we're talking about the heart of London. There's a probate evaluation in here."

Penny opened her mouth, closed it, and tried to control her jaw, which kept wanting to drop and wobble. She managed to say, faintly, "A theatre?"

"Yes, indeed. The property is located just south of Fleet Street, on a tiny alley called Hawthorne Walk. It's between Bouverie Street and Whitefriars; you can walk down to the river. I believe the nearest Tube station is Temple, on the District line. The theatre is called the Bellefield; that's the French spelling of *belle,* by the way, not the ding-dong sort of bell. I have no idea where the name comes from. Perhaps a good researcher could find out, if you wanted to know its provenance."

Penny said nothing; it was doubtful she was even capable of coherent speech, and for the moment, she had given up trying. Her eyes were wide with disbelief. She simply sat, and stared at him. He continued cheerfully.

"It's a very good area for this sort of thing, you know; theatres, I mean. It used to be absolutely dotted with little playhouses, and I suspect that's what the Bellefield was, about a hundred years ago. Vaudeville, 'knees up, Mother Brown,' all that sort of stuff. I'd imagine the theatrical license laws of the nineteenth century kept the big drama away from these little places, but they would have done lots of comedies, and lesser lights, and of course, revues. And now there are a few supper clubs and bistros that are actually open past teatime. Lucky for you, if you're doing evening shows. Nice to have a local for your cast and your audience, I imagine."

"Yes," Penny said, and wondered if anything had actually come out of her mouth. She tried again. "Of course."

"If you pop up a few Tube stations to the northeast, you're at the Barbican Centre." John-William had hit his stride. "And of course, half a mile dead east there's the Millennium Bridge, with the Globe and Shakespeare Exhibition just across the river. It's not the West End, but still, very nice for theatre indeed. Traditional. Are you all right, Ms. Wintercraft-Hawkes? You look awfully pale."

Penny shook her head. With trembling fingers, she opened the manila envelope and slid the contents on to John-William's desk.

A smaller envelope in expensive parchment paper, sealed with red wax; Penny's full name was written across the front in a flamboyant scrawl. A set of industrial-looking keys. Official documents: an insurance policy, an old receipt for new locks installed, a bill of sale, a transfer of title deed for a freehold on the commercial property, located at 1, Hawthorne Walk, London, E.C.4.

Penny looked at the signature lines, and saw Marie-Thérèse's name in that same flamboyant handwriting, next to the date. She had acquired the Bellefield less than a month after watching Penny's Edinburgh foray into the delights of Corneille and Racine. The purchase price had been over three hundred thousand pounds. There was a tax evaluation attached to the original documents, dated just five days ago, obviously for probate purposes. It had been issued by the Crown and the City of London, and it listed the current valuation of the Bellefield Theatre, 1, Hawthorne Walk, London E.C.4, as one million, one hundred thousand pounds sterling.

Penny swallowed something in her throat. This was too much. It was simply too much. She looked up and saw John-William's shrewd blue eyes fixed on her in complete understanding.

"I know," he said. "It's a corker, isn't it?"

"Dear lord." Penny found her voice. "Mr. Gunther, John-William, is this a joke? Any of it? All of it? Because I don't understand. I don't understand how this is possible. I didn't even know her! Why would she do this?"

"I suspect there's an explanation of sorts in that sealed letter." John-William remembered his coffee, and took a mouthful. "I'm just guessing, of course. She never communicated to me what her reasons were, so I don't know for certain. But that sealed letter is addressed to you, and you may want to open it before you do any additional worrying and wondering."

"You're right." Penny looked up and saw that he was holding out a silver letter opener. She steadied her breathing, took the opener from him with a murmur of thanks, and slit open the parchment.

There were two items inside. One was a single sheet of paper, addressed simply to "Niece" and written in English. The second was a personal cheque, in the amount of one hundred thousand pounds. Penny turned it over, face down, on the desk, with sweating hands.

Her heart was thumping erratically. She began to read aloud; she felt somehow that having another human being hear what was written would make it real.

"Niece," she read.

Having seen your passion for the drama of the written word, I feel that to give you a room of your own in which to perform will secure my place in heaven, if heaven there be. The Bellefield, at this reading, is therefore now entirely your own, or will be once the travesty of efficiency that is the British court system admits that I have actually moved on. The Bellefield has a history, as it happens. I leave it to you to discover this, for without it, none of your work within the Bellefield's walls will have any grounding. I am including sufficient money with which to accomplish restoration, which is to say, sufficient at this writing but of course, it is English money, not French, and may be worthless by the time you read this. If such is true, *j'offre mes regrets,* but you will have to cope. I wish to add that, having purchased this with my own funds and not inherited means, I am free to dispose of it as I choose. I discern in you an adventurous spirit, and to my surprise, am aware of regret that I will not be here to see how you and the Bellefield do together. I ask only that you perform to the top of your considerable bent, and that you will perhaps find a little season for the work of the greats, and dedicate that season to my memory's honour, if only in your mind.

Yours etc,

Marie-Thérèse Ysabel Lésurier Heatherington, wife of Stephen.

On the final words, her voice trailed away. She looked up and found John-William staring at her, his eyebrows raised so high they were nearly lost beneath the curls.

"Bloody hell," he said faintly. "No, sorry, I beg your pardon, most unprofessional of me, but, well, *bloody* hell."

Penny set the letter delicately atop the rest of the papers. She was aware of several things at once: a desire to laugh hysterically, an urge to get up and dance around the small office, an enormous weight of something that might have been tears pressing at the back of her throat. Most of all, she was aware of surprise at her own deep sense of loss. How had it been possible to have had this astonishing woman on the periphery of her world, and yet to have never gone out of her way to bring Marie-Thérèse inside?

She came to a decision suddenly.

"John-William, this isn't actually mine yet, is it? I mean, we haven't cleared probate."

"That's correct—I'd say another fortnight for that. It's a big estate, but a simple will. The Bellefield to you, one or two small bequests, and the bulk of her personal money to charity." He saw the question in Penny's eye and answered it. "No, your uncle Stephen won't contest it. I'm not breaking any professional behaviour code to tell you that. There's actually a notarised letter on file with the wills and estates people, waiving his rights to any of her personal money. They had an arrangement."

"How very French. And how very civilised of Stephen." Penny picked up the keys. "My reason for asking—well, is there any legal reason why I can't go look at the place? I know the theatre isn't officially mine yet—I don't want to break any dainty little laws, or get you in trouble, or jeopardise anything."

"The laws are not particularly dainty." There was laughter in John-William's face. "And I was wondering when you'd ask; good heavens, I'd think you were insane if you didn't want to go and have a good gloat. Take the keys, by all means, but I'll need you to sign them out, since they're technically the court's property, not mine. Just bring them back here when you're done. I'm assuming you don't want company, but may I call you a taxi? It's a longish walk from here, and the weather's rough."

"No, that's all right. It's kind of you, but I need to be alone for this. I have a conversation with my amazing French aunt moving around in my mind, and I need to commune. Besides, I expect I'll cry, and I only ever let people see me cry on-stage. And no taxi, thanks. The walk will do me good."

She emerged from John-William's office into a chilly drizzle of December rain. Water accumulated in glistening pools at curb and grating, and splashed her upturned collar from the higher sills and cornices of faceless office buildings. Penny never noticed. Her attention was focussed on convincing herself that this was not all some joke in extremely bad taste that some cruel and evil-minded creature was playing on her, with no better reason in mind than to snatch everything back again. The fact remained that, until she saw with her own eyes that there was actually a theatre in a tiny alley of which she had never heard, she wasn't going to be able to process acceptance of her own good luck.

The wind picked up and swirled damp city detritus around Penny's boots. She walked west, past the elegant curve of Sir Christopher Wren's famous dome, and continued on down Ludgate Hill, crossing the traffic snarl of horns and busy office workers darting across Farringdon Road on their way to and from their jobs. Ludgate Hill became Fleet Street as it crossed Farringdon; Penny jangled the heavy keys in her coat pocket and heard their metallic voice mingle with the bells of St. Paul's, tolling eleven o'clock behind her.

*Oranges and lemons,* she thought, *say the bells of St. Clement's,* and she was aware of tears on her face. She stopped abruptly, drinking it in, and then threw her head back and laughed aloud, earning the startled glances of a few wet, hurrying passers-by. She had begun to understand that she was wide awake, and that it was entirely possible something wonderful had just happened to her.

She saw Whitefriars on the south side of Fleet Street. Here it was, then; Hawthorne Walk was between Whitefriars and Bouverie. She sucked in cold air, savouring it, letting it burn her lungs for a moment or two. With a sense of one about to embark on something momentous, Penny crossed Fleet Street and walked down Whitefriars, heading south towards the river.

Hawthorne Walk began, or rather ended, with a pub at the corner. Penny took it in; a genuine Tudor building, from the look of it, three floors high, with an unexpected amount of its original half-timbering still intact. A small bronze plaque between the doors and the first set of windows informed the curious that the pub had been situated on this very site since 1608. How on earth had it survived the Great Fire, never mind the air raids of the Second World War? Penny wasn't a Londoner by birth, but she remembered enough modern history to be sure that St. Paul's had been a favourite target of the Luftwaffe; the dome had made both the cathedral and its environs disastrously easy to find from the air.

Penny stepped southwards across the narrow street and admired the pub. It was a pretty place, built in a modified U-shape, as is common to old corner buildings in London. It had a lovely old clock between the first-floor windows directly above the door, leaded glass in the upper windows, and a general air of quiet good cheer.

In contrast, the sign hanging from an iron crossbar over the green-painted door was startlingly macabre: This showed a heaped pyre of some sort, with a human figure bound to it, and muted flames jumping heavenwards in the background. Off to one side, a cloaked figure held up one hand in an indefinable gesture. Penny glanced up and read the name at the top of the sign. The pub was called The Beldame in Ashes.

"Good lord," she muttered, and shivered. As if she had somehow caused a disturbance up above, a thin stream of rainwater cascaded down and splatted on the cobbled walk beside her. She stepped back across the street in a hurry. It occurred to her that she ought to check the street number above the pub's red-painted doors. The Beldame in Ashes, purveyor of food and fine spirits, was at 20, Hawthorne Walk. She peered at the hours, and was pleased to see that the Beldame was open Mondays through Saturdays from half past eleven in the morning until eleven at night, and on Sundays until three in the afternoon. Not only would the cast be delighted, the audience would have a local at which to drop round for a pint of Everard's or London Pride.

Penny walked west down Hawthorne Walk, hands in pockets, touching the borrowed keys. It wasn't a long alley by any means, perhaps a hundred metres from end to end. The north side was an odd mix of a few small shop fronts—fancy lingerie, an antique shop, a custom bootmaker—alternating with the backs of establishments fronting onto Fleet Street, to the north. On the south side, where the theatre would surely be located, Penny passed a tobacconist with beautiful bow-fronted windows and a license from the Crown discreetly displayed in a corner, a small and expensive-looking stationer's, and then a long curve of wall. Her breath caught in her throat; here it was, then.

She forced herself to slow down, mentally stiffening, committing the physical reality of the Bellefield to memory. The stretch of wall was irregular, broken by brick arches seven feet tall, with curving timbers around and above each arch. Some of the bricks were a lighter colour than the rest, while others showed faint, elderly touches of black where fire had licked them and left them stained. *Hitler's doing, most likely,* Penny thought, *and not the Great Fire.* She brushed the bricks of one arch with a fingertip. The wall was cool to her touch.

She walked on for another ten feet; an oversized roll-up door, some twelve feet tall and several feet across, marked the westernmost curve of Hawthorne Walk. This would be the flat entrance, for loading and unloading scenery and equipment. Penny's mind, forced into practicality, filed it away. It would do, she supposed, although getting a lorry of any size at all down this curvy bit of road would be tricky. Perhaps there was another entrance around the back? She would check later. And surely, that corrugated metal rollup door was out of place on a building of this age. Presumably, it had replaced the more traditional pocket fold-ins as part of the post-war repairs.

More brick arches, running along the length of the theatre's front like a dancing Grecian frieze. All the bricks at the western end were a uniform colour, without the black fire stains. At the end of the arches, a boarded-up area, almost certainly the box-office window.

And here it was, the house entrance itself: tall, elegant double doors in black-painted wood, tarnished brass fittings at hinge and bar and, infuriatingly, plywood fixed over what was presumably the glass, as protection against vandalism. Around the push bars of both doors, connecting them securely, ran a length of good strong chain. This was twisted tight, allowing almost no slack, and was held firmly in place with a serviceable padlock.

Penny, hoping she wasn't going to need oil, pulled out the ring she had taken from John-William, found the padlock key, and clicked it home. The lock opened smoothly, cleanly, without a squeak or a hitch. She slid the chain off the push-bars, releasing them, pressed on the right-hand bar, and let herself into the Bellefield Theatre.

She stood in the foyer, breathing deeply, letting her eyes adjust. The interior was dim, but not completely dark; Penny glanced upwards and discovered a line of flip-up windows on the equivalent of the first floor. There were at least a dozen of them, set in along the length of the foyer, opening onto the street. The weak light of a winter afternoon spilled down onto Penny and her surroundings, and gave her enough to see by.

The first thing she took in was the foyer carpeting, decrepit and badly stained. Sometime during Charlie Chaplin's heyday, the floor had been expensively covered with a flat pile the colour of dried blood, decorated with a design of enormous purple cabbage roses. Penny shuddered and began a mental list, tentatively entitling Column A as "Things to Be Thankful For, But Which, Regrettably, Would Still Cost Money." The necessity to replace this hideous carpeting was going to make a satisfying first entry in that column.

The paint on the wall panels, between what looked like oak framing partitions, was also red. This was a far nicer colour, however, and Penny started Column B of her list, giving it the working title of "Nice, Keep If Possible, Use the Money for Something on Column A." The panels were ticked off as something to be checked into as a restoration project. At first glance, they seemed to be in surprisingly good shape.

There were a dozen sconces set into the panels, charming lily-stem designs in brass, that had once been gas and were now obviously wired for electricity. Penny saw that three were damaged at their base, with the fluted glass shades of at least two more either cracked or chipped. It would be worth finding someone to fabricate replacements for the damaged ones, if the rest of them proved functional. They were lovely, and perfectly harmonious with their surroundings. Yet another item for Column B; if the second list outnumbered the first, she was going to be a very happy woman.

Penny turned and walked towards the auditorium. Four tall doors led into the pit. She laid a hand on the nearest door, and pushed gently. It swung easily, first in, then back towards her. Pivot hinges, obviously, and someone had kept them reasonably well oiled. Yet another item for saving and restoration. All four doors were missing the kickstops that would have allowed the doors to be held open during play intervals. Those, at least, would need replacing. Penny shoved her purse under one of the doors, propping it open for some light from the foyer.

She walked into the pit and immediately knew where the bulk of Marie-Thérèse's hundred thousand quid was going to be needed. Swearing under her breath, her eyes watering and her breath stuck in her throat, Penny added a Column C: Things That Would Eat Up the Restoration Money at Light Speed.

Penny could smell the damp before her eyes had even begun to adjust to the heavier darkness. Oddly, there had been no hint of mould or, in fact, of any kind of water problem in the foyer. Yet, here in the pit itself, it was overpowering; it caught at the back of her nostrils, pungent and acrid. The place smelled as though a nineteenth-century naval battle had taken place here, the mental image of burning ships at sea impossible to avoid. She wondered if she was imagining the taste of smoke. It was strange, she thought, that water and fire should smell so much alike sometimes.

There were no windows in this part of the building, and Penny had no torch. Her only light source was the bit of greyness from the foyer. There was no point in risking a broken ankle or even a broken neck; without better lighting, exploration of the main part of the building was folly. The green room, dressing rooms, the scenery preparation areas, not to mention the stage itself and the upper levels—all these would have to wait. Besides, she wanted to get away from the smell, which was as depressing as it was unpleasant.

*I will no longer be my daughter's murderer.*

Penny paused, and shook her head. Where in sweet hell had that little thought come from? And why did it sound familiar? She thought for a few moments, chasing the elusive bit of prose down memory synapses. She knew it, that was certain, she might even have spoken it, but she simply couldn't place it; the source remained stubbornly just out of reach.

She turned back towards the swinging doors and stopped in her tracks. Something behind her, around her, had moved.

*Rats,* she thought, *oh God there's rats and I'm alone in the dark.* She sucked down the damp-scented air, feeling it stop at the top of her lungs. She stood perfectly still, trying not to whimper, willing herself to invisibility so that whatever moved in the dark places behind her might miss her presence here. . . .

The movement came again, and this time, there was a rustling sound as well. It was farther away, higher up; this time, it had come from the flies and rafters, high above the pit.

Penny slumped, putting a hand to her forehead, wiping away the sweat of true phobia. When she was a child, she'd watched her younger sister Candida startle a water rat in the reeds that flanked the river which ran past their family home. The rat had bitten Candida and the resulting nightmares, of her baby sister screaming as the rat bit and glared, had haunted Penny until she'd reached her university years.

But it was all right—this was only birds. That was all, nothing but birds. Not those horrible fanged rodents that predominated in older buildings near the Thames, with their biting fangs and red glaring eyes and horrible bald tails; nothing but a harmless bird or two. In the best tradition of an abandoned theatre, pigeons, or doves, or perhaps even an owl, had taken up residence in the Belle-field's upper reaches, setting their nest in a high dry place, away from the rigours of the London winter. One more item for the third column; if birds were nesting in the building itself, they had found an access point in, and that meant getting the roof checked for leaks.

*A mind unstable is an unjust possession, disloyal to friends.*

Penny put a hand out and touched the wall. She was thankful for the support it offered; something had washed in and out of her mind, a line, a bit of theatre, coming in from nowhere with an astonishing force behind it. She was dizzy now, a bit sick. She breathed deeply, nearly choked on the thick pungency of smoky wetness, and stumbled back into the foyer. The smell was completely absent in this part of the building, a bare yard away. How was that possible? She thought for a bit, but gave up; she couldn't place either line and she couldn't make sense of the difference in the air quality. She gave up, retrieved her purse from its duty as door wedge, and went out of doors.

Penny emerged into Hawthorne Walk and carefully secured the chain, as she had found it. Stepping across the street, she looked up at the Bellefield's frontage, taking note of what she missed at first look: the line of windows, the pleasingly silly cornices and curlicues over the doors, the way wall met roof in a solid unbroken line.

She lifted one hand to shield her eyes against glare and mist, and strained upwards. It honestly did look to be unbroken; no entry for those birds anywhere that she could see. That meant those rustlers in the rafters had either come in through the roof itself, or else the back side of the building was not in as good a condition as the front. There was only one way to tell, and she'd meant to do that anyway.

Penny walked to the western end of the street, and turned left onto Bouverie Street. A December wind blew north off the river, bringing with it a sharp clean smell of moving water. It lifted Penny's hair, stinging her eyes and deadening the surface nerves in cheekbone and jaw.

She nearly walked right past the service alley for the theatre without seeing it; for some reason, she'd been expecting another through street, a twin to Hawthorne Walk. Instead, the rear of the Bellefield was reached through a rectangular cul de sac, nine or ten metres deep, slightly narrower in width. There were two doors, one of standard height at the back of the alley; this was apparently the stage door. The other was what Penny had been expecting, a match for the loading rolldown at the front of the building. These had their original doors intact, customised pocket models of reinforced wood that secured where they met in the centre as well as locking at both edges, and that could be pushed into the walls of the building itself. Unlike its counterpart on the theatre's frontage, this loading door was secured with several lengths of sturdy chain.

As Penny stood, considering whether to see if anything on the key ring would fit the oversized lock, the skies suddenly opened. It began to rain in earnest, harsh needles of hostile water riding the wind from the Thames. Penny turned up her collar and headed for Fleet Street in search of a taxi.

# Two

*They couldn't do to me no harm*
*So they slew my baby in my arms*
*Left me naught to wrap him in*
*But the bloody sheet that he lay in*

One week before Christmas, Ringan Laine parked his battered Alfa Romeo behind a brand-new Mercedes, walked half a block against a howling gale, and rang Penny's doorbell.

"Ringan!" She opened the door so quickly that he knew she must have been watching for him through the curtains of the flat's front room. "Come in, you must be frozen."

He unbuttoned his heavy jacket with numbed fingers as Penny latched the door shut behind him. "Frozen? Lamb, you have no clue just how frozen I am. Something's gone wrong with the locking mechanism on the hood of the bloody Alfa. It went off on me halfway to the City. Mr. Toad's wild ride, that's what I had."

She slid the jacket, sodden with snow beginning to melt into the wool, off his shoulders, and headed off to the bathroom with it. She called back to him over her shoulder. "Do you mean you had to drive up here from Somerset with the top down? It's snowing like a Father Christmas wet dream out there. That expensive-looking blonde who does the weather for BBC says the southern counties are already looking at snow flurries until the weekend, and that Scotland's already buried."

"Flurries? That must be official BBC-speak for 'blizzard.' And no, love, I did not have to drive here with the top down." He headed into the front room, and saw that the gas log was glowing with bright warmth in the tiny fireplace. Calling down a silent benison on his girlfriend's head, he squatted to defrost his frozen hands. He thought, with lazy amusement, that he was very much like Pooh talking to Piglet: toes, nose, and ears were all blue with the winter's interior chill. He even had ice particles in his black beard. Surely, there was a song in there somewhere? "It was much worse than that. The damned thing kept sliding down when I'd hit a turn, and I had to stop and get out and put it back up again. If I'd left it halfway down, the wind would have carried the car halfway to France, and me with it."

"My poor darling. Still, it's not all bad news, is it? I mean, you get to spend the next two or three days in my bed, not wrestling with bits of uncooperative canvas roofing in a wet windy car. Well—maybe not all in bed. I have to talk to you." She emerged from the kitchen, carefully balancing a tray on which sat a heap of chocolate digestive biscuits and two fragrantly steaming mugs. Even from across the room, the scent declared itself: good dark rum, lemon, nutmeg. Ringan, stretching his legs out straight in front of him on the hearth rug and bracing his tired back against a chair leg, sniffed appreciatively.

"Here, have a hot toddy," she told him, and set the tray down. "This ought to warm you up a bit."

"Mmmmmm, rum. Or should I say, Yo ho ho, drop your main-sails and prepare to be boarded, lassie? And chocolate biccies! You're the best a man could have. You know that, don't you, wench?"

She grinned at him, a purely saucy twisting of lips and dimples. It was one of her most enchanting expressions, and Ringan felt himself relax a bit further. Home, no matter whose home, was always where Penny was, somehow. How nice for both of them, and how awfully lucky, after so many years together.

"I may or may not be the best a man could have," she told him, "but I'll thank you to treat me with respect, you uppity Scotsman, you. I am now officially a woman of substance. Kneel before me, pauper!"

"The Bellefield! I'd almost forgotten." Ringan sipped the

toddy, feeling the heat and alcohol slip into muscle, nerve, and bone. "I gather probate's been cleared?"

"This morning." A wide smile broke over her face. "As I said, it's official. I now own the theatre and the property. And that means I can start making serious plans for the future. Which, m'dear, is what I want to discuss with you."

"Congrats, love." He lifted his toddy glass to her. "You know, you haven't really told me much about it. Want to fill me in on the details? Or is there some reason I'm not to know?"

"I suppose I did stay mum about it, rather. Superstitious, like all theatre people. I didn't want to hex it by jumping the fence before I had it sewn up." She considered this wildly mixed collection of metaphors, shook her head at herself, and took a healthy swig of rum. "All right, here we go. Listen carefully, please, because not only do I want to tell you all about it, I want to offer you a job."

Ringan emptied his glass in one swallow and set it down beside him. "Well, that got my attention. Go on, darling. Talk to me. You won't mind if I munch biscuits while you talk, will you? I've had nothing since lunch, and that was bad pub food six hours back. Um—you did say a job?"

"Indeed I did. And actually, the biscuits are only to take the edge off; I got a couple of dinners from Marks and Sparks market section, the posh kind you just heat up. Very nice, too—rosemary potatoes and best Scotch topside beef and something green as well. They're in the oven. Listen now."

She gave him the story of how she'd come to inherit the Bellefield, complete with details. Ringan listened, interrupting once or twice with pertinent questions, and working his way steadily through the biscuits.

" . . . and that's the whole story, I think." Penny squinted down at the dregs of her toddy. "So there you have it. I took formal possession of the documents, the title, and the keys to the kingdom at eleven this morning, over a glass of mediocre but well-intentioned champagne at John-William's office. And I deposited the hundred thousand quid in the Tamburlaines' bank account this morning; good thing I'd had the sense to warn my branch manager ahead of time, or he'd have had an apoplexy. Very bad form, to kill your bank manager. Comments? Questions?"

"Just two. First of all, what's all that about being free to use her own money because it wasn't inherited? Why wouldn't she be able to leave you inherited money?"

"Oh, that's French law, or at least what used to be French law; I have no idea if it still applies. It used to be, in France, that inherited money couldn't be left away from the family. And yes, I know she was married to an Englishman and they lived in Scotland and French law wouldn't apply, but, well, she was French and old school and that's how she thought, I suppose. Did you say two questions?"

"Yes. Was your aunt as bizarre as she sounds?"

Something that might have been regret shadowed Penny's face momentarily. "I'll never know, will I? She was a complete stranger to me when she was alive. And it's too late to find out about her now."

"Don't beat yourself up over it, love." He touched her hand gently. "From everything you've said, intimacy with her husband's family was just about the last thing on earth she wanted."

"True. She'd likely have hated the idea. And then she'd have left the Bellefield and all that lovely fixer-upper lolly to a home for indigent punk rockers, or a society for the preservation of antique sheep dip bottles, or something." She glanced at him from under her lashes. "Speaking of fixer-uppers . . ."

"Ah, yes. This job." Ringan Laine, acclaimed folklorist, guitarist for the successful touring band Broomfield Hill, and one of the leading lights for Britain's National Trust in its quest to preserve and restore properties and sites of historical significance, grinned at his lady-love. "I'm always up for a job. Break it to me gently, I'm a wee delicate flower who needs careful handling. Just how bad a state is this theatre of yours in, anyway?"

"Well—it's not, that's the thing. That first day, when I went to look at it, I made a lot of little lists in my head. You know the sort of thing I mean: things to fix, things that can't be fixed, things in perfect repair that you're going to get rid of anyway because you happen to loathe them and you have enough money to replace them."

Ringan grinned. "Not to mention things to burn while cackling gleefully and rubbing your hands together and dancing around? Yes, indeed, I know all about those lists."

"Right. Well, that first day, I listed. The foyer carpets are wrecked and need replacing, but that doesn't break my heart, because they're ghastly. I'll need someone who can do replacement copies for the wall sconces. The panels are in superb condition, a nice clear red, though I suspect we'll need to jump through flaming hoops to get an exact colour match for touching up. But the one big problem I found that first day was in the pit itself—you know, the house, the auditorium? It absolutely reeked of smoky-smelling water."

"Not good." Ringan shook his head at her. "Not good at all. That hundred thousand quid won't leave enough left over to buy us each a pint at whatever the Bellefield's local is, not if we need to rebuild entire sections, and deal with mould, or wood rot."

"We don't, at least I don't think we do." In the kitchen, a timer pinged. Penny got to her feet, with Ringan following. "Ringan, it's the oddest thing. I went back this morning. I'd asked John-William to have the power turned back on, and they did, a few days back. So today I got my first good look at the place, under full lights."

"And?" Ringan set two places at Penny's small table, laying out napkins and cutlery. Behind him, Penny pulled on oven mitts and carefully slid two dinners from their plastic trays onto china plates. "Did you find the source of the smell?"

"There wasn't any smell. None at all. It was the damnedest thing; first time around, the pit smelled like a ship had burned in the Thames, a kind of scorched-soggy-timber effect. I kept thinking of Nelson at Trafalgar. It was very strong, it was quite nauseating, and it scared hell out of me. I thought just as you did: damn, there goes the restoration budget. Today? Nothing."

"Nothing? Are you serious?" Ringan forked a slice of hot beef into his mouth. "Mmmmm, good. This is just what I wanted."

"Nothing, except the same sort of dusty-musty sniffle-making smell you'd expect in a building that's only seen sporadic use during a century and a half. The foyer smelled like that, the first day I looked; it's what I think of as the basic old London building smell.

But there was none of that heavy wet-burn stink. I found two small patches of damp, one on the green room wall and a corresponding patch on the wall in the dressing room just the other side of it, so, really, that's probably just one patch of damp, sharing two rooms. I suspect a small plumbing disaster in the wall there; it looks as though someone had tried to install a back-to-back shared sink basin between the two rooms, and botched it. We may have to replace that wall, or a section of it, and a sink would be good. But I couldn't find a damned thing else."

Ringan chewed, swallowed, and reached for his water glass. "Odd. But I wouldn't look the theatre gods in the face, if I were you, lamb. A question: What were the conditions attached to that cheque she left you? Do you have to return the leftovers to the estate, or something, if you don't use the lot?"

"There aren't any conditions. The only thing was that letter she left, saying she was leaving me money for repairs, and if it wasn't enough, I'd have to cope. But I don't think she left any specific strings attached. Theoretically, I suppose I could drop the whole pile on a down payment for a little cottage in France somewhere, but I'm not going to. Why?"

"Because I'm curious as to whether you're legally justified in using it for production, or for setting up an interest-bearing fund for future theatre maintenance, or whatnot. I mean, that's assuming you don't find deathwatch beetles in the timbering, or something. I was just curious." He mopped up the remaining gravy from his plate with a bit of bread, and sighed, clear down to his boot heels. "Now, darling girl, a question: what exactly do you want to hire me to do?"

"Truth to tell, I was hoping you'd tell me, Ringan." She grinned wryly. "I've never done anything remotely like this before. I'm a— a property virgin, I suppose."

"Not completely," he pointed out in a fair-minded spirit. "You bought this place, didn't you?"

"Yes, through an estate agent. All I had to do here was sign papers and produce money, find a local place to house the Jag, and choose furniture. There was nothing that needed doing here; the previous owners had totally renovated. This, the Bellefield—it's different, you know it is."

"Yes, it is. But the question remains—I'd like to know if you have any ideas about what you need me for."

"I need you to act as a kind of consultant. I don't even know what questions to ask; is the wiring up to code? The plumbing? What about fire safety, where do I find that out? And of course, I'd like to get the place looking like a nice believable Victorian play-house again, insofar as that's possible within the limitations of meeting London's building codes. That's why Marie-Thérèse left it to me, and I'm damned if I'll let her down. But every time I think about diving in and starting, having to ring up officials and look at regulations and code specs and who all knows what else, my brain curls up and whimpers." She met his gaze, and held it. "This is your field, darling. My field is whipping an acting troupe into shape a few times every year, and taking them on the road, and giving paying audiences the best version of a given play that I can put on. I don't want to do this. I'm not equipped."

"Right. Well, come say hello to me and ask me properly, and we'll discuss it."

He pushed back his chair and smiled lovingly at her. She got to her feet and came to sit on his knee.

"I'll charge you the going rate." He nibbled her ear, pushing aside a cloudy mass of black curls. "You do realise that, of course? But don't worry, I'll stay within the budget."

"Good. Because I don't want to have to worry about it, and with you handling it, I won't." Her eyes half-closed, she let one hand rest against the small of his neck. Ringan was a furnace, always warm, never seeming to feel the cold the way she did. It must be something to do with the genetics attached to being a Celt, instead of an Anglo. "I had a nasty little thought this morning, standing in the pit. I was sniffing away, wondering where in hell the smell had gone, and I suddenly remembered smelling Betsy Roper's lavender this summer, down in Somerset—the way it filled the room, and then faded? Definitely not what I needed, all alone in the building, not even in broad daylight."

"Oh, God." Ringan went still. "Don't remind me. I manage to not think about those two ghosts in my house more than five times a day, and I manage to keep the nightmares about that exorcism to about once a month. Do *not* remind me. No more ghosts, please."

"Amen," Penny murmured. "But tomorrow, let's go down and look at the Bellefield together. We'll take notes. We'll climb up and look at light rigs and bridges and flies. Yes?"

"Yes." Ringan stroked her back, and felt it arch under his touch. "That's tomorrow, though. Tonight, there's other things I'd rather do."

The next morning, under a soft fall of damp snow, Penny and Ringan took a taxi from North London to Hawthorne Walk, to give Ringan his first look at the Bellefield.

The snow was ephemeral; London, a temperate city, is rarely cold enough to support such weather. The oversized white flakes drifted down to eye level and mostly dissolved, like sugar on a child's tongue. Those that completed their journey to the pavement melted on contact.

Ringan paid off the driver, and stepped back across the street. He took in the facade of the theatre with one quick, professional look of assessment, and gave a long whistle. Penny's French auntie had certainly done her proud.

"You know," he said, joining her on the wide, shallow stair and watching her wrestle with the chain on the entrance, "you can probably dispense with the chain now. We're going to have workmen coming in and out in a few weeks. It's not as though the place is deserted any longer. Vandalism shouldn't be a problem, now that it's going to be in use."

"You're right, and I'm quite happy about you being right, because this chain is sodding heavy and I loathe and abominate it." She coiled it, pushed open the doors, and led Ringan inside, dropping the chain in one corner, out of easy stumbling reach. "Foyer lights just inside the box office, where the Great Unwashed can't get at them and make mischief. Could you reach inside, to the left, and—ah, there we go. Brightness, falling from the air. Lovely. Ta."

"Welcome, ducks." Ringan stood in the foyer, gazing around appreciatively, taking it in. A small notebook sat ready in one hand, but he made no move to open it. "This is completely superb," he said plaintively. "Why don't I have a madly wealthy eccentric French aunt? Some people have all the luck."

Penny grinned and shook her head at him. "Behave yourself. It honestly is superb, isn't it? Seriously, first look, what do you think? Anything immediately grab your attention?"

"Besides the carpet, which ought to be shredded and used as cat-box filler, no. I don't think period carpeting is feasible, even if we could find it. My own take is a good industrial grade, in a nice solid colour, or something with a tiny dot, to echo the panels. You're right, that clear red is gorgeous. If there's no damp in those walls, we've got lucky."

"Tiny dots, industrial grade." Penny nodded. "Darling Ringan. See, I wouldn't have known where to begin."

"The sconces, now, I see what you mean. We need to find a good craftsman to do up some copies." He opened the notebook at last, and began to write. "There's a bloke I've worked with, top-notch fabricator, down in Kent. He'll likely give us a good deal on the lot. I throw a lot of business his way. I'll call him tonight. Nice frames on the panels, by the way. Interesting choice—this is Jamaican lancewood."

"There's something called lancewood? Huh—learn something new every day. I thought this was oak; it's very hard wood." Penny touched one of the two-inch-wide frames which encased the red walls and turned them into individual panels. "What do you want to bet one of the original backers who built this place had a nice share in a Jamaican hardwood plantation?"

"I wouldn't take the bet." Ringan looked up. "You didn't tell me about those gorgeous painted squares up there—my God, are those individual murals? Penny, that's amazing."

Penny craned her neck, her mouth open. "Do you know, I didn't notice that ceiling the first time around? Too dim; it was all natural light. And yesterday morning, I went in through the back. I never even came into the foyer. Besides," she added, "there was that smell. I wanted to chase it down. But are they really murals? How big do you suppose they are, Ringan?"

"Each square? Hard to tell from down here, but at a rough guess, about a half-metre square. The surrounds look like moulded plaster, just a classic Victorian bit of playhouse decor. It looks as though it might be wildly ornate, but we won't know until we see it up close and personal; might be worth spending a bit to gild the surrounds, might not. I don't suppose we have a sturdy, really tall ladder anywhere on the premises? Any way to get up and check out the condition of that lot up there? Because if the condition is good, it adds enormous value to the property. Original Vic painting!"

"I saw a ladder in the scenery prep room yesterday, but it's smallish. Nothing like tall enough for that." She turned her gaze and her attention back to Ringan, and watched him add a single word: *ladder.* "Your list increaseth," she said wryly. "And my restoration money runneth over. Ringan, if there's nothing immediate out here, I'd like to explore a bit in the house, and also in the backstage areas. And I haven't even been up to the bridges and rafters. Would you mind doing that bit next?"

"Right. Just remind me, when we do get the tall ladder in here, I want to check the windows. There's no way to identify things like pin cracks or missing caulk from down here."

"Will do." She pushed open one of the auditorium doors, heard Ringan mutter "kick-stops" under his breath and the scratch of his pencil, and grinned to herself. Nice to know she had hired the right man; nicer to know they could discuss it over breakfast while the work was in progress.

"Where are the house lights?" Ringan was beside her, glancing around in the dimness. The theatre, while not large, seemed cavernous with shadows. "Is there a lighting board set up somewhere, or are we talking about mains?"

"Mains, two sets—there's a master control in the lighting booth upstairs, and one over here by the backstage door. Stupid place for it." Penny made her way to the front of the house, and fumbled behind a tattered curtain for a moment. There was a gentle crackle as long-disused circuitry rediscovered forgotten connections, and the house lights came up.

The auditorium suddenly came to life, and Ringan glanced around, taking in the arrangement of overheads and floor spots. Lights, many of the bulbs either missing or broken, ran the length of the house from foyer entry to stage, on either side, halfway up the walls. The upper level, consisting of the first-floor gallery seats and six good-sized boxes on each wall, was lit from above by a similar line of bulbs in the rear gallery section, with individual small overhead fixtures in each box. Ringan saw curtains, rotted and mildewed with age, hanging in tatters from the front of each box. He made notes: box curtain replacement, check house and gallery bulbs.

Penny had disappeared, presumably backstage. Ringan walked into the heart of the house, checking the condition of the chairs. The frames were sound, and had obviously been a much later addition to the original Bellefield. They were sturdy metal, with what felt like cowhide leather on seat and back. They seemed to have seen virtually no use, a fact which surprised Ringan considerably. Except for a certain dryness of the leather itself, indicating a major need for oiling, they seemed to have suffered from nothing more than disuse. He did a brief mental count: there were ten rows of seats, each with a centre block of eight and two wing sections of three seats each. The gallery upstairs would be smaller. . . .

"You're looking thoughtful. Penny for them?"

Ringan jumped. Penny's voice, from where she stood at the edge of the proscenium, caught and spiralled eerily through the empty places of the pit. Nice acoustics the place had, he thought, and wondered briefly how those acoustics would be affected by a houseful of people. He moved down an aisle to meet Penny, and walked up the stairs on stage right.

"I was counting the house," he told her. "A hundred forty in the pit, probably another fifty or so in the gallery upstairs, plus those dozen private boxes."

"The Bellefield is rated for a maximum occupancy of three hundred, but that includes cast and crew. Good eye, you." Penny had an odd look on her face; her neck was taut, stretched out to-wards the empty auditorium. "Ringan . . ."

"Well, all we need for the house seats is some good leather lotion and a couple of schoolboys who want to make a few quid. They're in excellent shape, so there's money you won't have to—Penny? What is it?" His voice sharpened. "What's wrong?"

"Listen," she said, and the Bellefield's acoustics took her voice and sent it off into shadow, a thin echoing spiral of itself: *listen listen listen.* "There's someone here. A person. People. I can hear whispering."

Ringan felt something small and chilly close down hard at the base of his spine. "I hear damn-all," he said clearly. "What do you mean, you hear them? What do you hear?"

"French," she said, and she turned to look at him in surprise. "I heard someone speaking French. A patois, I think. From down below us. There must be someone in the basement. Maybe two people. And I heard footsteps, soft shuffling footsteps."

She looked down at her own feet, where the trap and old-fashioned prompt booth were. "Downstairs," she said impatiently, not understanding the look on Ringan's face. "In the basement. Come on, let's go see who's come in here. No reason to worry, really, it's likely just a few of the local beggars. Hello? *Bonjour?* Is anyone here? *Bonjour? Est-ce que quelqu'un est ici?*"

"There is no basement. And there's no one else here."

Ringan's voice was flat and cold, a sharp line of ice in the musty air. Penny stopped and went very still. A sudden memory came to her, too vivid, too clear: laying her hand on the side of a tithe barn, a building whose foundations had been laid long before the Conqueror brought his knights over from Normandy, and her eyes and ears flooding with pictures that no one else had ever seen, life and death within those walls, and the passage of fourteen hundred years.

The theatre was quiet. She stared at Ringan. There was a kind of awareness in his eyes, knowledge mixed with fear.

"There's a basement." Her voice was as thin as a reed, reaching no farther than Ringan himself, a scant few feet away. She gestured with one hand, and saw that her pointing finger shook. "Of course there is. The traps lead down there."

"No. Not a basement." Ringan pushed his awareness of a small cold knot in his stomach away. He spoke slowly, carefully. "The ground below this part of London is all damp river clay; that's why the Tube lines run so deep here. You have to go down sixty feet or more to get past the high water levels from the Thames. They didn't dig a cellar here. They just raised the stage. There's nothing below us but the floor of the building and an area directly below the stage that's probably only just big enough to hold the necessaries for raising and lifting. All the lighting and whatnot are up above, in the flies; I can see the rig setups from here. And I heard nothing, nothing at all." He tilted his head to one side, listening, hearing nothing, watching her. "I would very much like to know what it was you were hearing just now, Penny."

"I heard people talking, maybe just one person, but someone talking. French. Muttery, whispery, in French. I heard it, Ringan. I know what I heard!"

"I'll tell you what, lamb. I believe you did." Ringan stared around the building that would take the bulk of both their time and attention for the next several months. "Bloody hell," he said. "Not another haunting. Not again."

On Friday, 22 December, having arranged for workmen to meet them back in London after the holiday, Penny and Ringan headed off to Lumbe's Cottage, Ringan's house just outside Glastonbury, to spend Christmas together.

They were breaking with a ten-year tradition. Every Christmas since they'd met had been spent at Whistler's Croft, with Penny's family. Her parents were charming, amusing people, boasting brains and a vast tolerance. They were deeply attached to Ringan, liking him as much for his own sake as for their daughter's. If they regretted her staunch refusal to formalise the union with a marriage license, they were neither of them foolish enough to let on. Since the entire Wintercraft-Hawkes family, other than Penny, was musical, Whistler's Croft during the Christmas holidays was a celebration of music and art.

This year, however, marked a major change. Ringan wanted to spend his first Christmas as owner of Lumbe's at home, and his mention of the traditional mass held at the ruins of Glastonbury Abbey tilted Penny into joining him. They decided they would drive up to Hampshire right after New Year's and spend two days at Whistler's Croft. After all, as Penny pointed out, one really only needed an hour or so to get drunk on her sister Candida's homemade mead, and destroy the wrapping on one's presents.

The weather, grey-tinged and indefinably dirty in London, was prettier by far in England's southern counties. In Devon and Dorset, a light snowfall had stuck, dusting the great expanse of Dartmoor with feathery brushes of white, and sorely confusing the wildlife. The hedgerows along the country lanes of Somerset and Wiltshire were stark against the winter sky. Without crowds and traffic, the effect was very much as it had been a thousand years earlier. Winter in the countryside, just past the shortest day of the year, was something the Druids might well have recognised.

They took Penny's Jaguar, leaving Ringan's car in London with a mechanic who promised to have the faulty hood lock replaced by the time they returned to the city. Leaving London just after breakfast, they reached Glastonbury in plenty of time to catch the local shops before closing, and to stock up on basic comestibles. Luckily, Christmas dinner itself was not something they had to worry about; Albert Wychsale, Baron Boult and Ringan's landlord, had invited them up to Wychsale House. On the road back to Lumbe's Cottage, as Penny maneuvered the Jag down muddy cart tracks under the shadow of Glastonbury Tor, Ringan cast a sideways glance at her profile, intent in the car's dusky interior. "You know," he remarked casually, "you've been awfully quiet the whole way down. And you're looking far too thoughtful and considering. Come on, open up. Penny for them."

He saw her mouth curve up in a rueful smile. "Damn. You do know me rather too well, don't you? Actually, I've been running an idea around in my head, and I was going to tell you all about it a bit later. I do believe I want your opinion."

"Charmed, I'm sure. And delighted to oblige."

"We'll see about that. You may not be." Penny was still smiling. "I honestly don't know whether I've had a brilliant stroke of genius or whether you're going to end up wanting to have me committed. It's about money, for the Bellefield. I've got an idea that involves the Right Hon. Let's get to Lumbe's and get some dinner on, and I'll tell you all about it over dessert."

"Do we have dessert? Did we buy any?"

"Now you mention it, no. Damn! I could fancy a nice slab of something with too much chocolate in it. Ah well. Brandy, then."

They pulled up at Lumbe's without further conversation. For Penny, who had been on tour with the Tamburlaine Players the entire autumn season, this homecoming in deep winter raised mixed feelings. She had only seen this place in the full verdant glory of England's early summer, surrounded by roses and green herbs and apple trees, with Albert Wychsale's Persian cat, Butterball, stalking butterflies in the long grass. Her memories had left her unprepared for how charming, and how different, the cottage would look with a faint sift of snow edging the dormers and sills.

She climbed out of the car, reaching for a plastic sack full of groceries, and let her gaze travel to the old tithe barn.

Standing motionless, staring at it, Penny remembered her last encounter with that building with a sense of clarity that was nearly physical. It had been climactic and terrifying, as Ringan and his Broomfield Hill bandmates played Lumbe's two resident lost souls to their eternal rest. Since then, Ringan had adapted the barn as a wonderful work-space for the band, the members of whom had been down several times, for working weekends in the country and a good rehearsal. According to Ringan, their attempt at exorcism had apparently succeeded completely. There had been no sign of ghosts since that day in June.

Yet Penny had experienced something that none of the others had, and she was aware of a deep reluctance to touch any part of the tithe barn or, in fact, even to approach it. She didn't doubt that the shades of Will Corby and Betsy Roper had gone from Lumbe's and the barn. But she had seen other things in her brief contact with the place, lives and deaths before and beyond those two. She wondered for a moment why that memory was so strong in her mind's eye, and then remembered whispering, a rusty rasp of a voice, muttering away in some odd patois of a language that Penny herself spoke fluently, yet could not quite comprehend, the whispers echoing below her feet in counterpoint to a sly, furtive shuffling of feet in a place where no one should be. . . .

So strong was the hold of remembered horror that Ringan's touch on her shoulder had the effect of an electric shock. Penny lost her grip on the grocery sack; it slipped through her slackened fingers and fell, scattering half its contents. A small whistling scream forced its way out from behind her clenched teeth. Inside her leather driving gloves, her palms were slick with cold sweat. Breath, visible only as sharp jerky puffs of translucence on the cold night air, whistled through her nostrils.

"It's just me, sweeting." Ringan knelt and gathered the groceries. "It's all right, you know. It really is fine. Will Corby is gone, so is Betsy Roper. I've used that barn at least twenty times since the summer. It's clear. You don't need to be afraid to deal with it. And there will be no slinky Napoleonic era factory girls in our bed tonight, either. Word of honour."

"I know." Penny, regaining some control over her unruly nervous system, went back to lock the car. Her hands were infuriatingly unsteady. "I wasn't worrying about Will Corby or Betsy Roper, Ringan. It's not that."

"Those other pictures you saw, then?" He was quick, she thought, very quick. He was also frighteningly intuitive. She took a firm grip on herself and followed him as he opened the front door, flipped on the lights for the main room and hallway, and pushed the door closed behind them. "Or was it the whispering French whatever-it-was I couldn't hear, back at the Bellefield?"

"Both." There was no point in trying to hide it from Ringan, certainly not here at Lumbe's, where that first instance of her extreme sensitivity to things just past the edge of the natural horizon had manifested itself. "Perhaps they're really one and the same thing, though. Ringan, do you suppose I'm some sort of freak? You're the musician, not me. So why do I keep hearing these wretched things, and not you? I mean, it hardly seems fair. I can't even hum a tune without sounding like some sort of death drone, so why do I keep getting this happening to me?"

"I don't know, love. I wish I did. Do you know, I still find myself resenting the fact that you and Jane could both see and hear Will Corby, and I couldn't pick up so much as an echo? But that thing, back at the Bellefield—we haven't discussed that."

"No. I wasn't ready to. I'm not sure I'm ready now." She met his steady gaze, saw one eyebrow lift, and threw up her hands. "I know, I know, all right. I'm aware that I'll have to deal, and sort it out in my head, before we start work on the theatre. I will. I promise. All right?"

"Yes, if you mean it. And now let's rub up a steak and see if Butterball's waiting for us at the kitchen door."

The next two days passed pleasantly, and without disturbing incident. Ringan went into Glastonbury for some last-minute shopping; Penny phoned the core members of the Tamburlaines and told them about the Bellefield. Ringan sorted out the tapes he'd made of his own shows in the North Country, and burned them onto compact discs, to share with his bandmates; Penny e-mailed the producer in America to discuss bookings, and told Ringan, in broad outline, about the idea she had had concerning the Bellefield's financial future. Ringan went out to gather and stack fuel in the enormous fireplace, and dozed on the sofa for an hour afterwards; Penny secretly revelled in the imminent presentation of her Christmas gift to Ringan, which involved herself wrapped in nothing very much but a few strategically placed bows and ribbons. Together, they obtained a tree and strung it with a few shiny, locally themed baubles from the Glastonbury Abbey Barn gift shop.

In the early-falling darkness of Christmas Day, suitably dressed for the occasion, they climbed into the Jag and headed up the road towards Wychsale House. On the back seat of the car was their Christmas present for Albert Wychsale, a charming nineteenth-century watercolour of Wychsale House itself, that Ringan had found in a local antique shop. There was also a bottle of champagne, a *grand cru* vintage that would be their contribution to what would likely be an excellent dinner; they'd dined at the House before, and knew how dependable the cook was. Besides, as Penny pointed out, a few mouthfuls of the type of champagne that widened one's eyes would be a nice way to broach the idea she'd been mulling over for several days past.

Wychsale himself opened the door for them. The great house looked exquisite and serene, with the winter sky as backdrop. In each of the tall windows that flanked the main entryway and stone steps, two multi-armed Victorian candle trees stood. Framed by mulberry-coloured draperies held back with golden tassels, loaded with their full complement of lit and burning tapers, they shone brightly out across the lawns and drive. The doors themselves were draped with swags of holly and, as Penny learned almost at once, mistletoe from Wales.

"Happy Christmas to you both." Albert Wychsale, portly, sixty-ish, and referred to affectionately by Penny and Ringan's intimate circle as "the Right Hon," planted a resounding kiss on each of Penny's cheeks. She caught sight of the hanging mistletoe directly above her head, grinned, and bussed him back again.

"Hello, Albert. I'm assuming that kiss for Penny is for both of us? You don't feel any odd inclination to pucker up at me? Ah. Good." Ringan slid out of his coat. "We've brought prezzies, well, one prezzie plus some extremely good bubbly. Did you give the staff the day off as a holiday? That's very left and proletarian, for an old aristo."

"Yes, indeed. I answer my own doorbells and fetch my own food on Christmas night. No, I don't prepare it, don't look so worried. But the staff's gone off to have families and lives and whatnot for the weekend. You wouldn't believe the difficulty I had convincing them to go, either. They thought I was a complete communist, can you imagine? In fact, the housekeeper's insisted on coming back to clear the table when we're done. I may need help fending her off with a drumstick, or something."

He led them indoors, to the great room where an enormous tree, at least fourteen feet in height and decorated in a cascade of gold and scarlet ornaments, stood in solitary splendour in the bay formed by the tall French doors.

"Don't feel guilty about Mrs. Waring coming back to clear, Albert. Even money says she doesn't trust you not to leave filthy plates stacked up, and food stinking up the breakfast room. Bottom line, she's protecting her territory and saving herself extra work." Penny stood back, admiring the tree. "Gorgeous, that tree is. Did I hear you say something about a drumstick? Does that mean a Christmas goose, by any blessed chance?"

"Indeed. Green goose in a cherry glaze, with vegetables and dressing and things. It's all laid out—as you guessed, we're eating in the breakfast room. And John Wainfleet may or may not join us for an after-dinner brandy and a pick-at-the-carcass moment or three. That's one of the great pleasures of a well-roasted holiday bird, after all, or at least I've always thought so. And now I'm an adult, not to mention the lord of the manor, I can do it whenever I like."

"Or when you nerve yourself to demand it from your cook?" Ringan was laughing. "I hear you, mate. I've been known to eat leftover chocolate cake for breakfast, myself. Who's to stop me?"

Wychsale, who had taken the wrapped watercolour from Penny and held it up to the light in a frank attempt to see through the paper, turned his attention to the champagne. He gave a strangled shriek; his guests, seeing his reaction, looked pleased.

"Louis Roederer Cristal?" Wychsale exclaimed. "From 1990? My lord, you two must be solvent beyond the dreams of man. I'd kill to have a few hundred of these in my wine cellars. Or did you mug some wealthy eccentric Frenchman to get your hands on this? And why are you looking at me like that?"

"Because a wealthy eccentric person of the French persuasion is likely to prove the main topic of conversation after dinner, that's why. Be warned: I have a business proposition I want to put up to you." Penny was squatting down, shamelessly peering at the labels on the wrapped packages beneath the tree. "Gifts for the staff, and lots of them, too. Nice, kindly Albert!"

"If you're looking for yours in that pile," he informed her crisply, "you'll be there awhile. Yours are at table, the both of you, and that's where I'm bringing this mysterious thing you brought, which feels like a painting. Speaking of which, I am under instructions from the cook to take the lid off the warming dish and carve the goose at precisely five minutes past seven, and it's just gone seven now. Shall we?"

The goose, marinated and roasted to perfection in a glaze of brandied cherries, was a masterful exercise in culinary excellence. For several minutes, all conversation was suspended in favour of the carving, serving, and demolition of the Christmas bird. Small chafing dishes were uncovered to reveal roasted potatoes, a casserole of winter vegetables, and a loaf of aromatic warm bread. In a lordly dish on the mantel, a beautifully domed apple and plum pie awaited their attention. There was even a thermos of very good after-dinner coffee.

It wasn't until half the pie had been reduced to smears and crumbs on their dessert plates that Penny, drawing in air clear down to the goose and trimmings she'd consumed, brought up the matter that had been occupying her mind. Between sips of coffee, she told the story of Marie-Thérèse's amazing bequest. Wychsale listened with rapt attention. Long before she was finished with the story, it was obvious from the look in his eye that he knew just what sort of proposition she was likely to make to him.

"All right, then." Wychsale cocked his head at her. "You said a business offering, yes? Am I correct in assuming you're looking for an angel—a backer, that is, in the traditional meaning of the word?"

"Not exactly, no." As Penny marshalled her thoughts and words, Ringan swirled his wine in its balloon goblet, watching the pair of them. He never missed a chance to expand his knowledge of how Anglos did business; the subject was a never-ending source of fascination and mystery to him. "An angel, a backer, would be for one show," Penny explained.

"And that's not what you want? I see." Wychsale had an expression of concentration that gave his round face a very shrewd look. "What have you got in mind, Penny?"

"A business partner," she said slowly. "I want someone who will own a stake in the Bellefield's productions, for as many years as we produce shows. Because I'm thinking about an annual season at the Bellefield, one month per year of London home shows by the Tamburlaine Players. We've never had the means or the facilities to do that, we've always been a touring troupe. But now we can play London, compete with the Globe and the RSC and the Old Vic if we choose to go down that road."

"Why do you need a partner? I'd have thought you would infinitely prefer to have complete artistic control." Wychsale's tone was noncommittal enough to make Ringan nervous. He glanced at Penny, to see how she was taking this, and made an interesting discovery: there was a gleam in her eye, and it was answered by Wychsale's tone of voice. Something was passing between them that he himself had no part in. There was no point in resenting his own lack of comprehension, either. In theatre terms, he barely qualified as a walk-on for this conversation. He settled back in his chair to watch.

"Oh, I'd have complete artistic control in any case." Penny smiled, a rather sharklike grin that signalled her readiness to do battle at need. "That little option isn't on the table, now or ever. Financial control and input, though, that's a different matter. Why, don't you trust me to choose what the Tamburlaines produce? I've done quite well to this point, I'd say."

"I certainly do trust you." Wychsale was smiling back, a genuine look of amusement. "Just poking the bear, nothing more."

"Careful," Penny warned him. "The bear has been known to bite, especially when she thinks her creative expertise is being insulted. That's likely not the safest cave to wander into. So? What do you think?"

"Well. Let's see if I understand you. You've inherited a classic Victorian playhouse in the City—I'd want to look at the place before I committed to anything, of course. You've been left what you think will be more than sufficient funds with which to bring it back to glory, or at least utility. You want to make this playhouse the home base for the Tamburlaine Players, and your ideal route for doing that for a touring theatrical troupe is to dedicate a chunk of every year to a London season. Is that right, so far, at least?"

"Quite right, up to that point." Penny watched him, her expression inscrutable. "Do go on."

"Right. You've got the building. You've got the funding to restore and repair it. You've presumably already hired the best man for the restoring and repairing, that being our Ringan, here. You've got the world-renowned actors. You've got the reservoir of plays from which to choose. What you haven't got is the lolly to risk on those first few seasons. You need someone to share the risk, and making it permanent sweetens the pot. Yes?"

"Yes, yes, and yes again." There was admiration in Penny's voice. "Albert, if this was a coconut shy at a local fair, you'd have won all sorts of tacky plush animals with that explanation. Bravo! That's exactly right. How say you? Yea or nay?"

"Good heavens, I don't know. What sort of numbers are we talking about, on the investment and the production end? How much of it needs to be cold cash up front? When can I see the theatre?"

Ringan judged it time to make his presence felt. "We're meeting some of the potential artisans and workmen at the Bellefield on January 8. Why not come up then? No pressure, no commitment, just come and see. Even if you decide you're not interested for whatever reason, you ought to see the place. It's really something."

"January 8 it is, then. And now, all in favour of opening presents, and opening that bottle of Roederer?"

As they sipped champagne, and exchanged good-humoured comments about each other's taste in gifts, something occurred to Ringan: at no point in Penny's pitch to Albert had she mentioned the likelihood of the Bellefield being haunted.

# Three

*I cut my locks and I changed my name*
*From Fair Eleanor to Sweet William*
*Went to court to serve my King*
*As the Famous Flower of Serving Men*

On Monday morning, January 8, the long-deserted Bellefield The-atre found itself the scene of furious activity, hosting a throng of noisy humanity.

The visitors to the theatre comprised two distinct groups. At the head of a small but clamorous mob of potential workmen and arti-sans, Ringan Laine listened to suggestions, rebuttals, and impromptu cost and time estimates, on everything from cleaning the thirty-foot proscenium curtains to installing new plumbing in the dressing rooms. He made notes and tried to maintain some semblance of or-der. At the head of the second group, which was quieter, smaller, and visibly more eclectic, Penny Wintercraft-Hawkes donned the roles of producer, director, organiser, and queen, and took charge of intro-ducing Albert Wychsale to the other four core members of the Tam-burlaine Players.

After a few odd conversational crossovers had nearly left both groups in total confusion, it became obvious to everyone concerned that one of the two factions would have to go elsewhere for the duration, if anything was to get accomplished that day. Penny, with visions of hard cider and comfortable seats as an incentive, nobly suggested that the acting and financial end of this meeting move to the local pub, The Beldame in Ashes, to continue their conversa-tion. Ringan, furiously jotting down high and low bids for carpet replacement and new wiring, applauded this idea, and waved her on her way.

Staking their claim to a black-varnished table in one quiet corner of the pub, Penny sent her young leading man, Robin Sayles, to fetch a round of drinks for everyone. The rest of the group settled back gratefully in their chairs.

"That's a very handsome bloke." Albert Wychsale made this observation in a purely dispassionate spirit, a man stating a simple fact, leaving no room for misinterpretation.

The remark was met laconically by Robin's fellow actors. "Gorgeous, isn't he? *And* he knows it. Don't let those long lashes and amazing dimples fool you. It gives him this vaguely naive look. But he knows what he looks like. Old enough to shave, after all." Petra Morrison, who looked like a young, updated Pre-Raphaelite angel herself, grinned at Wychsale. "I'm teasing, you know. Robin's a sweetie, really."

"Robin's a love," Penny said absently. She was beginning to relax for the first time that day; the realisation that she would have to sell her idea to Albert Wychsale had left her tense and edgy. As she'd explained to Ringan that morning, she was used to having people try to sell things to her. This other-way-round scenario was off-putting, and very much not to her taste. "He's got less actorly ego than I'd have thought possible," Penny remarked. "Looking like that, you'd expect a spoiled brat, now, wouldn't you? I mean, good grief, you look up *heartthrob* in the *OED* and there's a picture of our Robin. But no. Not a hint of it. Brilliant actor, too."

"Not a hint of what?" Robin, carefully balancing an enormous tray laden with glasses, had edged his way back to their table. He accidentally brushed against a middle-aged woman just getting up from a neighbouring group, smiled bewitchingly, and apologised with his own uniquely genuine charm, then turned back to Penny without ever noticing the woman simper and melt.

"Conceit. You. Not a spot of it. Dear Robbie." Penny took the two ciders amongst all the beer, one for her and one for Wychsale, off the tray. "Ta, lovey. Here, take a chair. All right, now that we're all here, with no workmen shouting out laundry lists, let's get down to business. Your attention, please; first, let me make a proper introduction. Lady and gents, this is the Right Honourable Albert Wychsale, Baron Boult of Glastonbury, toff and all-around aristo. He's the high lordship of Ringan's little fiefdom, and I'm trying to sweet-talk him into parting with enough of his lovely inherited wealth to buy him a limited partnership in making a London season at our new home a reality. He's ever so posh and swank, so all you little plebes had best mind your manners, now."

"Cheeky. Naughty and cheeky." Wychsale, grinning, shook a finger at her. "Hello, people. My name's Albert. Could I get a round of intros myself? I'm aware of Penny, of course, and now of Robin here, but everyone else? Names, please?"

"I was just continuing on, Albert, but you interrupted me. Talk about cheeky!" Penny waved a hand. "Right. The deceptively fine-boned young lady with the glorious red-gold curls is Petra Morrison. Don't be deceived by how fragile she looks; she's as tough as old boots, honestly."

*"Enchanté,"* Wychsale took Petra's hand and kissed it, a courtly gesture which left her charmed.

"The gent at my left is David Harkins," Penny continued, "and beside him is Donal McCreary, who was the first actor to ever sign on with the Tamburlaines, nine years ago. David has a Golden Globe nomination for the film he did of *Lear*. Donal has starred on Broadway and in the West End, in the Scots play. Petra has an entire scrapbook of glowing reviews, of everything from school plays to a stint she did with the RSC as a child actress. And Robin, to go with one *Evening Standard* Award nomination and one Olivier nomination for Best Actor, not to mention many other fairly obvious attributes, has groupies for miles."

Robin blushed. "I don't, you know. Besides, I thought only rockers had groupies. Oi, Albert. Nice to meet you. Are you really Baron Boult of Glastonbury? Because my mother's mother came from an antique family in that part of the world, the Bedberes. They've all died out, of course—absolute dinosaurs. Not good, having first cousins exchanging vows and whatnot. Leads to early extinction, that sort of thing. And tails."

"Thinking of the Habsburgs, are you? Goodness. Your mum came from a much older family than mine—the Wychsales are upstarts, but we got to own everything, so, well, here I am." Albert was enjoying himself; Penny could see it. She was suddenly reminded of how easy he was with Ringan's bandmates, even the prickly fiddler Liam McCall. He was a likeable man, she thought. She hoped he'd see his way to signing on as partner.

"Well." She cleared her throat. "So, I spoke to everyone here individually during the Christmas hols, and you've all had the story of the Bellefield and how I came to get it. You've all heard that I'm hoping to have us be able to do a London season each year, or perhaps two short seasons, a winter and a summer run. Let's face it, it would be much nicer to not have to carry our own toilet paper to the theatre in mid-August, wouldn't it? And if we're home, here, I can guarantee an easier time than touring in Scandinavia, or Turkey."

"Sounds like perfection to me." Robin Sayles, relaxed and chugging his beer, had a remembering look in his eye. "Lord, two years ago, that drama festival on Sardinia—no more tropics in midsummer? I call that a bit of heaven."

"That's the general idea, Rob. And I wanted to lay my idea for the opening run on the table and get some feedback. Because, well, I think I have the perfect project in mind, but it's not what you might expect. So, your opinions are actively solicited."

"Oh dear." Petra bit her lip. "Penny, please tell me you're not thinking of something modern?"

"Just the opposite." Penny had an odd, concentrated set to her face. She picked her words carefully. "Here's the thing. That letter my aunt left me, along with the keys to the Bellefield, finished up with something about a little season of the greats, dedicated to her memory. Now, when she first saw me, and presumably when she got the idea to leave me this place, I was playing Corneille and Racine, up in Edinburgh."

David Harkins, greying at the temples and with the build of a boxer gone into retirement, looked apprehensive. "Penny, dear, surely you aren't thinking of opening in French?"

"Don't worry, David, I wouldn't do that to any of you. No, I want to go to the source here."

"Euripides." Donal McCreary spoke abruptly. "You did *Phèdre,* didn't you? And *Andromache,* in the French—Racine's stuff? It's all updates on the original, the Greek originals, that is. Is that what you mean by going to the source?"

"Clever Donal." Penny looked around the table. "I want to open with *Iphigenia*—the dark one, set in Aulis, not her among the Taurians. We could do a series, maybe three plays, ten nights each, all Euripides; there's at least ten to choose from. *Medea,* maybe? Or *The Trojan Women*? But I really want to do *Iphigenia*. That one, I just can't explain it. It's a very strong feeling I've had, ever since I first walked into that theatre. A couple of lines popped into my head, just planted themselves there; I couldn't track them to the source just then, but I did later, and it's grown into something like compulsion. I know it sounds peculiar, and hell, it should, considering that it really isn't what I'd usually think of last, much less first. But I did. I want to do *Iphigenia*. And every time I've been near the Bellefield, that idea's planted itself deeper. I looked at the scene rooms and thought, we could do flats for *Iphigenia* in here, easily. I looked at the stage and I could visualise what the backdrop would look like, where the Chorus would stand, the costumes, the altar where they sacrifice her for a fair wind to Troy. I kept trying to bring it back to our usual period, but no luck, ducks, it's *Iphigenia,* full stop."

"Brrrr. Sacrificial altars." Petra gave an elaborate shiver, but her eyes were gleaming. It had clearly occurred to her that she was likely to be tapped for the lead character, and that insofar as juicy roles went, it was a young actor's dream part. "Spooky play, if I remember it. Isn't that the one where they go through with it? I mean, it's the one where Agamemnon's actually willing to cut his daughter's throat so he can play soldier-sailor with his brother and Achilles and the bad boys? Have I got it right?"

"That's the one." Wychsale's entrance into the conversation was unexpected, and they all turned to listen. He spoke with tremendous authority. "The Atreus heads of household, that's Agamemnon and his brother Menelaus, go off hunting. They trespass in a sacred grove and accidentally kill a hind, a deer, belonging to the goddess Artemis. She gets shirty about it and calls in a favour from Poseidon; he obliges with a bit of wind control; and the entire Greek fleet fetches up becalmed at Aulis. A seer reads the oracle, says Artemis isn't amused and wants the sacrifice of Agamemnon's eldest daughter, Iphigenia, as payback for the deer. No dead daughter, no fair wind to Troy for the Atreus boys and their mates. It's the play where you really get to see what an iconoclast Euripides was. By the time the play's done with, the whole lot of those people, except perhaps Achilles and of course Iphigenia herself, have been shown up as spoiled arrogant louts, with no moral centres."

Wychsale suddenly realised that he'd been lecturing a tableful of world-class actors on the subject of drama. He glanced around the table, saw them all gaping in amazement, and the tips of his ears turned pink. "Sorry for the speech," he murmured. "I bankrolled a fund-raiser version of the play at my old school, a long time ago, around the time Petra and Robin here were in nappies, and even got a bit part. I played First Messenger."

"Don't apologise," Penny told him. "That was a very succinct summary. You got it precisely right, too. They'd been portrayed as heroic figures for a thousand years, and Euripides exposed them for what they were: greedy, no greatness of heart, liars, and oh, yes, murderers. Not my idea of heroic."

"I take it I'll be playing Achilles?" Robin had his perfect chin cupped in one palm. He looked devastatingly handsome, and frighteningly intelligent. "You know, I've always seen Achilles as a strutting little git. He really needed a slapdown in the *Iliad,* I thought—all that running about, posturing and waving his sword and being the child of a god stuff, how irritating was that? Couldn't wait for someone to nick him in the heel and shut him up. The problem is, if I recall him in this particular play, he's rather a sweetie-pie, you know, used and made a fool of by the Atreus brothers. Do you see him that way, Penny? I mean, you won't want me to pound my chest and declaim heroically, will you? Either way, I'll have to get to know the boy better."

"Robin, ducky, you read my mind, and we are firmly on the

54

same page. It is a bit tricky, isn't it? In the *Iliad,* he's annoying and arrogant; here, predating all that, he seems to have very good intentions, even if he's as stupid as mud. Have I mentioned how glad I am that I don't have to take a producer stick to you and beat you like a gong? I mean, to convince you to not play him as a comic-book superhero? And oh my, I get to play Clytemnestra, and won't *that* be jolly?"

"So I'm the infanticide-committing, not-nearly-tortured-enough-about-it-papa, Agamemnon?" David was looking enthusiastic. "Or is Donal? Would you rather I played Menelaus? I'll confess, I can see Donal quite clearly as Menelaus; he's got the physical pugnacity for it, not to mention the voice and the vigour."

"David as Agamemnon to my furious mum Clytemnestra, Donal as the warlike and ego-outraged cuckold Menelaus, Robin as Achilles who will be irritating as all get-out but have good intentions, and our Petra shaking her curls as the play's only genuinely noble character. My God, this damned thing casts itself, doesn't it? We'll have to rope in a few outsiders, messengers and Chorus and whatnot, but I don't see a problem. One booking request sent to the staff at the Royal Academy and we'll be swamped with would-be standard-bearers and singers lining up for the privilege of trying on thong sandals and white knee-length robes."

Penny shook herself suddenly, like a dog coming out of water. "Albert, I should probably apologise for subjecting you to so much purely technical talk. I know we said we were going to stay strictly on the subject of money and possible theatre operations, but you seemed to know as much about the play as any of us. So I won't apologise."

"No, don't apologise. You'd be a complete fool if you did." Wychsale got to his feet, and smiled cordially at his hostess. "I do believe I'm in, Penny dear. That's assuming we can work out the finances, but for now, let's assume yes, shall we?" He chuckled as Petra let out an enthusiastic cheer. Heads turned throughout the Beldame; behind his broad wooden counter, the barkeep paused in his drawing a pint of beer to grin. "Flattery will get a pretty girl like you everywhere. Penny, let me kidnap you away from our

Ringan this evening, and buy you dinner, and we'll see if we can hammer out a deal. If we can, I'll take it to my money people in the morning."

He glanced around at the Tamburlaine Players, all of whose faces wore varying shades of pleasure and satisfaction. "And I'd be a complete fool to not want a piece of this. It may be risky, but do you know, I do believe I'm going to have fun."

The workmen had gone, their bids submitted, and Ringan Laine was alone in the Bellefield.

He sat on the stage, letting his feet dangle over the edge into the pit. He ticked items off his list, muttering to himself as he did so: check references for wiring crew, get selection of fabric swatches for foyer carpeting and box curtains, check rafters and bridges for solidity, structural code, and safety issues, find out why one plumbing bid was two thousand pounds less than the other. The morning, while chaotic, had been productive; he had an estimated figure for Penny, one that would cover the bulk of the work needed to bring the Bellefield back to life. She was likely to be pleased with it, since it was about half of their first high estimate.

There were still the mechanics to check, however, and Ringan got to his feet. He wasn't going to do the flies and bridges without someone else along. There was no point in risking a broken neck. Likewise, the area below the stage would wait until Penny was back, since it was a two-person job at the least, one onstage and one down below, matching calls.

The Bellefield's sound system could be checked, however. One of the electricians who'd put in a bid for wiring had mentioned the forty-year-old speakers he'd seen mounted discreetly, just above the auditorium doors. It was conceivable they'd want to replace those in any event, considering their age, but if they sounded decent, and the wiring was sound and up to code, they could save a tidy bit of Penny's budget.

There was one easy way to check, and Ringan had come prepared. He retrieved his overcoat, which he'd stored in the green room, and rummaged in one capacious pocket. From this, he pulled a portable CD player and two lengths of coiled custom-made audio cabling, with connectors at each end. From under his coat, he pulled the small amplifier he'd brought for the purpose.

He stopped in the hallway just outside and hoisted the folding ladder, which was lying along the base of the wall, carefully under one arm. Although, at eight feet, it wasn't tall enough to check the ceiling murals in the foyer, it would reach the house speakers with ease.

Ringan, a ladder under one arm and the amplifier under the other, made his way to the front of the auditorium. He set the ladder up beneath one of the speakers. Even with the mains turned on, this part of the theatre was dim and shadowed; the only real source of light was provided by the few intact and functional bulbs on the underside of the theatre's upper level. His fingers traced the speaker wires to their source in the bottom rear of the speaker box itself. If he had to splice in this darkness, it would have to wait. . . .

But no, the wire was a plug-in. Ringan silently thanked whichever god of acoustics looked after musicians, and snapped the plastic connector free. Uncoiling his own cable, he checked the connector: a perfect match. Plugging that end into the speaker and the other end into the tiny jack in his own CD player, he found the outlet in the floorboard just behind his ankles, and plugged in the amplifier. It fired up with no problem. This was heartening evidence of sound wiring. It might even actually be up to present-day code.

Ringan used the second length of cable to connect the amp to the CD player. He looked at the playlist for the show he'd recorded: two, maybe three songs, ought to provide an adequate acoustics test for range and dead spots. He set the CD player atop the ladder, and pressed the "play" button. Whatever came out of the speaker would answer a few questions at once: not only would he get to test the Bellefield's sound system and musical acoustics, he'd be getting his first real chance to hear what some of his own live stuff, recorded up in the frozen north just before the Christmas break, sounded like in a natural theatre setting.

Pure, elegant musical tones poured out of the speaker. His Martin guitar, a jumbo-bodied D-45 that was famous in musical circles and known as Lord Randall, pumped its clear midrange and deep booming bass into the empty theatre. The notes rang out, a simple scale first as he tuned the instrument, filling the auditorium. Ringan tilted his head, listening. There were no real dead spots at either end of the audio spectrum, at least back at this end of the house.

The first song, done as he always did with no opening remarks to the audience, was short and simple: a classic called "Sovay" about a woman who dresses as a highwayman. It was played mostly on Lord Randall's midrange. He clicked the machine off, and considered. So far, so good; it sounded fine, but the crucial questions, the high- and low-end acoustics of the Bellefield's auditorium, remained unanswered. More information, and another song at least, were needed. He clicked the machine back on, and settled himself against the ladder.

Banter, tune-up, conversation with the audience. Ringan remembered that evening fondly; a man had yelled out for a crowd favourite, one that was very tricky to play and sing on the spur of the moment. The speaker above his head brought the memory to life, and gave it flesh. He heard the thick, nearly incomprehensible tones of the North Country accent, thickened even further by copious amounts of the local lager, calling out his request: "Oi, mate, give us 'Famous Flower of Serving Men,' then!" And Ringan's laughing answer, Have a heart, it's got about a hundred verses—would you take something a bit less wordy, as a favour to a man with a head cold?

More banter, some good-natured catcalling, laughter from audience and stage alike. What, are you fainting with fever, matey, and you a hardy Scotsman, come on then, give us the tune. Ringan's laughing capitulation. The opening guitar riff. Then Ringan's own voice, beginning the lyric.

*My mother did me deadly spite / For she sent thieves in the dark of the night / Put my servants all to flight; / They robbed my bower, they slew my knight.*

It came from the air, from everywhere and nowhere, slamming into the side of Ringan's skull. Something took him like a rush of solar wind, cold and heat, sharpness, pain in his face, the trickle of warmth sliding over his left cheekbone. He heard impossible sound, close to his ear, something from a million light-years away, something he could not be hearing in a balanced universe. He felt a flash of blinding heat and a pain in his back, and knew he had somehow come off his perch on the ladder and landed hard on the theatre floor. And the music played on.

*They left me naught to dig his grave / But the bloody sword that slew my babe / All alone the grave I made / And all alone the tears I shed.*

Ringan lay on the floor, fighting for breath. In his head, a mantra began to run in a continuous loop: *I am not scared I am not scared I am not scared.* From out in the foyer, he heard the hard ratchety *click* of the front doors opening and closing, followed, blessedly, by Penny's voice.

"Ringan? Hello, darling, are you still here?"

She came through the door where he lay, nearly hitting him. When she saw him on the floor, she cried out, a soft inarticulate exhale of sound.

"Ringan, oh God. Are you all right? What happened? You're bleeding, your face, it's bleeding—something cut you!" She knelt beside him, seemingly unconscious of the music. Ringan heard it again, the impossible thing that he could not, should not, be hearing, as it cut through the song and into his awareness. A blast of something as cold as winter wind lifted his hair in an invisible breath. It might have been a concentrated malice; it might have been simple hate. His nostrils, and then his lungs, filled with pungent smells: waterlogged wood, fire, and beneath it all, something sweet and rotten, unbearable to the senses and understanding alike.

*I am not scared,* Ringan told himself; somehow these words seemed talismanic, the only protection against the upsurge of panic threatening to swamp him. *I am not scared, I am not . . .*

*I cut my locks and I changed my name / From Fair Eleanor to Sweet William / Went to court to serve my King / As the Famous Flower of Serving Men.*

"I'm all right, at least I think I'm all right." Ringan, with a supreme effort, managed to keep his voice under strict control. *Not scared, not scared, not scared.* Somewhere in him was a kind of knowledge, the sense that he must not, under any circumstances, show weakness to whatever watched from the dark places of the Bellefield. As he fought for mastery of breath and muscles, he realised that whatever had been affecting him was fading out; his lungs cleared, and the ugly reek dissipated like thin smoke. "Will you shut that damned thing off, please? It's up top on the ladder. Ta. Oooof!"

Taking his time, he sat up gingerly. He prodded at different portions of his lower back, found nothing a hot bath wouldn't fix, and then discovered a very sore spot on his left hip. That was going to leave a thumping great bruise. Ringan felt the rags of his composure and his temper alike begin to disintegrate.

"What happened in here, for God's sake?" With the music turned off, the silence in the Bellefield suddenly seemed huge, menacing. It felt as if something, perhaps the building itself or the ground beneath it, was holding its breath, awaiting an answer. Penny's voice was knife-edged with concern. "I've just sent everyone off. We finished our meeting; Albert wants to take me to dinner and work out details. He says he's in, if the money's right. What happened here, Ringan?"

"Your muttering French intruder, the one I couldn't hear—I think I made her cross, that's what. Hang on a bit, I'm coming up." He accepted Penny's arm, and got shakily upright. "Christ, my wretched hip will be screaming for days. I'm too old for this rubbish, you know? Yes. Well. You do remember her, right? Your whispery French haunt, she of the odd version of the language and the slow shuffling footsteps in the basement that doesn't exist? Something I did seems to have got her back right royally up. I have the feeling I know what it was, too." As a muscle twinged in his lower back, he added grimly, "Damn! Is this going to happen all over again?"

"There's a scratch down the side of your face." Penny's own face was a white mask in the dusky light. "It looks deep. And it's still bleeding."

"I'm not surprised. She's a strong bit of ectoplasm, this one. Sliced me across the head and threw me off the ladder. Although, truth to tell, I doubt she threw me. Likely I just fell off the ladder and gashed my face on the way down. Maybe she didn't touch me. How the hell should I know? It's her doing, either way; if I fell, it's because I was dodging her. Whether or not she could actually hurt me, she wanted to."

He touched his cheek and looked at his hand. It had come away bloody. "Bitch," he said, with feeling. "Mean, nasty, unpleasant bitch. Definitely in a different class from the young lovers we had last time."

"Why do you keep saying 'she'? What are you talking about?" Penny's face was a study in denial, an unwillingness to know. "How do you know it wasn't one of the birds in the rafters? That scratch looks like a claw could have done it. And I told you, I heard them nesting up there. Flying about."

"Because, Penny my one true love, birds don't speak French. It's a damned shame I don't speak it, either, or I might have picked up some clue as to why a little bit of traditional music should have turned her, it, whatever you want to call it, into a homicidal maniac. But French it was. She was screaming at me. No mistake possible, dear. Nasty French ghost, we've got. And whether I got this cut from the ladder or a pair of mouldy fingernails, she meant damage. She wanted to do me harm." *Not scared, not scared, not not not . . .*

Penny stared at him, speechless. He noted, with detachment, that the smell which had threatened to choke him as he lay on the carpeted floor seemed to have passed by her completely. Whatever the revenant had been doing here, it had been aimed at him alone.

Ringan retrieved his CD player and slid his coat on carefully. The amplifier, he decided, could damn well stay where it was until he was inclined to bend over and pick it up. He unplugged it from the wall and let out a long sigh. "Can we go home now? I'd like to get some antiseptic on this gash and make damned sure it doesn't fester."

"Do you know what I'd like to see?"

It was nearly midnight, and Penny and Ringan were in her bathroom. Ringan was soaking in a tubful of water as hot as he could stand; in the hours following his fall in the theatre, several small bruises and one very impressive one had come to the surface. He'd rubbed the cut on his face with antiseptic cream, wincing at the sting and interspersing soul-soothing expletives with disparaging comments on the ghost's ancestry.

Penny, after being persuaded with some difficulty that Ringan was a grown man with a few bruises and could therefore be left home alone in her flat with perfect safety, had gone out to dinner with Albert Wychsale and sealed the partnership agreement she'd been after. She'd been under strict injunction from Ringan to say nothing about the possibility of a ghost haunting the Bellefield. Wychsale had reason to be leery of hauntings; he'd dealt with the first two. In any case, Ringan said, they had no idea what they might be dealing with. Not yet.

"What would you like to see?" Penny sat cross-legged on the bath mat beside the tub, nursing a glass of wine. She was very fond of the flat's bathroom; it was a good size and was properly heated, something of a rarity in a flat of its period. She had poured an entire package of mineral salts, a variety whose advertising claimed would draw the aches from tired muscles, into Ringan's bathwater. As she pointed out, this was a sure sign of her love and devotion, since the salts had been procured at an Austrian spa and had been outrageously expensive.

"That letter, the one Marie-Thérèse left you. Didn't you say there was some hint in there, about the Bellefield having a history? And how your work wouldn't be any good if you didn't track it down, or something? Because it seems to me, that's a statement we ought to be looking at."

"Damn. You're talking about doing research, aren't you? What a wretched idea. Not only wretched, it's one I don't have time for. I've got a new business partner, not to mention a play to produce and a restoration to pay for, damn it." Penny regarded the prospect of delving into historical documents and old parish registers without enthusiasm. "Oh, hell, of course you're right; we need to know more about the history of the place. Do you suppose she knew it was haunted? Marie-Thérèse, I mean."

"No clue. That's why I want to see that letter. Do you have it here, or is it safely tucked away in a lock-box somewhere, with the title deeds and Granny's secret recipe for kidney pie?"

"No, it's here. Half a tick, I'll get it." Penny disappeared and was back a minute later, envelope in hand. "Here we go. Shall I read it to you?"

"Yes please. Nice and slow."

Penny unfolded the thin, expensive paper. In the same clear, precise intonation with which she might have auditioned a young actor for a part, she read the letter aloud. The shade of Marie-Thérèse, her eccentricity, her oddity, her peculiar generosity, seemed to fill the room and become more vibrant with every word.

"Can you read me that bit again?" Ringan was frowning, his brows drawn together. "The part about the theatre having a history?"

" 'The Bellefield has a history, as it happens.' " Penny glanced up at Ringan, and he nodded at her to continue. " 'I leave it to you to discover this, for without it, none of your work within the Bellefield's walls will have any grounding.' " She stopped suddenly. "What a peculiar way to put it. I've only just noticed. I wonder why I didn't notice just how peculiar that was, the first time?"

"You were overwhelmed by the simple fact of the inheritance, that's why." The bathwater had cooled, and Ringan's extremities were beginning to wrinkle. He pulled the plug, letting the water drain away as he carefully rubbed himself dry and then reached for his bathrobe. "But you're there now, and I'm glad I'm not the only one who thinks it's an awfully deliberate way of phrasing it."

" 'I leave it to you to discover this.' " Penny had climbed to her feet, edging out into the hall to give Ringan room to maneuvre. "That's not even a casual mention, is it? More like a clarion call. Up and away!"

"It certainly is. Tag, you're it—it's like a child's game. She wants you to hunt it down, whatever it is. And if you follow on with that bit about having to do it, because otherwise nothing you do at the theatre having any worth . . . "

"No." Penny was studying the letter again. There was an intent look in her eye. "Not 'worth,' and not 'theatre.' She used two very specific terms here. She used the word 'grounding.' Strange choice for a woman whose native language isn't English, isn't it? And this is really bizarre, subtle, but still . . . she never uses the word 'theatre.' It's always the Bellefield, the Bellefield."

Ringan tied his robe and limped out into the front room. The gas log had been switched on, and the flat was toasty. He sank down into one of Penny's high-backed chairs. "What's your point, love? I just assumed the choice of idiom was because she was French. You think there's more to it? Perhaps something we need to know about why the place is called what it is?"

"Yes. I do. In fact, I think that's what she meant, when she said she wanted me to discover it." Penny tapped the letter with one hand. "I have the history of the theatre itself, Ringan. There's no mystery there. It was built mid-nineteenth century and there's nothing off; it was a playhouse from its inception. I did a bit of looking when I found out I was going to own it. It was built with money from a consortium of financial backers and one or two Victorian *nouveaux riches* types who fancied themselves artistic. There's no record of anyone dying on the premises, although I must say, I do find it puzzling that the place has spent as much time standing empty as it's done."

Ringan rubbed his beard. "You're right. London property doesn't just sit and decay for no reason, especially in the heart of town. It's far too pricey. That really is odd."

"Very odd, considering we're talking about a pattern here that goes back to its original opening night. It kept getting sold, there would be a month of shows and revues and whatnot, and then the run would abruptly get cancelled and the place would stand empty for a year or three, until someone else came along, bought it or leased it, and started the whole cycle over again. That's the thing I find puzzling."

Ringan slid a pillow up against his aching hip. His eyes were alight with interest. "I think I see where you're looking with this, love. What have we got?" He began to list verbally: "A theatre, not very old by the standards of the surrounding area. Said theatre's built in one of the oldest parts of London; there's bits of Roman wall there going back two thousand years. And a theatre with a very unusual name. Why the Bellefield? If it was b-e-l-l, I'd be looking for an ancient hole in the ground and a history of casting church chimes, but this is the French spelling, meaning a woman. And isn't the pub at the corner called The Beldame in Ashes? Here, pass me that wine, would you?"

She poured him a half-glass. "Just a wee drop for you, bonny boy; you took painkillers, remember? Yes indeed, a Frenchwoman, a *belle,* something burning which gets us to the 'in ashes' part, and again, beldame, a good old English version of the theatre's name: belle, beldame, variations of same. Do you sense a theme here, Ringan? A pattern? Because I do."

"Yes indeed, my lovely one. Not being an idiot, I am beginning to see where the dots might connect."

"Don't you snub me, my man." She smiled, but briefly. "Right. We have a newish theatre in a very old neighbourhood. No notices of anyone dying that I could find, when I looked at the title history. That's what I was checking into, by the way, just making sure there were no liens or outstanding claims against the property itself, or old suits for whatever reason, filed when Kaiser Wilhelm was alive and kicking. John-William seems like a thorough bloke, but he might have missed something, anyone might."

"Making assurance doubly sure? Wise woman. I expect John-William, if he's got half a legal brain, would be applauding your foresight." The wine was beginning to interact with the pain pills Ringan had taken, already established in his nervous system. He was drowsy, but with that physical state came clarity of thought. "So. We take all the factors and add them up. We remember to include the absurdity of a playhouse in excellent physical condition, and with a low rent attached, standing essentially empty all these years. What do we get?"

"We get something on the site of the Bellefield before it was the Bellefield, that's what. Something ominous happening there, something I suspect may well predate quite a few things. And we get a haunting that's likely been going on for centuries. I wonder if any of the people who used the Bellefield recently, I mean, before

Marie-Thérèse acquired it, would talk to us?" Penny hugged herself, suddenly cold. "We get a *belle* or a beldame, someone French, tied to that spot, and extremely upset about it. As a working hypothesis, I think it'll do. Ringan, half a tick—you said something, back there at the theatre, when I found you on the floor, remember? You said you thought you'd done something to make this, well, whatever it is, angry, and you suspected that you knew what it was you'd done."

" 'Whatever it is'? You don't like the word 'ghost'? I don't blame you, in this instance. Yes, I said that. I meant it, too." His gaze was fixed on the flickering dance of the gas fire. It was soothing, an invitation to doze. He yawned cavernously. "I think it was the song. Maybe I'm being paranoid, maybe I'm being predictable—but after all, that's what Lumbe's ghosts reacted to, so why not this one?"

"It sounds perfectly reasonable to me. Logical, at least. Let's assume you're right, for now." Penny curled up at Ringan's feet, her bare knees drawn up to her chin. "What was that song, anyway? The one that was playing when I came in?"

"It's called 'The Famous Flower of Serving Men.' It's about a woman whose daughter runs off with a man, and has a child. Mama, whom I suspect was one of those demented mystical Catholic obsessives they tended to breed back when the popes hung out at Avignon, gets so cross about her daughter running off that she hires some masked hitman types to kill the daughter for her sins. Good heavens, lamb, it's just a song. Why have you gone all white and trembly?"

"Are you saying this song is about infanticide?" she asked slowly. "About a parent killing her daughter?"

"Well, the infant she's trying to kill is probably twentysomething, but parent killing daughter, yes to that. Trying to, anyway. Mama doesn't actually succeed, and her failure comes back to, well, haunt her." He looked down at Penny, puzzled by the strength of her reaction to what was really nothing more than a scholarly footnote to a traditional folk song. "Would you mind telling me why you look like you just saw Medusa, up close and personal? All turned to stone?"

"An obsessive parent, a child she wants dead." The skin of Penny's face was drawn so tightly that every bone in her skull was visible. "I need to know more. Go on—what else?"

"Well, according to the song, the hitmen don't kill the girl, whose name, by the way, is Eleanor. They kill the boyfriend and the infant, and leave her the sword to kill herself with. Nasty touch, isn't it? But the idea backfires, because she doesn't kill herself. Instead, she uses the sword to bury her dead and cut her hair off. Then she goes into hiding from Mama, and into drag as well, and becomes the king's personal valet: Fair Eleanor becomes Sweet William. She's apparently pretty good at the whole cross-dressing thing, because the king believes she's a man, the Famous Flower of Serving Men. It's a good safe place to hide from Mum the Demented Psychobitch, but Eleanor, who is now running the king's personal life as William, keeps having nightmares. There's a lovely verse about that: *But all alone in my bed at e'en / Oh there I dreamed a dreadful dream / I saw my bed swim with blood / And I saw the thieves all around my head.* Nice and bloody. Very tasty stuff."

"Which king?"

Ringan blinked at her. Penny's voice was a laser. She had twisted around on the rug, her entire body speaking of tension.

"What, the one who hired Eleanor? From the feel of the song, probably a Plantagenet. John? No, he'd have been too early, and he didn't really like anyone very much. Out of character for him. One of the Edwards, maybe? The second Richard? And that's assuming the sovereign in question wasn't just some local toff, some wealthy Northumberland landowner called Walter or Hubert, who just liked to trot about his bit of bog, calling himself a king." Ringan caught himself. "What am I going on about? Penny, get a grip, will you? There's a small problem here: so far as I know, the song is entirely fictional."

"Humour me. What you don't know is that, from the first moment I walked into that place, I knew I was going to open it with *Iphigenia*." She saw his incomprehension, and sighed. "I take it you didn't do Euripides at your school? It's a play about the events before the Greek army got to Troy, and the subject is a father sacrificing his eldest daughter, cutting her throat, to appease an angry god. You probably don't realise what an unlikely choice of play that is for me. It predates my period by, oh, about seventeen hundred years. And do you know what, Ringan? It never occurred to me to open with anything else. Lines from the play kept popping into my head, from first contact with the Bellefield. And I never performed the damned thing in English."

Ringan stared at her. The dots were beginning to connect with a vengeance. *A song about killing one's child,* he thought, *an overwhelming need to do a play about a murdered child, a woman burning.* What had happened, Ringan thought, what unbearable human misdeed had blackened the very ground of Hawthorne Walk?

Penny was on her feet, pacing, alive with nervous energy. "I'm trying to get hold of something here. Come on, Ringan, help me concentrate, will you? What have we got? We heard French, both of us. We heard slow, shuffling footsteps, or at least I did. We've had this nasty phantom smell, big sea–battle smell of burning wood, or at least I did. . . . "

"We both did." Ringan had suddenly remembered. "I smelled it, as you were helping me up back at the theatre today. I forgot until just now. Nasty thick reek, and you're quite right, it stunk to the rafters; first thing I thought of was a burned wooden building, where they've put out the fire with more water than was needed for the job. A definite excess of smoke-saturated, scorched wetness. You didn't smell it, did you?"

"Today? No. Not a whiff." She sat down. "Fire. Water. French. Leaving the more subtle stuff aside for a bit, the infanticide and whatnot, does this sound sort of seventeenth century to you? London's Great Fire?"

"How should I know? I'm a Scot. You want to know about England, ask an Englishman. But if you want to match the song to the seventeenth century, I'll tell you straight out, I don't see it. I'm speaking as a folklorist and a musician as well, and trust me: the language and feel of the lyric are much earlier than that. By the Great Fire, we're well past the Plantagenets on the throne. This I am sure about, what with being a Scot. The English kings at that point were Scots as well—the Stuarts; I'm pretty sure London went up in smoke under one of the Charleses. The Great Fire was, what, late seventeenth century sometime, wasn't it?"

"Sixteen sixty-six. But can we begin there? After all, we both smelled signs of fire. And that was quite a fire."

Ringan's hip had stiffened into protest; it was time to move. He hoisted himself upright, planted his feet, and began to slowly rotate his lower back. "It's a good enough place to start winnowing, I suppose. But I'll say it again: if you're linking the song to the event, the Great Fire's all wrong. Still, let's have a go. First thing is to find out what was on that spot when the city burned. Council registrar, tomorrow morning? Or the archive people at St. Paul's might have records from the period."

"I suppose so, yes. They've likely got a pet historian on call, what with their being St. Paul's Cathedral. If they don't, we could call John Wainfleet down in Glastonbury, and get the best sources from him. He's a librarian, a historian; he'd probably know where we go next. Might save some work. Even more important, it might save some time."

Her voice trailed away. For a moment, their eyes met, and the unspoken message was clear enough. With the Bellefield about to be full of people, and a ghost whose spectral language seemed to be one of physical violence, time had suddenly become a precious commodity.

And Ringan, listening to the cycling words *I am not scared I am not scared* loop through his mind, admitted to himself they were a lie.

# Four

*So well I served my lord the King
That he made me his chamberlain
He loved me as his son
The Famous Flower of Serving Men*

Two days later, Ringan sat down with his final choices for the Belle-field restoration project, and began the excruciating process of nail-ing down firm dates and firm numbers. Penny, meanwhile, found herself eating onion soup at a fashionable West End brasserie, across the table from Dr. Richard Halligan, secular archivist and deacon emeritus for St. Paul's Cathedral.

Remembering long, tiring hours spent poring over old registers in search of any mention of the two ghosts who had haunted Ringan's Glastonbury property, Penny was pleased at how quickly her sources of information for this second, very unwelcome haunt-ing were declaring themselves. She had phoned the cathedral of-fices yesterday morning, had identified herself and explained that she had some questions about the history of the area, and had left her name and number with the docent. When she got back to her flat that evening, there was a message awaiting her: Dr. Richard Halli-gan had spent nearly thirty years as the deacon in charge of St. Paul's historical record keeping. He had recently retired, he lived just across the Thames in Southwark, he was entirely at her disposal, and could he buy her lunch tomorrow? And by the way, he had seen the Tamburlaines' production of Marston's *The Dutch Courtesan* in Rouen three years ago, and was she that Penelope Wintercraft-Hawkes? Because he was a huge fan, and really, it would be an honour to help her . . . After a consultation with Ringan, during which it was decided to tell Halligan as much of the truth as possible without mentioning ghosts, Penny had rung the retired archivist back.

Richard Halligan, doctor of both divinity and history, was a charming man, courtly, intelligent, with a gleaming mane of silvery hair. He confounded the young South London waitress by ordering off the menu in French, and he managed to do it without appearing pretentious. Penny liked him at once.

"If I understood you properly, you said you were curious about the general area around Paul's, in the years leading up to the Great Fire." Halligan noticed that Penny's wineglass needed topping up, and promptly poured some Chardonnay. He had a beautiful speaking voice, modulated and musical. "Did you have any specific times in mind? Or streets?"

"I did, actually." Penny dipped crusty bread in her soup. "You see, I've just inherited a theatre, the Bellefield, on Hawthorne Walk—that's a small alley that connects Bouverie Street with Whitefriars, just south of Fleet Street. I'd love to know something about what was there before the place became a theatre; it was put up mid-nineteenth century, and I'm curious about what predated it. I noticed what seems to be a theme, that I'd like to pin down—the theatre is spelled b-e-l-l-e and that seems to tie in with the pub at the corner of Hawthorne Walk. That's an early seventeenth-century building, with the most macabre pub sign I've ever seen, a woman being burned, and there's the name, The Beldame in Ashes. So, considering the theatre's name, I was wondering—coincidence?"

"Oh, you've discovered the Beldame! That's one of my favourite pubs—the locals simply call it the Dam. Whacking good beer. I know Hawthorne Walk reasonably well, as it happens, but the theatre—is that the big brick building on the southwest end of it? The partially boarded-up place with the handsome line of arches?" Penny nodded, and sipped her wine. "Nice to know someone has it who will actually use it and appreciate it," he remarked. "As to it being a coincidence? I doubt it, especially if you add the name of the street to the equation."

He saw her puzzlement. "Ah, so that's a bit of lore you aren't familiar with? Hawthorne Walk, the name of the street. Hawthorn was used extensively as an accelerant, back in the bad old days, when someone was burned alive. Hokey-gren is the old name for it. It burns very efficiently, and very hot."

"I didn't know that." *Hawthorn,* Penny thought, *beldame in ashes, belle-field.* "So, would you say the names were all connected? I mean, I'm not imagining a sort of continuity here?"

"Hardly. I think I see—you're looking for information about the physical history of the area, at least insofar as fires are concerned. Is that right?"

"Well, not the whole area so much as the street itself." The waitress bustled by, stopping to deposit their salads and a fresh basket of warm bread. Penny mentally added the brasserie to her list of daytime eateries; the food was good and the service, unusual for central London, was prompt. "I take it Hawthorne Walk survived the Great Fire? I mean, the pub predates it, and most of that half-timbering looks original to me."

"Yes, it survived 1666, which is more than I can say for St. Paul's itself. You do know that the present cathedral's a replacement, yes? The original was wood, with an incredibly tall spire. It went up like kindling, during the Great Fire. Wren built a new one, out of Portland stone. More fire-resistant."

"Thereby benefitting from the same lesson learned by the Three Little Pigs? Good for Sir Christopher. I sometimes wonder if city planners are capable of learning anything."

"Well, Wren was no fool, but in this case, he didn't really have a choice—a law was passed, banning things like thatched roofs, and mandating stone partitioning between buildings." He smiled at Penny, and she saw how friendly his eyes were; they also held considerable shrewdness. "It's not as though fires in London were something new to them. The city was always breaking out in local blazes; entire neighbourhoods regularly burned to the ground. That's the price they paid for living in one huge, overcrowded slum, with all their buildings leaning against each other, and all made of wood."

"Fire wasn't the only result of that reality, was it? I seem to recall a few little health epidemics. The Black Death, and all that." Penny had demolished her salad and was looking longingly at the neighbouring table, where a woman was steadily devouring a multilayered *gâteau* covered with whipped cream and shaved chocolate. She was going to have to head back to the theatre soon. She'd promised Ringan and, in any event, he might need her signature on cheques or contracts. "Actually, I especially want to know what used to be on the site of the Bellefield, and the rest of Hawthorne Walk as well. Can you recommend a source for me?"

"Several, but there's no need. If you'll trust me with it, I'd be delighted to do the research for you. It's my field, after all, and I have the time and access to the documents." He lifted a hand and cut off her thanks before she could begin. "Let me make certain I've understood precisely what you're after. We're talking about anything to do with Hawthorne Walk, with emphasis on the theatre end of the street, that might be in any way related to burning? Good. Now, a question: are you purely talking about the seventeenth century? Because E.C.4 is a very old part of town, and there's been something on that site, probably going back to the Conqueror in 1066." He paused for a moment, seeming to choose his next words very carefully. "If you're curious about the running mentions of burning, you might want to consider the other big historical blaze. There was one just as intense, and even more socially traumatic, in 1381."

"A big fire in 1381?" Penny wrestled to keep her voice noncommittal, but something inside had stiffened to attention. She was remembering Ringan's explanation of the song, the lyrics of which he believed had triggered the attack on him. What had he said? From the sound it, probably a Plantagenet king . . . "Was that during the Richard II years? Oh, and please do call me Penny. My surname's a bit of a mouthful for conversation."

"Yes, of course, I'm talking about the Peasants' Rebellion. The rebels marched into London and set certain political targets ablaze. The fire spread nicely; all that wood, you see." Halligan signalled the waitress. "May we see the dessert trolley, please? And we'd like two coffees as well, when you have a moment."

"The Peasants' Rebellion." Penny spoke slowly, staring off into her own memory. "I'd forgotten about the fire. Actually I'm not sure I remember it even now."

Her school history was coming back, clear in places, maddeningly fuzzy in others. Wat Tyler, wasn't it? The priest John Ball, travelling the south of England, calling for an end to serfdom? Every schoolgirl knew that much, but there was more, bits of pageantry stored in far-flung corners of Penny's mind; the boy-king, Richard II, confronting the rebels, telling them to trust in their true king, he would see right done, even as one of the king's own retinue pulled the rebels' leader from his horse and murdered him at Richard's feet.

And surely John of Gaunt, Richard's regent and chancellor, had played a major part in all that. The pedantic voice of a history professor from her university years, forgotten until this moment, popped into Penny's head: *The Peasants' Rebellion was the tap root not only for the Wars of the Roses but for the rise of the free market in a time when workers were scarce, and should have been valuable commodities.*

The waitress brought their coffees, along with the dessert trolley. They made their selections. "What went up in smoke?" Penny asked Halligan. "I'm not remembering details very well, for some reason. Too many years out of school, I suppose, but really, I ought to remember better than this."

"Well, let's see. A goodly bit of the south bank, for one thing, and a stretch along the north side of the river. Their main target was the Savoy, John of Gaunt's palace. It must have been a spectacular sight, when that burned; you'd likely have been able to see it from all over London."

"Of course, the Savoy." More bits of detail were coming back to her. "That was well west of Hawthorne Walk, though, wasn't it? On the Strand, where the Savoy Hotel is today?"

"Yes. But you know, Gaunt was one of the biggest landowners in London at the time of the uprising. He had vast holdings from his first two marriages; the Savoy was merely his town residence, all two thousand rooms of it. Undoubtedly one of many reasons the peasants loathed him so cordially. There's a good chance he owned the land your theatre's on, as well; in fact, if he did, it's highly probable he owned Hawthorne Walk, from end to end. London land grants from Crown to favourite tended to go that way. I can find out, easily enough, because the bulk of those records did survive the Great Fire. And the peasants thought Gaunt was a traitor, and went after what they thought might be his property." Halligan picked up a spoon. "Ah, chocolate mousse. A guilty little addiction of mine."

Penny was silent, thinking. She forked *gâteau* into her mouth, chewed, and tried to clarify her memories. The Savoy, the biggest Lancastrian holding in London, or at least the most visible. Was there something she should remember about it? Again, the overly smooth voice of the university history professor came, clearer than the facts and opinions he had stated: *It seems likely that the very size of the Savoy would have spurred the rebels into deeper fury at the inequities of the system.* She remembered him quoting the angry preacher, John Ball, speaking to the masses who were being denied freedom and a decent wage at a time when half the population had died from plague and their services were at a premium: "When Adam delved and Eva spun, Who was then the gentleman?"

She realised suddenly that Halligan was speaking, and that she had missed the first half of it. " . . . assuming any special time constraints?"

"I'm sorry, Dr. Halligan, could you say that again? My mind was elsewhere, in the fourteenth century, to be exact."

He waved away her apology. "I was just asking about time constraints. I know you said this was just curiosity, but for some reason, I'm getting a rather strong sense that you'd like this soon, rather than late. Am I imagining things?"

Penny opened her mouth, closed it again, and met his eye. She saw nothing there but good humour and patience. "You're very acute," she said simply. "No, you're not imagining things. I'm afraid I can't go into details, not at this point, but actually there is some urgency to this. Can I offer you your own private box at the Bellefield for our opening performance, by way of apology for having to be so secretive?"

"Indeed you may." He finished his mousse and set his spoon down. The waitress, as if on cue, appeared with the cheque. "I'll try to have as detailed a history of that bit of Hawthorne Walk as I can put together, sometime over the next few days."


"Penny? Can you spare me a moment?"

Penny, seated in the first row of the Bellefield's pit, glanced up with unfocussed eyes. A tattered paperback of *Iphigenia in Aulis* lay open in her lap. "Oh! David. Sorry, I was going over Clytemnestra's little how-dare-you-lie-to-me speech to Agamemnon. Listen to this line: 'We buy what we loathe with what we love.' Gorgeous, isn't it?"

"Very. It's a juicy play, all told." David Harkins sat down just behind her. "But I did want to ask you about it."

Penny had known since the meeting at the Beldame that this was probably coming, and she was still not really prepared to answer. She closed the book and met his gaze. "I was waiting for someone to hit me with it. Ask me, as in, why I was so adamant about wanting to do it?"

"That's it." He cleared his throat. "You know, I wouldn't have brought this up when you first announced it. After all, you were trying to nail down a partnership with Albert Wychsale, and none of us would have dreamed of arguing or questioning your decision under those circumstances. A solid attempt at securing financing is no time to have your authority or creative decisions challenged, and we certainly wouldn't have wanted to sabotage the chance. Besides, it's a marvellous piece, and we're quite excited over it. But . . . " His voice trailed away.

" . . . But it's off my usual lists and I seemed awfully set on doing it. Is that it?" Penny modulated her voice upwards. There was banging coming from backstage; the plumbers Ringan had hired were installing new pipes and back-to-back sink units in the two star dressing rooms. It was the first day of many in which the Bellefield would ring with workmen hammering, sawing, yelling from room to room. Since Penny had decided to begin rehearsals at once, the next few weeks were likely to be chaotic, even without taking a possible haunting into consideration.

"That's it," David agreed. "It's not just me, and please don't think we're objecting—we're not idiots, we love the play and the idea in general, and Petra in particular is over the moon about the part. But you seemed, well, almost fierce. And leaving aside that you're not usually fierce, I got the impression there was something else going on. Donal noticed it, too, and he's feeling a bit uneasy. Penny, be straight with me: is there something odd about this place?"

"Ah. Damn." Penny closed her eyes for a moment. Over the distant banging was that something else she was hearing? Someone whispering? No, surely not. It wasn't possible, not with the noise those workmen were producing. . . .

"Penny?"

"Sorry. I was distracted there for a moment." She wondered how much to tell him. None of the cast members knew anything about the haunting of Ringan's new home the previous summer; something in Penny had closed down at the thought of treating something so powerful as backstage chatter, mere gossip, or dinner table conversation. Betsy Roper, before her passage into whatever unimaginable corner of eternity had finally claimed her, had left a bit of herself with Penny. And Penny would not disrespect that memory, or take its results lightly.

"No. Penny—listen." David's head was canted sharply to one side. "Is there someone—Jesus! What on earth is that?"

Penny sucked in her breath. *No,* she thought, *no. Don't be this, don't do this. I'm not ready to deal with this.*

Whispering, harsh and guttural, rose from the floor, the seats, the ground beneath them. It gained resonance, lifting to a nearly metallic pitch of desperation. It filled the auditorium like a flood tide of dirty seawater.

*arrêtez mauvais mauvais j'ai offensé Dieu que vous avez offensé Dieu arrêtez libérez-moi trop chaud trop chaud les feux de l'enfer trop chaud me blesse me brûle arrêt*

The room filled with smoke. They could smell it, taste it on the still air; invisible, it forced itself into lungs, eyes, and nostrils. This time, the smell of water was entirely absent; here were wood and thatch, catching, feeding, jumping from joist to beam to eaves, taking and spreading. It was laced with ugliness, an unearthly barbecue neither meant nor fit for the human senses. Penny gagged, coughing, fanning at nothing, fighting for air. David Harkins, his jacket pulled up to protect his airways, was the colour of dirty ice. He looked blind.

"We have to get out." Penny, not knowing if her voice had sounded beyond her own bone-dry throat, got David by the sleeve of his jacket. Unheeded, the paperback Euripides fell from her lap to the carpet. "Hurry. Go. Come on, David, move!"

*Vite, je vous en prie, enlèvez-moi les dispositifs d'accrochage, s'il vous plait*

He came up limply, letting Penny drag him. As she pulled him up the aisle towards the foyer doors, stumbling and panting in whimpering breaths, she felt how physically unresponsive he seemed, heard his shallow gasps for air, and wondered if he was having a heart attack.

*un prêtre, je veux un prêtre, s'il vous plait, ne me laisse pas brûler. . . .*

The words, pulsing with tangible agony, crested and died as Penny kicked the foyer door open and wrenched David clear of the auditorium. Something, an audible memory or perhaps nothing more than an echo of those cries for pity and surcease, streamed out in a rush, through the propped-open front doors and into the chilly London afternoon, only to dissipate like burned-out fireflies as they met the reality of the modern world.

Into the absolute silence of the foyer crept the sound of hammering. Ringan's hired plumbers, working backstage, stolidly went about their jobs. Penny knew that the workmen had continued throughout the ordeal she and David had just come through; whatever had happened had happened only to the two of them. The pipefitters and solderers, fitting sinks into drywall, had been unaware and unaffected.

David's grasp on her arm, fingers digging nearly to the bone, made her jump and stifle a shriek of pain. She turned to face him and saw cold anger in his eyes.

"Did you know?" His voice was chilly, crisp, and held on a tight rein. "Can it be that you actually knew this theatre was haunted, haunted by something dangerous and potentially violent, and you didn't bother to tell us? Sweet Christ, Penny, how could you possibly have been so heedless?"

Amazed as much by his understanding of what had happened as by his unquestioning acceptance of a supernatural explanation for it, she gaped at him. Then she remembered: David Harkins was a devout Catholic.

"Get your coat and your bag," he told her tersely. "Come along. We're going down the pub and you're buying me a drink. You've got some explanations to make."

The Beldame was nearly empty when they arrived. The short walk from one end of Hawthorne Walk to the other had been made in absolute silence. Once established in a remote corner, Penny went to the bar, ordered two pints, and carried them back. David reached out, drained half his glass, and set it down again.

"Now then," he said. "Don't you think you'd better tell me a few things?"

"I'm going to." Penny had realised that the last thing in the world she wanted just then was beer; her stomach was unruly, whether from the encounter with the Bellefield's resident haunt or from the knowledge that she was going to have to explain to David, she wasn't sure. She took a tiny sip and pushed her glass away, shuddering.

"Right," she said, and squared her shoulders. "First of all, I didn't tell you because for one thing, we weren't sure what we were dealing with, and for another, it never occurred to me that anyone would believe it. That's my old Anglican bias. I have to see something for myself before I'll cope with it. But I'd forgotten you're Catholic—idiotic of me, I know. The Catholic Church believes in possession and hauntings and whatnot, doesn't it? You've even got an exorcism ritual, haven't you?"

"I believe we do." David was looking calmer, but no less intent; it was clear he was waiting, and would be satisfied with nothing less than the entire truth. Penny took in air, braced herself, and launched into the story of the haunting and exorcism of Betsy Roper and

Will Corby the previous summer. David listened without interruption, his face growing visibly more relaxed as the tale wound towards its conclusion. She finished up the Lumbe's Cottage haunting, and gave him a précis, omitting all detail, of what had happened to her and to Ringan at the Bellefield.

"So you see," Penny finished, "I wasn't planning on trying to hide it. I take it very seriously indeed—honestly, David, how could I not, after what happened last summer? I actually shared memories with that poor child. I just wasn't sure how to go about convincing all of you, because, let's face it, the bosom of the nice safe middle-of-the-road Anglican Church does not exactly welcome this sort of bump-in-the-night stuff. And I didn't even want to try and convince you until we had a better idea of what we're dealing with. Hopefully, I'll hear back from the man doing the research pretty damned quickly."

"Yes, I see. I understand, and I think you're probably handling it the best way possible." The taut, angry look was entirely gone from David's face. He merely looked interested. "Finding out who this person was—that part's being handled, you say? Are you sure the person researching is competent?"

"Retired deacon and archivist at St. Paul's for the better part of twenty years? I'd say we're in good hands." Penny's throat was dry from the long narrative, and she managed another mouthful of beer. "David, listen—do you think we should tell the others? And do you have any ideas about getting rid of this, well, whatever? As a practising Catholic, I mean."

"She's not a whatever, Penny. She's a ghost." His voice was very calm, very certain, and completely convincing. "A woman died badly, and from what I heard her screaming, I'd say she was a Catholic who was terrified of dying unshriven. I suspect that's precisely what happened, and that would be why she can't leave. She burned in there, inside the Bellefield, and she made no confession before she died, and now she's stuck in that moment, or at least that's what's happening if everything I've ever heard about hauntings is true. Dear lord, that poor thing. She was begging for a priest, and she was begging to have something—chains or shackles—taken off her. Were you able to hear that?"

"I heard it, yes. I don't know that I entirely share your sympathy, though. You haven't seen the gash she left across Ringan's face. I think she was a mean bitch, personally, although of course, I'd feel sorry for anyone or anything burning alive. And if she was shackled, she was likely under arrest for something, wasn't she?"

"It might have been heresy." David's voice was sombre. "Being burned for heresy, or even just for being Catholic, wasn't uncommon after Henry founded the Church of England."

Penny stared at the Beldame's plush booths and age-mellowed panelling, seeing nothing, trying to sort out the words that had slammed into her: *trop chaud trop chaud les feux de l'enfer trop chaud me blesse me brûle arrêt*—too hot, wasn't that? Too hot, the fires of hell, too hot, it hurts, stop . . . "This is the second time I've heard her, you know," she mused aloud. "The first time was a sort of muttery whisper, and it wasn't a variety of French I could really follow. Today she sounded a lot more clear. Right around the time the whole theatre started smelling like it was up in flames, I thought I heard something about someone offending God, but I could be wrong. I missed the last bit of whatever she was yelling; I was too busy being terrified that you might be having a heart attack. I'd never have forgiven myself."

"I know." He touched the back of her hand lightly. "I'm fine. Nothing wrong with my ticker. You asked two questions a few minutes ago. Should we tell the others? Yes, absolutely. Whether they believe it or not is strictly their business, but you'd best give them the option, for legal reasons if for no other reason."

"Oh, my God." She shook her head, dismayed. "The workmen, too. Lovely, perfectly lovely, just what I need, a lawsuit for being injured by being thrown off a scaffold by something they can hear but can't see. David, you're dead right, I'm a heedless idiot. I need to get back to the theatre. Ringan should be there by now. I'll let him tell them."

She began gathering her belongings. David held up a hand. "Penny, wait a moment, yes? Your second question—you asked if I had any ideas about getting rid of this ghost. I believe I do. But I think we'll need to wait until your deacon friend comes back with some solid information. An exorcism isn't something to be approached lightly, and you're quite right about needing to know just what we're dealing with."

It was not until much later that Penny realised she had never given David her reasons for wanting to do *Iphigenia*.


In a small, well-lit room in the bowels of St. Paul's Cathedral, Richard Halligan was taking notes.

The piles of books, documents, registers, maps, and papers that surrounded him in every direction would have seemed like total chaos to the casual observer. In fact, they were sorted to their last possible category subdivision. Halligan had thirty years of experience behind him as a researcher, and his methods were as logical as his work was meticulous.

He was writing in longhand, in an old-fashioned lined notebook. Several pages were already covered; at the top of the page on which he was presently working was a header, in bold black upper case: **HAWTHORNE WALK—14th CENTURY.**

Halligan leaned back in his chair, put his hands behind his head, and allowed himself a good long stretch. He took his glasses off and laid them aside, as he rubbed his eyes and closed them briefly. In his opinion, hunching over a desk for hours at a time was something too many people did without considering the implications for their health in later years. He had trained himself to ease his attention at reasonable intervals, to rest his eyes, to let his muscles relax. It was doubly important to relax when working with material of the kind he was presently using; a large register, bound in leather, opened to a page of tiny handwriting. The task was further complicated by the bulk of the information having been written in Silver Period Latin. Halligan, unusual among his peers, had never quite mastered the intricacies of Latin grammar. Translation was, for him, a tiresome and careful labour.

Presently he sighed, retrieved his glasses, and straightened up in his chair. Working slowly and methodically, he read a few words of tiny, back-sloping script. This had obviously been transcribed by a clerk of Richard Plantagenet's court. Halligan consulted a Latin grammar text on one corner of the desk, and jotted down notes. Gradually, the page in his notebook took shape as something legible: a land grant, from king to duke.

> Granted, from His Sovereign Most Gracious *(memo to self, "gracious" probably wrong, check if needed)* Richard Plantagenet to his Most Worthy *(note, Worthy improper word most likely, confirm)* Uncle and Regent, John, Earl of Richmond, Duke of Lancaster, King of Leon and Castile, un seigneur royal et puissant *(note to self—why the sudden switch to French?)* in service to the Crown, the land called the Hawthorne Way *(note: printing faded here, could be "field" or "walk")* from the Fleet to *(something something)* bordered southward by the Thames, for the erection of dwellings *(something something— "buildings of purpose"? check this)* that might house those Officials of our Laws, answerable to our gracious Uncle. Dated this third day of April, 1380.

Halligan sat quietly, staring in fascination at the original for a moment. On the page was a thin, wavering signature: "Le Roy R.S." Beside that, the boy-king's heraldic shield, beautifully drawn in miniature, vivid in scarlet, blue, and gold. *Richard would have been thirteen at the time,* Halligan thought, and felt an odd lump in his throat. There was something moving about that careful, uncertain spider scrawl, from a child dead these six hundred years.

He sternly swallowed the lump. It was silly to feel sorry for kings. They were who they were, there were personal power and bottomless wealth and unthinkable benefit to match every drawback attendant to their birthright. Besides, hadn't this one tried to get rid of parliament entirely, and install an absolute monarchy in its place? Personal power, indeed.

True, the son of the Black Prince had been born with a hard row to hoe, with an imperious uncle, vast changes in a world he was too young to comprehend, and the justifiable rage of reformers such as John Ball and Wat Tyler to cope with. His own death, too, had been horrific: left to starve in one of his own castles at the age of thirty. He'd lost his beloved queen as well, hadn't he? Anne of Bohemia, dead of plague at Sheen Castle. If the story was true, Richard had gone insane with grief, so much so that he'd burned Sheen to the ground.

But here, in that clerk's careful transcription of a royal decision, was confirmation of one thing Penny had wanted to know, and Halligan, that veteran researcher, was surprised to feel a surge of pride at having found it. One year before the peasants had poured across the Thames and set London's North Bank afire, Richard II had indeed granted the patch of land called Hawthorne Walk to his overpowering Uncle John. Interesting, though, an interesting thing: it seemed to be a specific charter, for the building of homes for— who, exactly?

Halligan checked the original, and translated it once again, aloud, slowly and carefully: "that might house those Officials of our Laws, answerable to our gracious Uncle."

Officials of our Laws. Now, what on earth did that mean? Bailiffs? Magistrates? Warders, perhaps? There were no police, as such, not in the fourteenth century; Robert Peel wouldn't set up London's police force until a few hundred years after that.

Halligan considered the question, and found no immediate answers. Surely Richard hadn't been referring to the notorious and infamous Cheshire Guard? He dismissed the idea at once. Those marauding thugs answered to none but Richard himself; three hundred men wearing Richard's personal emblem, the white hart, raping, looting, and taking what they wanted, with no one to stop them. They would never, as the land grant clearly stated as a condition, have been answerable to John of Gaunt. If Richard had been denied his absolute monarchy by Parliament, he had come awfully close to achieving it with the Cheshire Guard.

Halligan closed the register and set it carefully atop a stack of others on the floor. In its place, he set the pile of maps, many of them originals sealed in double-sided protective plastic, others modern reprints of ancient drawings too fragile, or valuable, to be handled.

Halligan loved maps. There was something about a good map, particularly a lovingly handcrafted one, that was, to him, humanity at both its cleanest and its most self-deluding. On the one hand, here was love of the earth below the mapmaker's feet, respect for the curve of river and hill, the atavistic understanding that as this land went, so went the life and death of the people who worked it. On the other hand was greed for that same land, a need to mark territory as one's own, to erect fences, to stake a claim and keep others out. Here were the very seeds of war and discontent.

He gently and lovingly sifted his way down the map pile. Southwark, his own neighbourhood, in a lively little drawing by an unknown cartographer from the year 1622, nearly derailed his search; completely charmed, he spent five minutes trying to pinpoint where his own three-room flat, with its high ceilings and commanding views of the river and City skyline, might be. After a few minutes of self-indulgence, he set the Southwark map reluctantly back in its place and continued his methodical hunt, down the stack, chronologically backward in time.

He had nearly reached the bottom before he found what he'd been after: a smallish, faded map on what looked to be a good heavy vellum, at least so far as he could tell beneath the map's protective plastic. With a feeling of deep satisfaction, he slid it free from the others.

The map had been drawn in ink, and it had been drawn well. The method used was, in itself, rather surprising; most maps of the period were woodcuts, made with the predetermined purpose of being bound into volumes. A brief examination of the map's clean, uniform edges showed no sign that this charming piece had ever been bound into anything. Yet another small mystery; this particular project seemed to be accumulating rather a lot of them.

Halligan adjusted his glasses and studied details. Here was the northern curve of the Thames, serpentine and graceful. Southwark dominated the bottom half, the borough's name written carefully and rather elegantly in a straight line, accentuating the sloping eastbound curl of the river above it. To the north was a detailed welter of information and images: borough names, from Shoreditch in the extreme northeast corner to Tyburn in the extreme northwest.

Halligan shuddered, without quite understanding why, and then remembered: Tyburn Hill was the killing field, the site where those who had fallen from grace under the Crown's definition of law had once been publicly hanged. That was well after the time he was researching, of course. In any case, it didn't apply if you were unlucky enough to have been sentenced to burn. You would have met that barbaric death at Smithfield, across from St. Bartholemew's Hospital, a bare stone's throw from where he now sat. Tyburn was marked on the map with nothing more than a careful rendering of its own name.

He returned his attention to the map. Here was the Tower of London at the northeastern edge of the river. Beside it, London Bridge, bewilderingly solitary to an eye accustomed to modern London's plethora of bridges. Between London Bridge and the ancient home of the Knights Templar lay the detail Halligan sought.

Here were individual streets, carefully rendered: the Strand, Fleet Street, Arundel. Some spots bore tiny landmarks, crafted as sharply limned flags to catch the eye: at Smithfield Market, for instance, was a tiny heap of something that looked like a bound sheaf of wheat, until he looked more closely and saw the flames leaping from its crown. Something cold moved down Halligan's back; why did this exquisite bit of priceless nonsense seem so familiar?

He peered at the area of interest to Penny. Here was the alley, unnamed on this map; clearly, this was Hawthorne Walk. And though the street itself was unnamed, there was something drawn there, taking up half of the south side of the Walk, from about the centre of the street to its southwestern edge. It looked rather like a series of brackets, back to back, linked in a line like can-can dancers. Was there something else there?

He moved the map carefully, trying different angles, shifting it by degrees. It was no good; try as he might, Halligan couldn't decipher the drawing. The protective plastic reflected too much of the overhead light, the drawing was faded and tiny, and his glasses simply weren't up to the task. This would require a good magnifying lens; hopefully, the current deacon would have one and be willing to lend it. Otherwise, a trip across the river to his own flat would be needed.

Halligan turned the map over. There was writing on the back, small, careful calligraphy, in a style he recognised as typical of an educated man of the fourteenth century. There were several lines of it, in fact, beginning with the cartographer's personal information. He had a moment of lightheadedness. This looked to save him rather a lot of hunting.

"*Delineavit et descripsit, Humphrey Lynde, 1381,*" Halligan muttered. "Drawn and mapped by Humphrey Lynde. All right, then. Must have been just before the rebellion. What have we got?"

He read a bit further. His brows drew together. A bit below Lynde's name was a small drawing, an echo of the linked brackets on the map's face, that marked Hawthorne Walk. The inscription that followed, tantalisingly incomplete, was in English.

"By charter, this Purview of Johannes of Ghent, herein is Residence of Martin Saxton, Wardour of those Womyn who have thyr God and King offended. Never by law to be commingled with . . . " and here, faded with age and the grime of centuries, the finicky script became illegible.

Halligan set the map down. His palms had gone a bit clammy.

*Wardour to those Womyn.* Answerable to Johannes of Ghent—John of Gaunt. A woman's prison? Had there been a prison at the Savoy Palace itself and, if not, where had it been? It would take a bit more digging, but the plain fact seemed pretty clear and was, after all, corroborated by both map and register. The section of Hawthorne Walk that now held the Bellefield Theatre had once housed wardours of women prisoners. Presumably, the chief wardour had been one Martin Saxton. . . .

"Richard? How are you doing?"

Halligan swivelled in his chair. The present deacon, Roger Clarrey, had stuck his head around the door.

"Afternoon, Roger. Come in, do. I was actually about to come upstairs; I need a bit of backup, if you wouldn't mind."

Clarrey grinned. "And I was actually just coming down to see if you wanted to break for some food. You've been down here five solid hours, did you know? Come have a cuppa and a sandwich and tell me how I can help."

Half an hour later, sitting in the office that had for so long been Halligan's, the two men pushed their empty cups aside and got down to business. Between mouthfuls of ham sandwiches and swallows of tea, Halligan had given his successor the story of his meeting with Penny, her request for information, and where his own research was leading him. Clarrey, twenty years his junior and with a nice edge of fortyish energy to balance his scholarly bent, was clearly enthused by the project.

"So," he said, when Halligan had finished, "you need, what? A good magnifying lens, for closer work on that map, that's one thing. Some deeper identification, any pertinent details, on the wardour that's mentioned, and also about that particular mapmaker? Have I got it right?"

"Martin Saxton, wardour, and Humphrey Lynde, mapmaker extraordinaire. Yes, please, and seeing as how much stronger at Latin you are than I am, I may well plead for a bit translation help there, as well."

"But of course." Clarrey reflected briefly that one of Richard Halligan's nicest personality traits was his willingness to admit a weakness. "All the translation you need."

"Thanks. One more thing—I'd appreciate anything you can come up with about the Savoy Palace as a home for 'those Womyn who have thyr God and King offended.' I never knew there was a women's prison at the Savoy, never came across anything about it that I can recall. And it appears to be vital to whatever's going on at the Bellefield Theatre, Hawthorne Walk."

"Well, I can help with information on your two blokes, easily enough. But—'going on'?" Clarrey's eyebrows lifted. "What a peculiar way to put it, Richard. You think something's happening there? Isn't this all history we're talking about?"

Halligan was silent. He felt a strong reluctance to betray anything that Penny herself might have considered a confidence when she made it. Was it necessary that Roger be told of his own suspicion, borne of Penny's own veiled urgency and secrecy, that something of the past was refusing to relinquish its hold on Hawthorne Walk?

He opened his mouth and closed it again. As he did so, he caught Clarrey's eye, and saw shrewdness and sympathy there.

"Not to worry," Clarrey told him lightly. "I'm acting just like one of my own cats, all curiosity and whatnot. Very rude of me. Let me hunt up a good strong lens for you to work with, and I'll get onto Saxton and Lynde. As a matter of fact, I should have something for you quite soon, because if I'm not mistaken, I recognise one of those two names. We'll rescue your mysterious thespian on Hawthorne Walk from whatever's bothering her, never fear."

# Five

*But all alone in my bed at e'en*
*Oh there I dreamed a dreadful dream*
*I saw my bed swim with blood*
*And I saw the thieves all around my head*

As roofers carefully checked the Bellefield for holes and patches, and fabric specialists measured rail-to-floor length for new curtains in the theatre's first-floor luxury boxes, Penny assembled the Tamburlaine Players for their first serious group discussion of the upcoming production of *Iphigenia*.

With Ringan and David Harkins beside her, she had summoned up her courage and told the players the full story of both hauntings to date. Nothing pertinent had been held back; Ringan had offered corroboration and David Harkins had lent additional weight by relating his own experience. If the two younger players took the threat of being haunted lightly, Donal McCreary did not. Penny was aware of a feeling of relief; the knowledge that the Tamburlaines' two senior statesmen would at least help keep the children in line was very reassuring.

Ringan had done the same with the workmen, bluntly telling them a truncated version of the Bellefield's situation. With Penny's authority as backup, he'd insisted on signed waivers, and offered to void their contracts without penalty or prejudice if they were uncomfortable with either the waiver or the ongoing situation. Whether from reluctance to walk away from an easy job and lucrative contract or from personal disbelief in the situation as stated, no one had taken Ringan up on his offer. The restoration of the Bellefield was proceeding on schedule.

The Tamburlaine Players, as a group, had set up shop on the stage itself; Penny had brought in folding chairs and a small, sturdy wooden table. Sides of the play, which would be each cast member's working copy, were being printed. Once the electrical systems were confirmed as safe, Robin brought in tea and an electric kettle, and Petra contributed disposable cups and a tin of shortbread. Fortified with food and drink, notebooks ready, Penny and her troupe got down to business.

Outside, things were less cosy. The January weather was miserable, a howling wind buffeting the city, carrying with it a dismal sleety rain that needled and stung, and refused to soften into proper snow. Since outdoor work was clearly impossible under these conditions, the three roofers had moved indoors. They could be heard moving about overhead, looking for rot in the timbers, checking load-bearing beams for strength and soundness.

Penny, who usually stuck to a tried-and-true routine for pre-production cast sessions, was deviating from the norm this time. She was, after all, scarcely more familiar with the play than her cast was. Although she always sought input from the actors on how they perceived their individual contributions, issues such as set design and costuming had, for the ten years of the Players' existence, been her exclusive purview.

Everything about the situation was new, however, and Penny knew it. She had thrown the doors wide for any ideas anyone might have on any aspect of the upcoming production: costumes, set design, the number of outsiders that should be cast for the Chorus, and most vitally, where the rest of the cast felt the play should be trimmed for the modern ear. On that subject, at least, there was complete agreement among everyone concerned: Euripides had written a wonderful play, and as it stood, it would take five hours to perform, cost a fortune to produce, and leave a modern audience snoring in their seats.

"If we were doing it in Greek, I suppose that would be entirely different." Robin sucked down the dregs of his lukewarm tea, twisted his classic features into a small-boy grimace, and got up to make himself a fresh cup. "But right now, we've got five-minute declamatory speeches which are promptly recapped, in full, by the Chorus. It feels—what's the word? I don't know—redundant, ponderous. Something, anyway. Not flowing."

"Unwieldy, possibly." Penny nodded her agreement. "Wordy? Top-heavy? The language is glorious, mind you, but I feel quite strongly that we want a very streamlined version—almost sleek in feel. You know, taking it down to the nub: A parent who is actually willing to murder their own daughter to get what they want, the rage, the lie, the willingness of Iphigenia herself to offer up her throat for her father and the honour of Greece. Honour, naïveté, personal interest, and murder. Bare bones."

"Can we stress the fact that just because Artemis swoops her off to hang out with the Taureans, that doesn't let Agamemnon off the hook as a murderer? Without me having to play the girl as the sort of noble virgin I always wanted to slap at school?" Petra, in black jeans and an oversized sweater, looked young, small, and as tough as shoe leather. "You know what I mean—dainty lace collars and pearls? I really don't want her to come across that way. It would be too easy, to play her smug."

A banging from behind the proscenium, followed immediately by the emergence of Ringan and an unknown workman from the backstage area, pre-empted Penny's reply. The two men carried a long collapsible ladder between them, each holding an end.

"Half a tick," Penny told the troupe, and jumped down from the stage to talk to Ringan.

"Hello," he told her. "It's all right, you go back to whipping the play into shape. We've got a ladder that opens to thirty feet, so we're off to check out the foyer murals. Oh, this is Ray. He restores gilding. Ray, this is Penny, our boss."

"Hello, Ray, lovely to meet you. Keep me posted, Ringan, will you? I'm dying to know what they are—still haven't got a good look, you know." Penny planted a quick kiss on one bewhiskered cheek and went back to the on-stage group, who were, depending on their bent, either displaying a well-bred pretence that they hadn't seen the kiss or frankly grinning.

"All right then," she told them austerely, "you lot just behave yourselves. Now. Where were we? Right, the girl herself and stream-lining everything about the play. I have some ideas about the design for the backdrops. . . ."

In the foyer, Ringan and Ray set the ladder down. Even with the wall sconces turned on, the foyer ceiling was impossible to see in any detail. Ringan, craning his neck with no better result than a blur, wondered why they'd bothered putting a gilded mural up there in the first place. Wasn't the idea for people to actually be able to see it? Once the design inside those gilded squares was identified and restored, he was going to suggest to Penny, rather strongly, that they spend a few quid on installing a discreet row of spotlights along the halfway point in the walls. Surely, whatever was up there deserved a decent view, especially since it would basi-cally be the first thing the paying public saw when they entered the Bellefield.

"I wonder what they are?" Ringan craned his neck. "Damn. It's too dark in here. Ray, do you want to go up, or should I?"

"Doesn't matter, mate. Either way." Ray Haddon, a hefty man in his early fifties, was a taciturn Geordie who had never, during twenty years of living in London, become acclimatised to life in the south of England. He had managed to tone down his original Newcastle accent to the point where people other than his fellow Geordies could understand more than one word in five. Since he rarely used more than five words unless he was discussing his work, this was just as well.

Between them, grunting and puffing, they got the ladder erected. Opened to its full height, it was perfect for a good viewing, al-though a bit short for actual touch-ups or genuine work. They stood at the base, regarding the distance between the ladder's top-most step and the ceiling.

"About seven feet, I'd say," Ray announced. "It's me up, then. I'm taller than you."

Ray went up with the ease of long practice. Ringan, never really comfortable with heights, watched thankfully from below. After a minute or two, he got impatient.

"Ray? What have we got? Talk to me, mate."

"Sorry—I was having a good look," Ray called back down, craning his neck casually over the ladder's back end. He sounded, for him, wildly enthusiastic. "We've got tragedy and comedy masks. Gorgeous ones, too, perfect late Vic. Whoever the artist was, he had a nice touch. These are a checkerboard pattern—they alternate. Comedy, tragedy, one to a square. The gilding's lovely, but it's a bit worn. Shouldn't be hard to fix up, or too pricey, either."

"Penny's likely going to kiss you and then dance a bit when she hears that." Ringan grinned upward, and tilted his head. "What? What did you say?"

Ray didn't reply. From thirty feet below, Ringan wondered why Ray's voice had dropped so low, and strained to hear. But when words came clear to him, they made no sense. And there was something odd about Ray's stance, a rigidity that looked as unnatural as it did uncomfortable.

*Sortez! Vous êtes mauvais! Vous devriez être dans l'enfer! Sortez, sortez! Allez loin d'ici! Vous n'êtes pas mon enfant! Mon enfant est morte. Je l'ai tuée et l'ai envoyée à Dieu.*

Too late, Ringan understood what was happening.

High atop his ladder, Ray Haddon heard a voice. He spoke no French; the words meant nothing. He would have paid them no attention in any event, for he had none to spare. Above him, just out of reach, something was happening that was not possible.

*Sortez, sortez, sortez! Le diable rit de vous!*

Smiles. There were too many smiles. Curving painted white mouths that had been turned down to weep for tragedy were grinning, leering, stretching in ghastly grimaces. Fire came from those mouths, fire that led into the pits of hell where someone, something, was burning and waiting. . . .

At the base of the ladder, Ringan stood helpless. He couldn't see what was happening to the ceiling; he was too far away to make out details. But there was no missing the light, a cold hellish light, bright, intolerable, that poured from the ceiling like streams from a pulsar. It snaked down the foyer's pretty crimson walls like evil rivers, and it enveloped Ray Haddon, standing on a ladder in its path.

"Ray! *Ray!*"

Ringan was shouting. He was unaware of this until shouting, making any noise at all, became something his body could no longer accomplish. The simple act of drawing breath became nearly impossible; the air in the room was suddenly as dense as sea-water. It was rank, hideous. Ringan felt his lungs clog with a smell that was as close to living flesh burning as anyone who had not lived through a war could know.

In the auditorium, Penny was on her feet. They had all heard it, the woman's voice, the crying out in French, the statement of murder. There was no way to say where that voice came from: it was above them, below them, all around them.

And Ringan was shouting. While the rest of the cast sat frozen, Penny was already moving. She vaulted from the edge of the stage to the pit below, narrowly missed breaking an ankle as her foot turned on impact, and, ignoring the pain, ran like a deer towards the house doors.

Halfway between the stage and the doors, she stopped as if she'd been shot in the back.

Pictures flooded her mind—huge, bright, blazing with light and unearthly colours. The aisles and carpeting of the Bellefield faded into nothing more than a backdrop for incomprehensible images: a young woman screaming in a canopied bed, a dead man beside her in a pool of his own blood, an infant with its throat slit. Above all, surmounting the intolerable carnage that moved mercilessly behind Penny's vision, a woman's face: older, sharp, with a lush wide mouth that pinched hard and tight at the corners, pushing itself closed against generosity or warmth, the face of the evil twisted witch in the fairy tale, something tainted, something mad, something who had lost all love and all warmth and everything she had ever loved . . .

"Ringan! Oh God, oh God—Ringan! Make it stop, make it

stop, someone make it stop." Penny took a single faltering step, stumbled, and sank to her knees. The pictures streamed on, inexorable, unbearable: the sharp-faced woman in chains now, a distant shouting of a thousand voices, crashing, the sounds of carnage and the trampling of an army of feet, fire erupting, flame, the building was ablaze, it was burning, she had chains that bound her tight and she couldn't run, she couldn't flee, she was going to die here, she was going to burn as she would burn in the fires of the Devil, burn because she had tried to give her own guilty child to God and had given God the blood of an innocent instead, burn because she would die unshriven of that crime, burn because she had led an innocent into death, burn in the pits of Hell.

*Eleanor, j'ai voulu que vous comprissiez. J'ai voulu que vous sentissiez le feu. Pourquoi suis-je ici, brûlant au lieu de vous?*

She was burning alive, the shackles were hot against her flesh and the leg irons burned like the Devil's brand into her ankles, she was on fire, the hawthorn stuffed into the cracks of this little house was greedy flickering tongues of pain sent to take her, wanting her, reaching for her. . . .

Penny was unaware of herself. She was unaware of her troupe of actors, all with watering eyes and clogging lungs, forcing themselves up the aisle towards her, through an atmosphere that felt at once as thick as quicksand and as lacking in air as the upper reaches of Everest. She was unaware of herself, hunched up and whimpering on the aisle floor, eyes wide open because closing them blocked nothing, unaware of her own living hands pressed against her ears to somehow muffle the agonised screams of the dead murderess as she fought through the smoke and flames that engulfed her, six centuries away.

Just beyond the swinging house doors, Ray Haddon's heart stopped. He came off the ladder, a dead man and a dead weight, crashing thirty feet to the ugly carpeted floor below.

"Apparently, it was a massive heart attack. The hospital's been on to his doctor. Turns out he had a family history of heart trouble—high blood pressure, cholesterol, the lot. His father died of a coronary."

Penny, her face drawn and colourless, looked up at Ringan from the sofa in her living room. Several hours had passed since the ambulance had screamed off into the afternoon, bearing Ray Haddon towards the nearest casualty ward. It was useless, of course; he'd been dead at the scene, and all attempts at restarting his heart had failed.

"She killed him." Penny's voice was flat. She had barely recovered from the events of the afternoon; moving was an act of will, and she felt as though she might never have any energy to spare again. She had a headache, as well, a deep grinding pain behind her eyes. It frightened her; everything about this ghost frightened her. Nothing in her previous exposure, to Betsy Roper and Will Corby, had left her feeling like this. "He had a heart attack because of her— Eleanor's mother. He'd have died without a weak heart. She wanted him to die, and he died." Her voice cracked suddenly. "Bloody evil murdering *bitch*."

Ringan made no reply. He picked up her cup of tea and headed into the kitchen with it. A few minutes later, the homely sound of a whistling kettle echoed through the flat. Ringan returned with a fresh cup, and set it down on the table beside her.

"All right," he said quietly. "She killed him. We can't fix that, Penny—it's done. And you know, I sort of get that you don't want to allow youself any sympathy for this woman at all. I understand that. . . ."

"Do you?" Penny looked up at him. "How, Ringan? You haven't been the one hammered by this. None of it's got inside you, has it? All your witnessing's been done from the outside, looking on. You think I'm being hard-hearted? I'm not giving her any sympathy? I felt her burn, love. I felt it in my flesh. But I also felt what she'd done, to get there. Don't forget that."

"All right," Ringan repeated. That Penny was wrestling with her own feelings was patent; trying to make her feel guilty about lack of compassion, when she'd been so much closer to the fire and so scored by the unknown woman's memories, would do nothing but make the situation worse. All he could do was to be there for

Penny, and offer support as needed. "The thing now is, how in heaven's name do we get her off the premises? Because you can hardly expose any more workmen to the risk—the next victim might be a twenty-year-old pipefitter who runs marathons on Sundays, with no heart condition to explain it away. And are you going to expose the Tamburlaines to more of this?"

"Of course I'm not. Are you insane?" Penny eased herself upright and took a cautious sip of tea, wincing as her head gave a warning throb. "God, my legs feel like blancmange right now. I'll call the cast tomorrow and tell them the play's on hold, and Albert as well—and may I say, I am so not looking forward to talking to the Right Hon about this? Lovely business deal I've got him into. Of course, I'll offer him the option of backing out. Even if I were callous enough, or ambitious enough, to risk people's lives over this, I couldn't bank on bad publicity not killing the production anyway. If the papers get wind of it . . ." She shuddered, and sipped her tea.

"I wish I spoke French." Ringan sounded regretful. "I heard her say the name—Eleanor—and I know that she was yelling about God, and doesn't *sortez* mean 'get out of here' or something like that? But the rest of it . . ."

"*Sortez,* get out. It's a command, an order. She was talking to someone, Ringan—maybe to more than one person. I can't quite sort it out. When I first heard her, she was yelling at someone or something to get out—and she also said something about the Devil laughing at whoever she was talking to." *That voice,* Penny thought, *that awful voice; if grave mould could speak, surely it would sound like that voice.* "But then she told whoever it was that they weren't her child, because her child was dead, she'd killed her child and sent it to God."

"But wasn't she talking to the woman called Eleanor? Her daughter? I couldn't have imagined that, Penny; you don't imagine speeches in languages you don't speak yourself, not unless you also think you're Catherine of Aragon and converse with the ghost of St. Vitus at the weekend."

Penny grinned, a small genuine smile that died away at once.

"That's why I said she was talking to more than one person. First she said, You aren't my child, I killed my child and gave it to God; then she turned around and spoke to Eleanor. I remember exactly what she said there, Ringan, word for word. She said, *Eleanor, j'ai voulu que vous comprissiez. J'ai voulu que vous sentissiez le feu. Pourquoi suis-je ici, brûlant au lieu de vous?* And that roughly means 'Eleanor, I wanted you to understand. I wanted you to feel the fires of Hell. How is that I must burn here, in your place?'"

There was a moment of silence. The skin around Ringan's mouth was blue-white as he pressed his lips together. There was nothing to say; the picture conjured up by the words alone was sufficiently ugly to stifle speech. That Penny had been forced to witness the visual as well left him helplessly enraged.

"And then she called on the Virgin Mary for help." Penny pursed her lips and blew air out of her lungs, as though she wanted to expel the sour memory of those unnatural visions along with her breath. "So—she was talking to at least two people. Or else she was completely loopy, and talking to herself the whole time. Oh dear. Nasty idea."

"Very. I'm so sorry you had to deal with that, love." He forced his mind back to practicality. "D'ye know what I find odd? The fact that none of the roofers heard her, or felt anything strange. Apparently, they came down just because they heard me yelling for Ray and thought there must be a problem. Whereas your actors all got broadsided with the whole package: maniacal on-fire lady screeching away in French, smell of burning, lungs refusing to function, the lot. It strikes me there's something awfully selective about this ghost."

"Broadsided? Good word, that. It doesn't even come close to describing what hit me, though." Penny's pupils contracted with a remembered horror. "I wish I could make more sense of whatever came ramming through my head, but those pictures were so confused. . . . I do know that the girl in the bed, the one I saw holding the murdered baby, was called Eleanor. And the ghost, the Bellefield's bitch-haunt, was Eleanor's mother. And from what she was saying—she ordered her daughter killed, Ringan. And the men she hired to do it, they didn't. They slashed a baby's throat, Eleanor's baby. I saw it bleeding. It was so blue, and cold-looking, and so tiny . . . oh, God, *God*."

The china cup began to shake in Penny's hand, sloshing a few drops of tea over the rim. Ringan took it from her, set it down, and covered her hands with his own, stilling them.

"It's all right." Ringan kept his voice very calm, very quiet. "At least, no, it's not all right, but it happened a very long time ago and there's nothing you can do about it now. It's history. What we need to do now is to find out who this woman was and why she's hanging about your theatre. And then we're putting her out on her arse. I refuse to worry about this one's soul."

Penny shivered suddenly, felt around, dug a soft fleecy shawl from where it had got wedged between the sofa cushions, and draped it over her shoulders. "I wish I could get warm. You realise, don't you, that what I saw is an absolute mirror of that song, the one you were playing when she attacked you? What's that thing called, again?"

" 'The Famous Flower of Serving Men.' Yes, indeed. We're going to need to go over that again, verse by verse, I think, and trust me, lovey, it's got masses of verses. Still, I think the story's all there, or most of it, anyway." Ringan sat down beside Penny; the emotional horrors and physical rigours of Ray Haddon's death were taking a cumulative toll.

"Penny love," he said gently, "I know this is hard. But can you tell me what else you saw? I know you've told me what you heard, but the visual, well—I want to see if what you saw is really reflected in the song; we could save ourselves some trouble, if it is."

"I saw her in chains. I saw *myself* in chains. She was me, or I was her." The picture came back into Penny's mind, the smell, the crackle of flame, the nauseating pervasive reek of death and terror and insanity. She steadied herself, and tried to speak calmly and flatly. "Some kind of leg irons. There was someone in the room with her—a man. He wasn't clear, not very, just bits of him through the smoke. Oh!"

"Something? What is it?"

"On his chest—he was wearing something, I don't know if it

was sewn on, or painted, or what. A badge? Anyway, it was on the left side of his chest, high up, near the shoulder. I don't know why I didn't remember this earlier; it was one of the most vivid things, clear as anything, right through all the smoke."

"Really? How odd. What was it? The badge, I mean?"

"A picture of some sort of white animal, it might have been a deer, or a stag: I remember seeing very long straight golden horns. It looked like one of those lovely bits of stylised fluff you might see in a family crest. You know, the whole heraldry thing—a white deer dancing with a bar sinister and a bend unguled, or whatever the terminology is. It seemed to be prancing, with its front legs all tucked up, really rather sweet. And it had a crown around its neck, a golden crown."

"Oh my." Ringan's head was tilted and his beard was jutting, a sure sign of interest. "Penny, have you got an encyclopaedia here? I do believe we've got something."

"Bedroom, small bookshelf by the window. Right down at the bottom, last two shelves—there's an old edition of the *Britannica*. Help yourself." She leaned back against the sofa, closing her eyes and trying to decide whether a glass of brandy was in order. She heard Ringan go and return, and opened her eyes as he sank down on the sofa beside her.

"Look." A volume lay in his lap. He flipped it open, one fingertip resting beside a small picture, a reproduction of a two-sided painting. "Look, and try to remember. It's important. Is this what you saw? The badge, I mean?"

Penny glanced up at him, puzzled by his intensity, and then obediently down at the picture. Her eyes focussed on a tiny little man, kneeling; behind him were three men or angels, complete with halos. He was facing what was obviously the Virgin and Child, flanked by saints or archangels. On his breast was a minuscule device of some sort; the device was echoed on the robes of the Virgin's entourage. It was a classic work of its period, and it was very familiar.

"What is this?" She bent her head farther, moving the book on Ringan's knee, trying to catch the light from the ceiling fixture, cutting down the glare. "I've seen this before, I know I have, but I can't place it—Oh! Yes, that's what I saw. It's a deer, isn't it? With the crown around its neck?"

"Reproduction of the *Wilton Diptych.*" Ringan was deeply satisfied. *Got you,* he thought fiercely, *got you. We know where to look for you now. There's nowhere to hide, not for you. We know when you lived, we'll find when you died, and we'll know who you were.* "The diptych was a portable altar, actually made for Richard II; the white hart with the crown was his personal emblem. His guards all wore it. And yes, you've seen the *Diptych* before; it's in the National Gallery."

"Then—we've got her. Or at least, we know where to look for her. You were right about it not being the Great Fire, Ringan. It must have been the Peasants' Rebellion, the fire I saw." Penny was on her feet, heading for the phone, displaying animation for the first time since Ray Haddon had crashed to his death. "I need to find Richard Halligan's number. Oh lord, my message light's blinking up a storm—tomorrow, I'm not dealing with it tonight. I wonder if there are any records that didn't go up in smoke, of prisoners' names and crimes and such?"

"And I wonder who the bloke with Richard's emblem was, the one you saw. One of the king's men, obviously, if he was wearing that badge, but what was he doing guarding a woman prisoner? Richard's guard had a very specific purpose, and that wasn't it."

"That's what we've got to find out. And it seems to me Dr. Halligan is just the man who'd know."

As Penny reached for the phone, it rang under her hand. She jumped, gasped and steadied herself, and clicked it on. "Hello? Oh—Donal. I was going to call you all in the morning. It's about the play. After what happened at the Bellefield today, I think we need to call a moratorium on . . . what?"

Ringan, absent-mindedly helping himself to the remainder of Penny's rapidly cooling tea, heard the emphatic crackle of Donal McCreary's voice through Penny's phone. Busily gloating over the tiny reproduction of the *Wilton Diptych,* wondering where to look for the records that would give them the name of the ghost who had killed Ray Haddon, he barely heard Penny's end of the conversation as it washed over him.

"Donal, that's absurdly brave of you, but—no, listen, there are safety issues we have to keep in mind—look, I know you're all being supportive, I understand that and I appreciate it, but really—are you joking, you can't honestly think I'd consider exposing you all to— you all saw what happened today, what this thing is capable of— besides, Petra, Robin, David—no, wait—Donal, are you sure? It could be dangerous. . . . " Ringan closed the encyclopaedia and returned it tidily to its place on Penny's shelves. When he came back to the living room, Penny had rung off.

"That was Donal." She looked stunned. "He's had a meeting with the others. They want—no, they're insisting on going on with the production. They want to get together at the Beldame tomorrow for steak and kidney pie, and tell me why."

"Is he barmy?" Ringan was as startled as Penny. "Christ, Penny, he was in the theatre today. They all were. They saw what happened to Ray. Don't they realise how iffy this is? Especially if the play is likely to provoke more of the same?"

"You'd think so, wouldn't you?" Penny was clearly amazed. "What with none of them being stupid? But when I say insisting, I mean precisely that. He sounded quite fierce about it. I mean, it seemed—I don't know, a personal issue, or something."

"Good heavens, a show of suicidal loyalty. Do you know, I find that remarkably sweet, all things considered." Ringan shook his head. "Insane, mind you. But still sweet."

Penny opened her mouth to reply, but was forestalled by the phone ringing yet again.

"Oh criminy, now what? The place is like Victoria Station tonight." She lifted the receiver. "Hello? Richard! My word, either you're psychic or else you've got remarkable timing. I was literally reaching for the phone to ring you."

The phone crackled at her, and she lifted her brows. "Message? No, I wasn't returning your call—I haven't checked my messages since this morning. Yes, of course you can—No, it's not too late for you to come by, not at all. We weren't considering sleep for the next little while, anyway—something horrible happened today and we're wired and edgy, which is why I haven't checked my messages; I simply couldn't deal with things tonight. Come around, by all means. You can meet Ringan and I'll fix you a drink. No, truly, I want you to. Do you have the address? Good. See you in a bit then."

As Richard Halligan and Ringan Laine shook hands, it was abundantly obvious to Penny that she had just introduced two friends for life. Richard and Ringan were two of a kind, separated by age, the inherent reactive differences between the Celt and the Anglo-Saxon, and by not much else.

Halligan had an attaché case with him, held carefully in one gloved hand. That he brought news was obvious; it was there in the gleam of his eye, the set of his jaw, a slightly edged tension he had not displayed during his first conversation with Penny. He was also drenched from head to foot, thanks to the earlier intermittent rain having become a hard, ice-touched downpour that hissed and slammed against the windows, rattling them in their sashes.

Penny hung his coat by the electric fire, poured him a cup of strong black tea with a shot of cognac added to take the chill off, and generally fussed over him.

"Here." She set a hastily assembled plate of biscuits and cheese on the living room's low table. "Have a bite. The weather out there looks to be a taste of some Nordic variety of Hell. Did you drive here? Any trouble parking?"

"I took a taxi, actually. Thanks—cheese and boozy tea are just what was wanted." Halligan rubbed his hands together. "I know this must seem odd, me wanting to come over this late, but I found out something, and for some reason, it set off all sorts of little alarm bells in my mind. But lord, I'm being awfully rude—you said on the phone something unpleasant had happened today. Are you all right?"

"We are." Ringan snagged the bottle of cognac from Penny and added a dollop to his own cup. "A gilding restorer named Ray

Haddon isn't, though—he died at the Bellefield this afternoon. Had a heart attack and came off a nine-metre ladder."

"Oh dear, sorry to hear that. How wretched for everyone concerned." Halligan hesitated and then, visibly, came to a decision. "This death—was it natural causes?"

Something in his voice, a sort of underlying awareness, brought both their heads up. "Why do you ask that?" Penny asked sharply. "Do you have some reason to think it would be anything except natural causes?"

"I don't know—that's something I'll let you tell me when you're ready. But I found out some things today, a few quite extraordinary facts about Hawthorne Walk and the site of the Bellefield in particular, and they're peculiar enough to be forcing me into a kind of imaginative overdrive."

He set his cup down and reached for the attaché case at his feet. Penny and Ringan hastily cleared a space on the table.

"Ta. First thing: a photocopy of a map of the street. The map was actually larger; this is a close-up of the area in question. This sheet shows the front, the one clipped to it is the back. Can you read Latin? I want to see if I got it right."

"Created and drawn by Humphrey Lynde, 1381." Penny turned her attention to Halligan. "Do we know who Humphrey Lynde was?"

"Indeed we do—he was half-brother to Geoffrey Chaucer. Born out of wedlock but given a nice little living with John of Gaunt nonetheless, thanks to the Chaucer connection."

Ringan blinked. Penny was quicker on the uptake. "That's right, Chaucer was connected to Gaunt, wasn't he?"

"Brother-in-law, by marriage. Chaucer's wife, Philippa, was Katherine Roet's sister, and Katherine was Gaunt's third wife and the mother of the bastard Beaufort line. They became the Tudors, by the way."

Ringan, looking frazzled, hunted around for the cognac. "Right," he said. "So we've established a map, drawn by a bloke called Humphrey Lynde, who was related to Chaucer, who hung out with John of Gaunt. And this is important—why, exactly?"

"Look at this." Halligan tossed another photograph on the table. "The original was far too valuable to photocopy; I couldn't talk the verger at the Westminster archive into letting me make off with it, not for one moment. We had to settle for a digital photo and a printout; I hope the quality's good enough to read. Do you see what this is?"

"It's an arrest warrant." Penny's voice was trembling. "Signed and executed by Martin Saxton, Wardour Royal, servant of Richard Plantagenet, King of England. It's on the charge of murder—oh, my God."

Her voice faded, as the paper slipped from her suddenly nerveless fingers. Halligan, unabashedly pleased with the sensation he'd caused, stooped and retrieved it.

"What is it?" Ringan craned across the table. "Come on, don't tease, what do we have here?"

"I'll read it, shall I?" Halligan cleared his throat. " 'By order of his Most Puissant Richard Plantagenet, to be committed for trial in defence of her life for the most heinous Murthers of James Caulfield, age two and twenty summers, and of an unbaptised Infant, aged three days only, and for the hiring of armed men who might so slay said Victyms. Also will the prisoner speak to a charge, that she did send hired men to slay the Lady Eleanor Caulfield, in defiance of all known law and rightnesse. For this Most Unnatural offence against God and Man is the Prisoner to the care and safekeeping of Martin Saxton committed for trial, this fourteenth day of May 1381.' "

Ringan sucked in his breath. A young man, an infant, a female defendant. Hiring armed men to commit murder. *My mother did me deadly spite, for she sent thieves in the dark of the night, put my servants all to flight, they robbed my bower . . .*

" 'They slew my knight,' " Penny said softly, and Ringan realised that, unknowingly, he'd quoted the lyric aloud. "Lady Eleanor—she was Lady Eleanor Caulfield. A dead husband, a dead infant. Ringan, it's the song, 'The Famous Flower of Serving Men.' It's all there in the song, the whole story. You were right. And I think Richard deserves to hear the entire story."

She turned to Halligan. "Richard," she told him, "I don't know if you're remotely likely to believe it, but I think I ought to tell you why we needed to know all this."

"You're being haunted. No need to tell me, not the bare fact, anyway. I found out something today, one of several things, that made me fairly sure that was the case. For one thing, did you know that The Beldame in Ashes has apparently been haunted since the day it was built?" He watched their jaws drop, and grinned. "I expect I looked like a stuffed cod myself, when Mike—he's the barkeep at the Beldame—let that drop today. Purely accidental; I stopped for a pint and we got to talking. They haven't got a solid ghost, nothing well defined, but a documented history of bottles flying off shelves, sudden unexplained fires breaking out, whispering when no one's about, things like that. Mike told me other spots along Hawthorne Walk have reported years, decades, of the same sort of thing. So I wondered. And that was one reason I wanted to come over and see you. The other reason is here, in the papers."

For a long moment, Penny and Ringan simply stared at him. Then Penny began to laugh, and Ringan joined her. If there was a tinge of hysteria in their joint reactions, Halligan was too polite to say so.

"Beautiful." Ringan wiped tears from his face. "Perfect. Here we've been trying to figure out who this is and what to do and all the time, all we had to do was go get snockered down the local pub and the bloke behind the bar has everything we ever needed to know." He sobered suddenly. "I wish I'd known before Ray Haddon was frightened to death. We might have stopped it."

Penny was on her feet, pacing, trying to deal with a sudden upsurge of nervous energy. "Richard, this prisoner. Do we have any information about her? I want to know who she was, what happened to her, why in sweet hell she's hanging about Hawthorne Walk making everyone's life miserable, and scaring people so badly that they come crashing off ladders and die."

"Oh yes." Richard lifted his face and they saw his eyes gleaming. "Yes, indeed, we do. This was no ordinary murder case, no ordinary trial, because this was no ordinary prisoner. She was never in the dungeons at the Savoy, so far as I can tell. I still haven't found any trial transcripts, so I don't know if she was tortured or not. But considering who she was . . . no, they couldn't simply rack her and brand her and break bits off her to get a confession. Not with this one."

"She was French," Penny said slowly, "wasn't she? We've been hearing her voice in the Bellefield, you know. It's always in French. And I know that French was one of the languages spoken at court, but this isn't formal French we've been hearing, it's fluid and fast. French was her native tongue. Wasn't it?"

Ringan, on his feet beside her, was holding his breath. If, in fact, Richard Halligan said she was English, or Welsh, or even German, they would be back at square one.

"She wasn't merely French," Halligan said clearly, "she was France. The lady's name, at the time of her arrest and trial, was Lady Agnes Maldown. She was the widow of one of the more dissolute English nobles of his time. But her maiden name . . . "

"What was it?" Ringan asked. "Who was she? Why was her arrest so extraordinary? What was her maiden name?"

"Her maiden name was Belleville, Agnes de Belleville. And Belleville was the name given to legitimised bastard children of the de Valois."

*"What?"* Penny shrieked. "She can't have been!"

"Wait a minute," Ringan said disbelievingly. "I know that name, de Valois. That was the French royal family. Wasn't it? Queen Margot and that lot? I saw a nice little film about her."

"Well, Margot, Marguerite, was rather later, sixteenth century and whatnot. But yes, same family. Your child murderer, the Lady Agnes, was an illegitimate daughter of the King of France. Child of John II, John the Good, to be exact."

"Wait, wait." Penny was breathing through her nostrils, rather like a thoroughbred horse scenting the finish line. "All right, look. This is amazing, it's fascinating, we'll get back to it. But first, my brain wants a bit of closure here. Can we tie this up, loose ends and whatnot? First of all, what does the Lynde map have to do with the rest of it?"

"You only looked at the back." Halligan grinned. "And we got rather stuck at the Chaucer part. If you read down, you'll see that name: Martin Saxton. And if you look at the copy of the front half of the map—well, you tell me. What do you see?"

"It's Hawthorne Walk." Ringan had got his hands on the map and was poring over it. "And that's the site the Bellefield's on, where all those little semi-square bits are drawn on. Oh, look! There's that little burning wheatsheaf thing, the one over the Beldame's door. What's it doing in the middle of North London?"

Halligan jumped. "So that's where I saw it! I spotted the pyre— it isn't wheat, Ringan, it's an execution bonfire—on the map as well, and couldn't understand why it looked so familiar. Of course, it's the pub sign at The Beldame in Ashes." He shook his head. "My word, that's embarrassing, missing a connection that obvious. I must be getting rusty with retirement."

"Ringan, you lout, come on, share!" Penny held the photocopy of the map's text side up beside the graphic side, forming one map. "Oh. Oh my, yes. Little brackets to show the location of Martin Saxton's house on the front, and his name, nice and clear, around the back, with the same dear little brackets. So there's our connection: Martin Saxton."

"The wardour's house." Halligan was nodding, satisfaction in his eye. "The site of the Bellefield was the home commissioned by the king for his uncle John's wardour of women prisoners, Martin Saxton." He quoted the text Penny held. " 'By charter, this Purview of Johannes of Ghent, herein is Residence of Martin Saxton, Wardour of those Womyn who have thyr God and King offended.' And this, my dears, is where they would almost certainly have housed a murderess of the prestige and birth of Agnes de Belleville."

# Six

*Our King has to the hunting gone . . .*
*He's stayed all day, but nothing found*
*And as he rode himself alone*
*It's there he spied the milk-white hind*

"You must be Mike. Have you got a moment?"

The middle-aged man in the oversized apron and dark fisherman's jersey paused, and looked up at Penny. He'd been busily polishing the bar's venerable wooden countertop until it gave off a dull gleam under the muted afternoon lights. The air in The Beldame in Ashes carried a curious, and very appealing, mixture of scents: lemon, beeswax, ale, and something that smelled like shepherd's pie, cooking in the kitchen just out of view of the pub's customers.

"Right you are. I'm Mike Dallow, proprietor of this charming establishment." He set the waxy rag down on a shelf on his side of the bar, wiped his hands carefully on his apron front, and offered one to Penny for shaking. "And you're the distinguished lady who's bought the old Bellefield Theatre, at the end of the Walk, if I'm not mistaken. Pleasure to meet you. How d'ye do? The name's Penelope, isn't it?"

"Penny, please. People only call me Penelope when they're trying to put me in my place." She shook his hand. "I didn't buy the Bellefield, though—it was a legacy. I was wondering if I could place an order before the place gets too filled up; my theatre group's coming in, and we need to have a serious talk about a few things. They'll be wanting lunch, and lots of drink."

"Serious? Ah, that poor chap at the theatre, with the dickey heart, yesterday." Mike's face, designed by nature to be rounded and cheerful, thinned out into sober lines. "I heard about it, not much, just the bare fact. Sorry; that's a hell of a way to start off in a new place. And yes, of course I can do you some lunch. Shepherd's pie, salad, and chips, for how many?"

"Five, please." It could have been six, she thought, but she had decided to postpone talking to Albert Wychsale about his participation and its status until she heard what her troupe had to say. "I was also hoping to be able to talk to you, when you've got a moment free. I know this isn't the best time, but a friend of mine, who was doing some research for me, told me you might be willing to share some stories about the Beldame's history."

"You mean Doc Halligan, used to be the librarian or whatever it was, over at St. Paul's? That's right, we had a nice rabbit about the Hawthorne ghosts, over a couple of beers. He didn't know anything about them. A bit surprising, that."

"I know. He seems omniscient, doesn't he? Nothing hidden, nothing left undiscovered. It's a bit terrifying, really, but I suppose that's what makes a good researcher." Penny glanced at the clock on the wall behind Dallow's head. "Might I get a half-pint, Mike? We're into licensing hours, yes?"

Dallow nodded and drew off the rich golden brew, letting the head settle before setting the glass on the bar. "Here you go, this one's on the house. A welcome to the neighbourhood. Anyway, I expect you'll be bringing the old Beldame a lot of custom."

"That's the general idea, yes. It depends, though, on the conversation I'm about to have with my cast. We may have to postpone things for a bit, until we get this sorted out." Penny, who tended towards small tasty mouthfuls when she ate or drank, found herself gulping her beer. She realised, with some surprise, that she was nervous. That was absurd, surely? Since she'd been planning on putting *Iphigenia* on hiatus until they could eject the unwanted Lady Maldown *née* de Belleville in any case, why be nervous? Was she afraid the rest of the cast would yell at her? Ridiculous. After all, who, precisely, was in charge around . . .

"Penny for them?"

Busy with her own thoughts, she hadn't been paying attention. She jumped suddenly at the touch on her shoulder, and at an unexpected voice in her ear.

"Ringan!" She pulled herself together. "What are you doing here? I thought you were going to send the workmen off?"

"I did. They've all gone home, and they're all coming back again the moment we call and say we're ready for them." He planted a quick kiss on her cheek and slid onto the stool beside her. "Cider, please. Oh—wait a bit, are you Mike?"

Mike handed him a glass. "Here y'are. Right, I'm Michael Dallow. Another friend of Doc Halligan's, or have you been round before? Because you look familiar."

"My significant other, actually, and the man in charge of the Bellefield's restoration. He's also a musician. Mike, Ringan Laine." Penny swirled the remnants of her beer around the glass.

"Criminy, you're Ringan Laine? This is a pleasure, and no mistake." The barman pumped Ringan's hand enthusiastically. "You're the front man and the guitar player for Broomfield Hill, aren't you? One of my favourite bands, that is. I saw you at the Isle of Wight Festival last summer. So you're restoring the theatre as well? I heard about that poor bastard yesterday—not so good, that. How'd he come to have a heart attack, anyway?"

"He was frightened to death." Penny set her glass down. "The ghost—we're pretty sure now that we know who she was when she was actually alive—she scared him so badly, he went into cardiac arrest. And now he's dead. She killed him. Or at least, he died because of her." She saw Ringan lift his head to regard her, and met his eye squarely. "Well, she did. The Beldame's got a ghost, maybe even the same ghost; she seems to—I don't know—hover over the entire street like a bit of dirty mist. And I want to get rid of this ghost, rather badly, because she's hurting people and mucking things up all over the place and anyway, I *hate* her. I completely and totally loathe her and I can't produce my play until she's gone. I know you think I'm being heartless and that I ought to feel sorrier for her, but right now I want her out of here, I don't care where she fetches up, anywhere will do. I just want her gone, the sooner the better."

The two men were silent. Penny picked up her glass, drained it in a single gulp, and slapped it down on the counter. She rarely drank alcohol at this time of day. "When are you free, Mike? Would your own significant other spare you for a meal?"

"I expect she'd be all right with that. Tonight?" Mike lifted a brow at her empty glass. "Another?"

"No. No, one is more than I'd generally drink before dinner. In fact, I think I'm a bit wavy. Not tight, you know? Just a bit of assertiveness I don't usually display at midday, unless I'm on-stage. And any assertiveness there, well, that's usually not due to beer."

Ringan touched her shoulder. "Look, love, Donal and your lot will be along in a bit. I'll finish my cider and clear out. Leave you a clear field, yes? Meantime, I'm off to the British Library—I called this morning and spoke to someone called Maddy Holt who specialises in what she calls 'historical documents of the courts.' Seems to be a fancy way of saying she likes famous trials. Anyway, I told her what we were after and she was right on it. Says they've got a few bits we could likely use."

"What, they did your looking for you? Aren't we lucky, you being the National Trust's pet folklorist and restoration bloke? Maddy Holt—Madeleine Holt? I wonder where I know that name from?" Penny planted a beer-scented kiss on Ringan's lips and glanced at the clock. "They should be here any minute now. Are you heading home to my place afterwards? Check the answering machine when you get there—I'll leave a message, saying where and when for dinner with Mike tonight."

Ringan headed out. The weather, which for two weeks had been as evilly dank and icy as winter gets at London's latitude, was showing signs of breaking; while it was still indecently cold, the solid grey facade of sky that had hunched over the city like unbroken ramparts for two weeks past now showed small chinks in the dullness. Clouds moved, slow and stately, from west to east, and a certain lightening of the grimness showed that, behind the dark density of winter, the sun would indeed keep its ancient bargain, and come again.

Inside a warm scarf and a pair of good gloves, Ringan was comfortably toasty. He walked into the wind, shoulders hunched, wondering if this trip to what was likely to be the intimidating confines of the Library would get him what he needed. A gust of wind laced with the remnants of a salty North Sea squall lifted the ends of his scarf and wrapped them around his eyes. As he stopped to untangle himself, he reflected that at the very least, he'd be indoors with some interesting reading material.

Ringan battled the wind until he reached the Embankment Tube station. Heading thankfully down the stairs, he caught a train to Kings Cross and mentally girded his loins to deal with the unknown terrain of the British Library.

The directions Maddy Holt had given him were simple enough; off at Kings Cross Station past St. Pancras, across the road on the same side, through the main portico and piazza into the Library itself. Ringan, despite having lived in London for years before acquiring his Glastonbury weaver's cottage, had never been near the new British Library. For a moment, he stood on the street, staring in disbelief. The sheer size of the place was overwhelming: looking through the portico, past an enormous bronze statue of Sir Isaac Newton, was an enormous piazza in patterned brickwork. Beyond that, a structure that soared and towered and seemed to cover as much ground as the vast railway station of St. Pancras across the road took the eye and hammered itself into the visual memory. Ringan, who had been expecting a nice, if imposing, bit of white stone with perhaps a pair of carved lions out front, consulted the directions again and made his way across the piazza and up the front stairs.

Madeleine Holt, who had until now been a briefly encountered well-bred voice on the phone, turned out to be a stately blonde in her early thirties. Ringan blinked away yet another mental stereotype; clearly, his perceptions of libraries and librarians were going to need drastic revision. He'd been expecting a sedate matron, not this runway-model child.

He offered her a hand. "Ms. Holt? I'm Ringan Laine. Thanks so much for making time to see me." There was an odd look in her eye, and he wondered if perhaps he'd dropped a brick. "You are Ms. Holt, aren't you?"

"Well, it's Lady Holt, actually, but I prefer the title I've earned, which is Doctor. Still, Maddy will do. Hello, Mr. Laine—this is a pleasure." She shook his hand lightly, and smiled, a bit nervously. "You likely won't remember, but we've met once before. About three years ago, you consulted on the restoration of an old meeting hall in Kent. . . . "

"What, Barris Hall? I remember that project, only too well. It was horribly underfunded, and the local Preservation Society hadn't a clue. They got in the way at every turn." Ringan cocked his head at her. "Call me Ringan. Were you involved in that, Maddy? I'm surprised I don't remember you."

"I suspect you do remember me, really." The nervous smile metamorphosed into a cheeky grin. "Do you remember a hot cup of coffee being spilled on your shoes? And a red-faced stammering woman, mortified almost unto death, with spiky black hair? Rather seventies-punk hair?"

"Oh, dear. Yes, indeed. Was that really you? The safety pin and mohawk-looking girl?" He grinned back, but in truth, he was a bit disoriented; the girl he vaguely remembered had sported a black-hennaed, partially shaved head, a pierced left eyebrow, and Doc Maarten boots laced to the knee. The sleek fashion plate he now found himself confronting, honey-blonde and designer-clad, might well have come from a different planet. Maddy Holt, it seemed, had a talent for self-reinvention. "The shoes got over it, never fear," he said. "In any case, it's nice to see you without soggy footwear being involved."

"I couldn't agree more. And it would seem I can atone for past clumsiness with some information. You said you were interested in a very special prisoner—the Lady Agnes de Belleville Maldown—and as it happens, she's a particular fascination of mine. Her daughter was astonishing, as well—the Lady Eleanor Caulfield, that was. I discovered the story a few years back, completely by chance, when I was doing my doctorate on the de Valois family, and I've been gathering information about her ever since. Fascinating woman, the Lady

Agnes, even though she was, well, completely insane. So, if you'll just tell me what you need, it's likely I've got it."

Ringan blew his breath out. "You've just made me extremely happy. I think this is my lucky day. What I need on the subject is anything and everything you've got: documents, transcripts, memoirs, records of any kind. I particularly want to know when and where she died. And how she died."

"Well, let's pop round to my office, then; I've got a cubbyhole behind the King's Collection." Her face, elegantly angular, suddenly plumped into that saucy grin again. "I can even offer you a cup of coffee, although likely not on your shoes."

Her cubbyhole was in fact a small, light-filled office with a staggering view. The room was pleasantly tidy, with neatly arranged books and fresh flowers in a vase; there were also an electric kettle and an espresso machine on a bookcase along one wall. Yet this was unmistakably the quarters of a working scholar. The volumes in those shelves spoke for themselves; here were the arcana of the researcher, laid out for utility and immediate use, rather than for effect or to impress.

"Have a seat." Maddy slid into her own chair. "Did you want to take notes? Have you got what you need? Ah—silly question."

Ringan had pulled a small, tattered notebook from his jacket pocket. "Don't leave home without it. This one's actually got most of my notes on the restoration I'm doing for my girlfriend's theatre, and trust me, this is the appropriate notebook for the job. The two subjects couldn't be more closely matched up."

"Your girlfriend is in the theatre? She must be awfully close to my own age. Would I be out of line to ask her name?"

"Penelope Wintercraft-Hawkes," Ringan said, and saw immediate recognition and delight on her face. "She said your name was awfully familiar, and was wondering where she knew it from—I take it you know each other?"

"Her sister Candida's one of my best friends. Candy and I were at school together, and university too. Penny was invited to my wedding, but her troupe was in America on tour. Oh, lovely! I've only met her once, at Candida and Richard's wedding, and she absolutely terrified me."

Ringan blinked. "Terrified you? Penny? That's beyond my imagining. Why?"

"She was so damned competent." Maddy straightened her shoulders. "Ah well, I've grown up reasonably competent myself. Let's get down to business. This adds a sort of personal twist to a professional request. Did you say the life and death of Lady Agnes were somehow related to Penny's theatre? That's fascinating, because considering that Agnes was what you'd have to rightly call a religious maniac, I can't think of a single circumstance under which she'd have set foot near a theatre. Can I ask how the two subjects intersect?"

Ringan was silent. He looked at her for so long that she blushed. Just as she was beginning to stammer something, an apology or a justification, she realised that he'd been staring through her, that he was considering something, and that whatever that something was, it was of vital importance to him. Just as clearly, she saw him make up his mind to trust her.

"Let me ask you something, Maddy," he said quietly. "Do you believe in ghosts?"


When Ringan let himself into Penny's flat a few hours later, clutching an overstuffed manila envelope under one arm, he was surprised to hear the murmur of voices coming from the front room. A clear, resonant male voice nearly stopped him in his tracks: Robin Sayles's beautiful tenor. *Do not bring your child into my sight, lady. Incur not the reproach of the vulgar. Hear one thing, and be assured: As I live, I will save the girl. . . .*

Putting his head around the corner, Ringan discovered not only Penny and Robin, but the entire Tamburlaine troupe crammed into the small space.

"Ringan, love, hello." Penny bore all the signs of a director deep into theatrical considerations; her pupils were narrowed to feline slits, her hair was messy, and her mouth was purposefully set. She looked completely distracted, and a bit deranged. "We were just rehearsing."

Ringan's brows went up. As he lifted his free hand in a general wave, he took in the paraphernalia of a working troupe: pencils, printed sides, reference copies of the play with visible slash marks through particular sections done in black marker and yellow sticky paper bristling along the margins, half-empty cups of tea, reading glasses pushed up above hairlines. Penny was serious. He had walked in on a rehearsal.

"So I see." He cocked his head. "Hello, Petra—you're looking delicious today, and hello, Rob, Donal, David. Shall I go away again, Pen? Am I going to be underfoot while you declaim?"

"No, of course not." Penny pushed stray hair out of her eyes. "Have some tea or a biscuit or something. Dinner at eight, with Mike. We're going to his place in Camden Town."

"Lovely. Then I won't have a biscuit." He sat down on a floor cushion and settled comfortably. "If you don't mind, I'll just sit and listen to you for a bit."

"You'll listen to us? Seems to me the shoe ought to be on the other foot. Penny said you were off getting the goods on the Bellefield's Demon Queen." The overhead lights glinted off Robin's cheekbones as he twisted to face Ringan. "Penny—can we take a break from the woe-is-me's and the rosy-fingered dawns and whatnots, and get a bit of news? Or are you going to wait until you've learned everything in the world, and then spring it on us all at once? Because frankly, I'm tired of being Achilles right now and I want to know what Ringan's got in the folder."

"I think we all want to know that, Rob." David Harkins stood up and stretched his shoulders. "Damn, I'm stiff. You know, before Ringan tells us anything at all, I think we ought to tell him why we're spouting bits of Euripides all over Penny's lounge. Quid pro quo, you know?"

"Well, since he's not a complete twit, he's probably sussed it out by now." Penny, who had pulled herself upright, was demonstrating her flexibility by doing some graceful yoga bends, touching the floor between her feet with knees straight and spine curved. "In brief, darling, we had a confab at the Beldame, complete with hot meat pies and lashings of liquids and a lot of other nosh—"

"They do tasty nosh," Petra interpolated. "Very tasty indeed. Mike and his wife, they can absolutely cook."

Penny shot her a look—"and we discussed Lady Maldown the Demon Queen, and Donal and David and Petra and Robin all made touching angry speeches about how this was our theatre and not her theatre, and how we were going to hunt her down and get her out and be ready to have a hugely triumphant opening the minute she's vaporised or transmogrified or whatever it is evil ghosty bits do when they've been exorcised. And in the meantime, since no one here is stupid and none of us fancies being burned or smoked or shoved off ladders or whatnot, we're going to get the basis of the play down here, and wait until the Demon Queen is off the Bellefield's premises before we set marks and adjust the production to full court staging. Anyway . . . "

Her voice tapered off as she met Donal McCreary's eye. Ringan saw a subtle change move across her face. It was a discomforting look, familiar, evocative of something he couldn't quite place. Then she lifted her head, tilting it towards Ringan, and abruptly he knew where he had seen that look before. Somerset, two seasons past. Lumbe's Cottage. She had looked like that as the first touch of a ghostly voice, singing a quarter mile away, met her ear. This was what Ringan was coming to recognise as Penny's ghost-look, an awareness that something not natural must be dealt with.

"I nearly forgot." Her voice was low. "Donal told us why he accepted the news of the haunting so easily. He's had an encounter of his own, and you've got to hear about this one, Ringan, if Donal can bear to tell it again. It happened at the Callowen House Festival."

Ringan, his back propped in a lazy curve against the nearest hard surface, straightened up in a hurry. For a working British performer of any calibre, the words "Callowen House" constituted a kind of Holy Grail. Every year, for two weeks sometime between spring and the end of summer, Lord Callowen held an arts festival at his ancestral home in Kent. Performers were paid huge fees, and the small, select audience was by invitation only. One Shakespearean actor had missed the Academy Awards (and watched the presenter accept the Best Actor award on his behalf) because the event had clashed with his invitation to read the St. Crispin speech to an audience of three dozen or so handpicked listeners. Ringan stared at Donal with a kind of awe.

"You did Callowen? When were you there?"

It had happened, Donal told them, eleven years ago, shortly before he had joined the newly formed Tamburlaines. He and his late wife, Sinead, had been names in Irish repertory and leading lights at Dublin's Abbey Theatre. They'd prepared and done a piece, based on fictional letters between W. B. Yeats and Maud Gonne. The applause had rattled the stately home's cornices and dropped plaster from the ancient mouldings, the pay cheque had been half a year's earnings, and they'd retired to bed after their first performance, flushed with accomplishment.

The sense of triumph, along with any good memory of Callowen House that Donal might ever have cherished, had dissipated abruptly during the small hours of the night. Donal had woken up clammy and trembling, and heard Sinead beside him. She was having some kind of seizure.

"A seizure? Jesus."

"A seizure, yes. Or that's what I thought for the first few minutes." Donal, long years after the event, had a faint imprint of that far-away helplessness and terror on his face. "I was in a flat panic. Sinead was in her late thirties, she had no history of illness of any kind, and here she was with the full moon shining through the window onto her face, foam on her lips, not blinking at all, muttering under her breath. I leaned over to take her pulse and touching her, just touching, was horrible. Can't explain it, really—it was like touching a slug. Hot, cold, it just—didn't feel like her."

The description, for Penny and Ringan alike, was a physical sense memory. Both of them knew precisely what Donal meant; both of them had come in contact with abnormally inhabited flesh, with muscle and tendon used by a girl killed two hundred years earlier, and neither was likely to forget the sensation. Their glances met, and each saw comprehension and remembered horror in the other's eyes.

"So I jumped out of bed. I'll never stop wondering if I couldn't have changed things if I'd made myself hold on to her, but that road's closed, and regretting what I didn't do is pointless; I couldn't have touched her." Donal took a mouthful of liquid from the nearest cup and swallowed it down. His voice was raspy, his eyes were full of pain. "And she sat up, and started talking. Except she wasn't talking to me. She was telling someone to get stuffed, go away, leave her alone, just not in any words I'd ever thought to hear come out of her. It wasn't her language, and it wasn't her voice. It just—*wasn't her.* And whatever it was, it was damned ugly, a mean tight little spirit."

"Possession?" Ringan asked quietly. "It sounds like it. God, Donal, how horrible. How long did it last?"

"Bloody long enough." Donal's face was pinched and shadowed. "About three minutes, I'd say, but it might have been three centuries from the way it felt. And then whatever it was let go of her, and it floated off into the wall."

"Floated—are you saying you saw it go?"

That, it seemed, was precisely what Donal was saying. Something misshapen and gaseous and wrong had come floating out of Sinead McCreary, paused for a moment as if to take stock of where it was and what it had accomplished, and then wafted into the wall that led to the outdoors. And Sinead herself, when Donal ran back to the bed to check on her, had seemed to be sleeping normally, but breathing in short, shallow gasps.

"The thing is, she was never the same after that night." Donal's mouth closed hard, and then relaxed again. His face had taken on a chilly, austere set. "She didn't remember anything odd, but she was never able to really focus on anything, and she'd lose her attention span—it was as if something in her had got lost, or been taken away from her, somehow. And it happened overnight—we had no warning."

Donal's remembered pain, even after the passage of years, was tangible in the crowded room. In the face of that pain, they were all silent. "She had some sort of stroke a few months later, and died of it," he said finally. "The doctors did an autopsy. They found a small tumour on the pituitary gland, said it looked to have been there for a few years. Maybe it was why she died, maybe not. They never could agree on it. But I've always thought it was triggered by that, that thing—by whatever happened that night, at Callowen." He looked pointedly at Robin and Petra. "So you'd best believe I'd take a haunting seriously. If anyone alive has got reason, it's me."

Petra reached out and covered his clenched hands with her own. "We take it seriously too, Donal." Her voice was gentle. "We were there, in the theatre yesterday. We saw what happened. We saw Penny, curled up on the floor, screaming. We saw the ambulance take that poor bloke away. And we're not likely to forget it, believe me."

"Not to mention that we heard it." Robin shuddered. "We're believers, Donal. If we took the story with a cellarful of salt before, and I have to confess that I did, yesterday changed all that. There's no one here who doubts the existence of the Demon Queen, and no one here who doesn't know she's dangerous."

For a moment, they were all quiet, remembering the events of the previous day. Then Ringan picked up the folder from the floor beside him, and stood up.

"If anyone's interested," he said clearly, "I can tell you all about her. Well, not all about her, but a lot more than you know right now. Gather round, ladies and gents, step right up. I've got the goods."


In spring of 1993, Madeleine Valroy was a history student at Goldsmiths College, University of London.

Maddy had chosen Goldsmiths from a long list of available options. Her punk-rocker persona, complete with tattoos, spiked dyed black hair, and multiple body piercings, was an interesting, if distracting, complement to a brilliant mind, a retentive and near-photographic memory for detail, and a fascinated commitment to the study of medieval France.

She came by her interest honestly; somewhere in the mists of centuries past, her paternal bloodline had come from the French upper classes, and Villeroi had got anglicised to Valroy. The additional information that a second ancestor had married a bastard child of an obscure fifteenth-century French duke had laid a spark to the kindling of Maddy's fascination with this part of her own history. From that point, there had been no stopping her. Her path had been chosen early.

Maddy opted for the University of London's history department at Goldsmiths for her graduate studies. It was a sensible choice. Proximity to the English Channel meant weekend trips to Paris and environs for research purposes as well as for decent Greek food, while Goldsmiths' location in southeast London allowed Maddy to keep her small flat near Wimbledon, and continue dancing the night away in the Soho clubs. Oxford, Cambridge, the Sorbonne offered up their siren songs and blandishments in vain; Goldsmiths College and Madeleine Valroy were a perfect match.

Halfway through the leisurely first draft of a paper on the long-term effects of the Hundred Years War, Maddy came across a casual mention of a royal death in England that sent her veering down a side path in history.

She'd found it buried in a mind-numbingly dry monograph someone had written on Charles VI of France. Maddy, after scrawling an optimistic heading on her notepad in bold letters, had not taken long to realise that her enthusiasm for this particular information source wasn't going to last long. The writing style alternated between timidly florid and turgidly academic, whoever had written it hadn't bothered with footnotes or source credits, and to put the tin cupola on it, the author couldn't spell anything properly, either in English or in French. Looking wistfully at the spring sunlight through the college library's big windows, Maddy convinced herself, with very little trouble, that there was nothing here she could use.

Still, personal responsibility is a strong spur, and Maddy had a powerful sense of duty where her work was concerned. She doggedly slogged her way through the dull prose. She was about to give up when something caught her eye and focused her attention.

. . . Charles was not the only boy-king of the period. Across the Channel in England, his young counterpart, Richard II, was forced to face down the insurgent Wat Tyler and the recusant preacher John Ball during the Peasants' Rebellion shortly after Charles himself took power in France. Whatever sympathy one child king may have felt for the other was surely tempered by several circumstances: Charles's grandfather's capture and long imprisonment by Richard Plantagenet's father Edward the Black Prince, the effects and ill-will generated by the Hundred Years War, and the peculiar circumstance of Richard having recently approved his Uncle Gaunt's order of execution of Charles' illegitimate aunt, the Lady Agnes, on the charge of murder and attempted infanticide. . . .

Maddy's eyes opened wide. What a very odd tidbit to find in the middle of a boring screed on the Hundred Years War. Murder, attempted infanticide, illegitimate aunt? Was it even possible to be somone's illegitimate aunt? It read like something that ought to have a jacket cover with a woman in a low-cut Regency gown, being menaced by a randy nobleman, or something of that sort.

Maddy, up to her elbows in research on this very period, had never seen a word written about this woman, until she found it here. Who in the world was this Agnes person, and why wasn't she famous? Why wasn't this the plot of a dozen films?

Maddy Valroy, without even realising the fact, had just embarked on a quest.

The first part, identification of the murderess herself, was simple enough. After all, if you're doing research, and you start with the precise time span and location in which your event occurred, you have a good idea where to begin hunting. It was all there, in that single paragraph: the Peasants' Rebellion, John of Gaunt, even the lady's Christian name. Maddy had an excellent starting point: June 1381, London, and an accused and convicted murderess, most likely a French royal bastard, called Agnes. Maddy reasoned that she had to have been the bastard child of one of the period's French kings; there was simply no other way to arrive at the phrase "illegitimate aunt" and have it make any sense at all.

She tried all the obvious sources first, and mostly drew a blank; the Savoy's surviving records were locked away and it would take time for her to procure credentials. Then she had a minor brainstorm, and it occurred to her to check the publication date on the dull monograph in which she'd first seen the story. Here she got lucky; it was only four years old, and the author was a fellow at Magdalen College, Oxford. One phone call, and just the right balance of serious scholar with tender young flirt, got her the information she wanted: the lady's full name.

Maddy, armed with an unarguable excuse and a spiral notebook, then went off to Paris for a weekend of information hunting through the likely sources, leavened with some mild nightclub debauchery, quantities of Pernod, and several scoops of *glâce à la cannelle,* sold by the ice cream vendor at the Jardins du Luxembourg.

A hunt at the Bibliothèque Nationale afforded her nothing but a long drool over some truly exquisite illuminated manuscripts. Frustrated and a bit hungover, she was about to return to London a day early when she noticed some flyers on the hall table of her 5th arrondissement hotel: the Musée de Cluny, not five minutes walk from where she now stood, was having an exhibition of borrowed artifacts and memorabilia, concerning or belonging to the de Valois dynasty.

Maddy made her way to the museum. She'd been there before, and loved the ancient abbey; certainly, as a setting for the *Unicorn* tapestries, if for nothing else, the medieval cloister was as close to perfection as was possible. Cluny had an atmosphere common to religious centres of great age: a combination of quiet, avoidance of the outside clamour, and a feeling of sanctuary from the mundane pressures of the modern day. Maddy had noted this about Westminster Abbey and Notre Dame. Even a steady, constant flow of tourist traffic through the stone arches and the display cases housing the carved reliquary caskets never seemed to make a dent in the quiet detachment. Had she been allowed to do so, she would have done all her research and writing in a cloistered cell.

Maddy followed the discreetly placed signs to the de Valois exhibit. The collection was eclectic, and perfect for a scholar or researcher. It ran the gamut from a precious two pages of commentary on the St. Bartholemew's Massacre of the Huguenots, written in

Queen Margot's own hand, to a necklace of harsh yellow gold and rubies, the relic of an earlier de Valois queen. The exhibit was fascinating, but Maddy was on the hunt, and she allowed herself only a minimal amount of time to linger over items not directly related to what she wanted. She'd nearly given up hope of finding anything connected to the mysterious murderess when suddenly, in a case near the exit, there it was.

The object was gold, incised with an image Maddy had seen before but couldn't quite place: a deer or hind, knee bent, horns straight, a crown around its throat. It lay in solitary splendour on a plush scarlet cushion, the gold gleaming dully. It was a medallion, and had obviously been meant to hang from a heavy chain; the goldsmith who had made it had crafted a large sturdy loop at the top, through which the chain would pass.

There was a printed information card on a stand beside the case. Maddy, fluent in French, knelt and read, translating as she went. Then she glanced down and discovered the entire text in English, printed directly below:

Badge of office, c 1380, given by Richard II of England to Lady Eleanor Caulfield. Lady Eleanor entered Richard's service dressed in male attire after fleeing her mother, Lady Agnes Maldown. The Lady Agnes, *née* de Belleville, had planned for Eleanor to enter a nunnery. When Eleanor defied her by becoming pregnant and subsequently marrying her lover, Sir James Caulfield, her mother arranged for her daughter's murder.

Events did not go as planned, however, the assassins instead killing Sir James and the couple's newborn son, while leaving the intended target untouched. Eleanor fled to London and by unknown means became Richard's personal servant, until her gender was discovered. At that point, upon Richard's demand, his uncle John of Gaunt arrested Lady Agnes, who was tried and convicted of murder.

Little is known of Eleanor after Richard's discovery of her gender; while she would not have remained in service to the

Crown, she would likely have received a pension from Richard. There are indications that she may have returned to France and remarried in later life.

Maddy straightened her back and stared off into space. Her mind, stoked with information, had clicked into high gear and was busily processing and placing what she'd just read into some sort of perspective. A young girl with, apparently, a nutter for a mum; she had to have been off her nut, the Lady Agnes, because what sane person would try and have her own child killed, just because the girl hadn't fancied becoming a nun? A religious fanatic, it sounded like. And Lady Eleanor, now; if one was to believe the little history on that card, that was a very spirited girl. Her own mother had tried to kill her and what had she done? Gone into drag as a bloke, got safe away from her loony mum, changed her name, and been given one hell of a great job. Great while it lasted, anyway; and after that, even when she lost the job, she'd got her mother arrested for murder.

This was an amazing bunch of people, with the makings of an incredible story. But why was the story set out here, among the priceless papers and tats and bobs of the de Valois family? Where did that "illegitimate aunt" thing come into play? Whose child had Agnes been, to qualify as . . .

"Excuse me. Is there something I can help you with?"

Maddy jumped and turned. A pleasant female voice at her left shoulder, speaking unaccented English, resolved into a tiny middle-aged woman with a crisply official air.

"Thank you—I don't know. I mean, I'm doing my doctorate on the de Valois family and I've got a bit sidetracked on someone called Agnes Maldown. I've heard her referred to as Charles VI's illegitimate aunt, and I gather she was a raving nutter, and a murderess as well, but . . . "

"Ah, yes, Agnes de Belleville, later Lady Maldown of Hertfordshire, England. Out of her mind, and a murderess? She was all of that, if the few remaining records are accurate." The woman smiled, and held out a hand; she was a foot shorter than Maddy, but her air of authority was tangible. "Angela Duperres. I'm in charge of the exhibition."

"Madeleine Valroy." The women shook hands as people drifted around them. "How in the world can one be an illegitimate aunt? The best I could come up with was that she was actually an illegitimate daughter, which I suppose by definition would make her an illegitimate aunt to legitimate nephews and nieces."

Angela laughed. "I wondered about that myself, when I was asked to put together this collection. But yes, that's it precisely. Agnes was one of two known royal bastards born to John II, Jean le Bon, and they were both out of their minds. Her brother, François, fetched up in a locked room near Chambéry; someone poisoned him for his twentieth birthday, or so the story goes. The de Belleville name was given to all the de Valois royal bastards."

"Wow. You're an expert on this woman? I couldn't be that lucky, not possibly."

"No, not an expert on her specifically. I do have rather a lot of generalised information on everything to do with this exhibit. You can't answer questions unless you do your homework, you know, and I've done my homework on all of it. Why, did you want to know more about her?"

"Yes please. Anything at all would help."

"Unusual. Most researchers seem to want to study the actual royals. Well, the known details are rather sparse, alas. We do know that Agnes herself was born in 1342, shipped off to England and married to an absolute horror at seventeen, produced Eleanor late in 1361, and possibly murdered her abusive wastrel whoremongering husband in 1368. That's when he died of something called the 'bloody flux,' anyway."

"Oh, my God. Wait. Wait, please?" Maddy was scrabbling frantically for her notebook. "Would you mind terribly—I want to get this all down."

"Certainly," Angela said crisply. "Whenever you're ready? Excellent. So, to continue: born 1342, child of an unknown mother and John II—he wasn't king at the time, by the way, he only got the crown when she was eight years old, and she was given the de

Belleville name later, sometime before she got sent off to marry Sir Hugh Maldown. Married in 1359, probably at the Maldown demesne in Hertfordshire."

"How in the world did you find all this out?" Maddy blurted.

Angela lifted one eyebrow. "I used the Internet, for a start. Anyway: Local parish records show baptism of one child, Eleanor, New Year's of 1362. There's nothing much about Agnes herself from that period, but there's quite bit on her husband, who appears to have impregnated several village girls and left them to starve. He was also censured several times by the local duke for whoremongering and gambling parts of his land away while gaming with his cohorts. He had a reputation for violence, too, if the records are to be believed." Angela lifted one eyebrow. "You're looking at me very oddly."

"Am I?" Maddy asked. "I'm simply in awe. I've been hunting through libraries and whatnot, and finding absolutely nothing."

"Well," Angela said easily, "that's what research is. You find something that interests you—and I'll admit, whatever else the story of Agnes may be, it certainly isn't boring—and you go on from there. That's what I did, and what I do every time. I use the tools I have to find the truth, and if those aren't sufficient, I hunt for more tools." She was quiet for a moment, and then added thoughtfully, "You know, I've always thought there was something more to the story. Something that never came out. Because even if Agnes was one of those hysterical religious types, why would she have gone to those lengths? The usual course, once Eleanor got pregnant and ran off to get married, would have been to blot her out, disown her, never speak her name again. You know—to eschew her, as provided for in the Bible, as one who had done evil. But to take the kind of risks Agnes took? Hiring killers for money, hunting down her daughter and new family, risking a horrifying death if the truth came out . . . no. I simply don't believe it. There's something else in there, something we'll probably never know."

# Seven

*Oh the hind she broke, the hind she flew*
*The hind, she trampled the brambles through*
*First she'd melt, then she'd sound*
*Sometimes before, sometimes behind*

In the top-floor flat of a converted Georgian house, Mike and Lily Dallow had put together a very nice dinner.

Ringan and Penny, both under the impression they were to be the only guests, found their arrival coinciding with three other people. Two of them, both women in their early sixties, were complete strangers; the third, to their delight, was Richard Halligan. Halligan was as pleased to see them as they were at his unexpected presence. The two unknown women smiled generally around the room, and awaited introductions.

These came shortly after everyone had arrived, and it became clear immediately why the two women had been invited. One, a Mrs. Alexander, was the owner and longtime proprietress of Hawthorne Antiques, at No. 10, Hawthorne Walk. The other, a Miss Radleigh, ran "Lucy's Inexpressibles," the toney lingerie shop at No. 16. Performing the introductions, Lily Dallow informed them that John Roberson, who owned the bootmaker's shop at No. 22, was in Scotland for the next week, which was the only reason he wasn't joining them for dinner. Penny privately thought that the unknown bootmaker would be missing a treat; whatever else was intended for the evening, an excellent meal was apparently going to be provided. The flat smelled of minted lamb and roasted potatoes. She glanced over at Ringan, and caught him in the act of sniffing appreciatively.

Lily Dallow was a large, comfortable-looking woman, with a wonderful mass of curly grey-streaked ginger hair and an air of someone who stands no nonsense. She thanked everyone for coming at such short notice, asked the guests to name their choice of liquid refreshment, and led the entire group off towards the dining table.

Unlike Penny's Muswell Hill flat, the Dallows' apartment had a formal separate dining room, as large and gracious as the dining rooms of the Georgian period generally were. Since the party was an uneven number, it was lucky the table was round. Everyone settled into their seats and dug into dinner.

Petra had been right: both Dallows could cook, and cook well. There was little conversation for the duration of the meal; everyone was concentrating on tender meat, crisp-skinned potatoes that flaked when broken with a fork, fresh green beans, and hot bread. It seemed almost unfair that the wine and beer were as good as the dinner itself, and Penny thought for a few moments that Lily Dallow was almost too much of a good thing. Then she remembered that the Dallows ran a public house; of course the alcohol would be the best available. She allowed herself a small grin, chided herself for having uncharitable thoughts, and forked up the rest of her second helping of lamb.

After dessert, Lily shepherded her guests into the living room and got them settled. When she was satisfied everyone was comfortable, she sat down herself and got straight to the point.

"You know," she told the room at large, "Mike and I have been holding down the fort at the Beldame for a good many years now. And until fairly recently, we thought we were the only ones who'd run into some odd things—hearing whispers up against your ear when there's no one there but you, little shoves in the small of one's back in an empty room, having to run up and down the stairs because there was a smell of smoke, enough to make your eyes water, but the smoke alarm system never seemed to trigger and you couldn't see anything. We always thought whatever it was, was confined to the Beldame. We even wondered why none of the earlier owners had used that, you know? Turned it into a publicity thing for the pub. After all, it would have been a nice selling point—our own private ghost." She turned her head towards Penny and Ringan, with Richard Halligan seated on the far end of the same sofa. "We found out, oh, maybe two years ago, that we were wrong about being the only ones affected," she continued. "It isn't just us. It's all of Hawthorne Walk."

"It's a pity we took so long to start comparing notes." Lucy Radleigh's voice, London on the surface, held distant overtones of a girlhood spent in England's North Country. "I'd kept my mouth shut about the things I'd heard and come up against in my shop. I couldn't see anyone believing a word of it, and I didn't much fancy fetching up in a crazy house."

"I'm in the same boat." Chrissie Alexander's voice was a shock; the woman herself was fashionably underfed, elegantly coiffed, draped in upper-class tweeds, but her accent was purest Cockney. She had the air of someone who diligently listens to herself, so as to keep her language on an even keel. "I mean, I come in and find tats and bobs moved from one place to another, smell of smoke but no smoke or fire anywhere about—one morning, I come in and there's a seventeenth-century silver sauce-boat gone missing from its locked case, and where do I find it? Halfway across the room and upside down in the cat's dish, that's where."

"How long has this been going on?" Halligan had discreetly pulled a small notebook from his jacket pocket. He had a snifter of brandy on the small table beside him; it glowed amber under the chandelier bulbs. "Actually, if I can ask this first—how long has everyone been at their various businesses in the Walk?"

Lucy Radleigh, it seemed, had been producing pricey silk knickers and lacy little cami sets at No. 16 for the best part of thirty years. Chrissie Alexander, born and raised nearby, had married a local man with an eye for collectibles; they had opened the antique store together in 1971. Her late husband—he had died while alone at No. 10 of an unexpected heart attack, in the early nineties—left Chrissie the business. Having learned the antiques trade as well as she could, his widow carried on successfully. The Dallows had taken over the Beldame in 1983, making them relative newcomers to Hawthorne Walk; the absent John Roberson's custom boot-maker's shop had actually been opened by his grandfather, in the final days of Victoria's reign.

Halligan nodded, making the occasional note. Ringan and Penny, seated side by side on a comfortable plush sofa, listened silently. Ringan touched the manila envelope at his elbow with nervous fingertips. And the others told their stories.

Although they were newest to the street, other than Penny herself, the Dallows had the richest history of haunting on their premises. Among the papers they'd inherited, after taking on the Beldame's license, were notes and memoranda from previous barkeeps. The earliest went back to the days of George III, and mentioned a mysterious breakout of fires, two of which had been damaging enough to force the Beldame's closure while the lower levels were repaired. And one note, dated 1822 and quoted by Mike, had mentioned "a ghastly stench, that brought to mind that smell of flesh burning, yet no fire to be seen, though we did search the premises in their entirety, from cellars to attics."

"Smoke, again." Lucy Radleigh was nodding. "The whole street sometimes smells like smoke. We've all come up against that—I know John Roberson even called a company in to see if rotten insulation could be causing the smell. They found nothing. No reason for it. I've smelled it, walking up to Sixteen. It gets strong enough to choke you, sometimes even on rainy days. Makes no sense, that. There's nothing burning in the Walk."

"And nothing outside the Walk, and no burning smell once you've gone past the Beldame or the old theatre at Number One, over at the Bouverie Street end—what's it called, the Bellefield?" Chrissie shivered, and forgot her careful grammar under the stress of memory. "Cor, I hate that smell," she said. "I do, really. First time I ever smelled smoke in the shop, that was the night I went to get my Phillip and found him slumped over the counter. Never had a moment's trouble with his ticker, not Phil, but he did that night, and it did for him." She blinked hard, and her mouth trembled. "I thought the whole shop was afire, the smell was that strong. But no—nothing, no fire or even smoke."

"Fire and smoke," Penny said dreamily, and Ringan's head jerked around. She sounded too far away for his liking; it brought back memories of their haunting by Betsy Roper and Will Corby the previous summer, and those bad moments when she'd seemed to want to be taken over by the very ghosts Ringan himself so desperately wanted gone.

But her eyes were shrewd and clear, and her next comment was completely in the present. "Or rather, smell of one but neither cause nor result to be seen anywhere. That's what you mean, isn't it, Mrs. Alexander?"

"That's it. And call me Chrissie, do. I can't do formal names with my neighbours. That's just silly."

"And I'm Penny. I can't do formal names at all, unless I'm trying to score points with someone. My name's far too much of a mouthful to be useful in conversation." Penny looked around at the assemblage. "So we've all had the recurring smoke thing, then? The sense that whatever or whoever was hanging about Hawthorne Walk, there was some traumatic connection with fire?"

"I never thought about it that way, but yes, of course, that sounds dead right." Ms. Radleigh smiled suddenly. "And call me Lucy, do. We're neighbours now. Has anyone said, welcome to the Walk? If not, I'm happy to be the first. We're all looking for great things from the Bellefield—shameful, that it's stood empty so long."

"Thanks, Lucy. I've got every intention of giving you great things from the Bellefield, once we nail down Lady Agnes the Demon Queen, and put her out on her bum."

Halligan's head snapped sideways. "The Demon Queen—that's definite, then? You've confirmed that we're dealing with the ghost of Lady Agnes de Belleville?"

"Agnes de Belleville Maldown, widow of Sir Hugh, mother and attempted killer of Lady Eleanor Caulfield," Ringan replied. "She's our resident haunt, all right. That's about as definite as we're going to get without a time machine, or a message written on the wall in ectoplasm. Child murderer and nutcase. That's our Demon Queen."

Everyone was suddenly talking at once, the room coming alive in a spontaneous outbreak of excited chatter. Ringan held up a hand.

"Look," he told the room generally, "I've got most of the back-story on this woman right here, in this envelope. I only came up with it late this afternoon—we'd planned to call Richard, here, and let him go over it first, but here we all are and everyone in this room is directly concerned in this. So, if no one can see a problem, my thinking is to give you all a thumbnail sketch of what I found out today. Penny's already heard the bare bones, as we were leaving to come here. Shall I go ahead?"

"Yes, please." Lily Dallow, who had been curled up in a Queen Anne chair with her feet tucked under her, got up and handed Ringan a fresh beer. "Start at the beginning. Who in heaven's name was this Lady Whatsis?"

Ringan opened the manila envelope and slid a stack of papers into his lap. "Before we get into the details, let me ask you all something. Is anyone here familiar with a very old traditional song called 'The Famous Flower of Serving Men'?"

Amid the general shaking of heads, Mike Dallow lifted a hand. "I am. Brilliant song, that is. All about a girl with a crazy mother who tries to have her killed . . ." He stopped abruptly, his eyes widening as the meaning behind Ringan's question met his own knowledge of the song and visibly produced a bright white light in his mind. As everyone watched in fascination, he opened his mouth, closed it again, shook his head, and then emptied his beer in one long swallow. "I don't believe it," he said when he could speak again. His voice was weak. "That song? It's based on a true story? On our story?"

"Apparently so. Don't feel bad, mate, it never occurred to me either, and I sing this stuff for a living." Ringan lifted a single sheet of paper. "This came off the computer of Dr. Madeline Holt, at the British Library. She specialises in the de Belleville family. Back when she was a student, she came across a casual reference in someone else's paper, mentioning that Richard II had signed off on the execution order of a member of the French royal family."

"This woman was a royal, then?" Lucy's eyes were alight with interest. "A French royal?"

"Not a genuine royal, a royal bastard. Daughter of a French king called Jean le Bon. Here's the chronology, and I'll keep it short: She was born in 1342, her father became king in 1350. Not sure when she was renamed de Belleville and officially acknowledged as a royal bastard; I don't think it matters, not for what we need. Her father arranged a marriage with an English knight called Sir Hugh Maldown, of Hertfordshire, who sounds like the villain in a bad romance novel. She came to England and married Maldown in 1359."

"I don't know very much about this sort of thing," Chrissie said slowly. "But—was that normal? Shipping off your kids?"

"Not only normal but standard." Richard Halligan took a mouthful of brandy. "I'm surprised they waited until she was seventeen; usually that would have been set up a good deal sooner than that."

"Would the fact that she was of, er, questionable mental balance have posed a problem?" Penny asked. "I mean, enough of a problem to offset her connections and presumed dowry?"

"I've no clue, love. Of course, from the look of Maddy Holt's notes, Sir Hugh wasn't the most stable thing on two legs, either." Ringan glanced down the page. "Ah. Her only surviving child— no, I don't know if there were other births, so don't ask me—was baptised Eleanor Marie at the Maldown family chapel, New Year's Day, 1362. And then nothing about the woman herself, except that she was probably absolutely miserable. Sir Hugh, from all accounts, was a complete sod. There are photocopies in this stack, of notes from the local parish records, and in this day and age he'd be taking court-mandated anger management courses and having restraining orders sworn out against him. He looks to have brutalised his wife on a regular basis, and if some of the reported whispers were true, he had a taste for little girls that doesn't bode well for Eleanor's happy childhood. I haven't found anyone with a good word for him. Even the monks sound completely unforgiving."

"I'd like to know—is there anything in there about whether this woman was always off her nut, or whether it came on later, after she'd got here?" Chrissie Alexander was clearly fascinated. "And what happened to him? To Sir Hugh?"

"He died."

Ringan's hands closed too tightly on the sheaf of papers he held. There it was again, that distant, dreamy voice that somehow wasn't completely Penny's own. A momentary touch of something, a channel opened that she couldn't or wouldn't close? Whatever it was, Ringan hated and feared it.

Coming hard on the heels of Donal's revelations about his late wife's possession and subsequent death, it was almost too much to take. He reached out one hand and poked her, hard, in the thigh. Her eyes cleared, and she turned to look at him with honest surprise.

Whatever it was, she wasn't aware it was happening. And that was the scariest thing of all.

"He died," Penny repeated, but this time her voice was normal, conversational. "Ringan, didn't you say he'd got some intestinal thing? In 1368, wasn't it?"

"The bloody flux." Ringan swallowed hard. Had no one else noticed that Penny had left them, not once but twice? Was he imagining things? "Details not really suitable for after-dinner conversation. A kind of inflammation of the bowels. Some modern researchers suspect bad water, dysentery, some hideous bug they couldn't treat. He died in the nick of time for whatever was left of Agnes's and the child Eleanor's well-being, too. Had he continued on the way he'd been going, there would have been nothing left of the Maldown estate within a year. The parish registry records Sir Hugh's death on Boxing Day."

"So the beastly Sir Hugh went to his just desserts in 1368, leaving a nearly impoverished widow with a small daughter. Eleanor would have been about seven." Richard Halligan finished writing and turned to a clean page in his notebook. "What then? Anything about the Maldown women we ought to know?"

"Not really. Agnes managed to bring the estate back a bit, with him gone. There are some sales recorded of crops sold at the local market, and of some sheep bought. For a crazy lady, she did seem to have a head for business." Ringan kept casting sideways glances at Penny. She was her usual self, right down to the physical posture he recognised as her wanting desperately to kick her shoes off and tuck her feet up under her, but restraining herself because she was a guest in someone else's home.

He caught her eye, and she smiled at him. "Go on, Ringan," she said encouragingly. "What's the next bit we ought to know?"

"The next bit happened in 1378, when the prioress at the local nunnery spoke with Lady Agnes about receiving her daughter Eleanor as a postulant, prior to taking the veil. There were four visits, two per year from 1378 to 1380 according to the convent's records; there's no mention of Eleanor being present for any of them. After that, nothing—total silence until 1381."

Chrissie and Lucy were leaning forward in their seats. Lily Dallow spoke up.

"And what happened in 1381?"

"The arrest of Lady Agnes on the charge that she hired three men to track down and kill her daughter Eleanor. Eleanor had declined to take the vows—she ran off with a bloke called Sir James Caulfield, a local knight with a small property, got pregnant, married him, and had a son." Ringan looked at his notes. "That was in 1379. The son was less than a week old when three men burst into the house, cut Sir James and the newborn's throats, dropped the bloody sword in Eleanor's lap, and left. Presumably, they figured she'd do herself in. Instead, she went into drag and got a job being a valet to Richard Plantagenet. All of this came out later; Eleanor was William Caulfield, the king's favourite dresser, basically, for at least eighteen months."

"My God." Lucy was open-mouthed. "It—no, really, it sounds like a movie plot. Or . . . "

"Or a folk song? Not surprising—it is one. I've got the song lyrics back at Penny's flat. I'll be happy to have them copied and drop them off with everyone." Ringan consulted the final page of Maddy Holt's information. "Eleanor's gender and personal history were apparently discovered by the king in 1381—he was just a boy himself, and likely wouldn't have considered whether she was male or female, because, well, women didn't apply for valet jobs. She served him under her late husband's name, or actually his father's name—Caulfield. There's nothing in here about how her identity was found out. But when the story came out, Richard told his uncle John of Gaunt to go bring Agnes in, and Gaunt did precisely that. She confessed to the entire thing, and was sentenced to death by beheading at Smithfield."

There was a long silence, as the guests to whom the story was new absorbed what they'd just heard. Finally, Mike Dallow asked the obvious question.

"Right," he said slowly. "So we know who she was, we know what she did, we know she was sentenced to die by having her head cut off at Smithfield. So what in sweet hell is she doing draped in fire and smoke, haunting Hawthorne Walk, a good two miles from where she was supposed to have died?"

"That," Ringan said slowly, "is what we need to find out. I mean, she obviously died right here, but we need to find out why she died right here. We do know that during and right after the trial, she was living on the spot of what's now the Bellefield: she was a royal, after all, and they wouldn't have left her in with common women prisoners at the Savoy dungeons. Richard, here, found a note about how she'd been consigned to the care of Martin Saxton, John of Gaunt's keeper of women prisoners. So she lived on Hawthorne Walk. That much is definite."

"That doesn't explain why she's haunting us up and down Hawthorne Walk, instead of making life miserable for the vendors over at the Smithfield market," Penny pointed out. This part of the story was new to her. "I know there was a fire on the Bellefield site, I know she was there, all the evidence and everything I saw and felt say she was trapped in there. But—look, this is insane. She wasn't just anyone, damn it—she was a royal. There would have been questions by the French Crown, records somewhere. She simply wouldn't have been left to die—my God, that could very well have triggered a war! Surely, if she was sentenced to be beheaded . . . ?"

"Well, that's the thing." Ringan's voice was very quiet. "There doesn't seem to be any record that she was ever actually beheaded. And we know she wasn't, don't we?"

As they left the Dallows' flat, it began to rain, a thin, dreary, weeping downpour that left streaks of winter dirt on everything it touched. Penny and Ringan sprinted for the car. As they hurriedly climbed in, the rain intensified.

"Damn." Penny turned the wipers on. "I hate this January weather."

"I know. I'd almost prefer a good hard freeze to this rubbish." Ringan looked at her out of the corner of his eye, debating with himself. At some point soon, he was going to have to raise the question of those two moments at the Dallow flat when she had seemed to be lost, somehow. He considered it for a moment, but decided that while she was navigating the car through horrendous weather in the dark wasn't the time. "You're looking awfully preoccupied," he said. "Penny for them?"

"My thoughts? Not sure they're worth a penny; they're awfully jumbled up. I don't feel very well, actually. I'm wondering if something in that gorgeous dinner could have disagreed with me. I hope not—I wouldn't have missed one mouthful." Penny pulled out into the sparse traffic, heading northeast towards Muswell Hill. "Ringan, what could have caused Martin Saxton, or anyone else, to abandon that woman to burn? How could anyone be so heartless? Maybe he didn't abandon her. Maybe she was deliberately put to death there. Doesn't the song say she was burned, by the king's order?"

"Yes, dear, but the song also has the king being led to the truth by a couple of magical animals. All things considered, I don't think we can take the entire lyric as gospel."

"Magical animals?" she said slowly. "What sort of magical animals?"

"A hind and a dove." Ringan's voice took on a bardic undertone as he sang the verse in question: "*Oh the hind she broke, the hind she flew / The hind she trampled the brambles through / First she'd melt, then she'd sound / Sometimes before, sometimes behind.* That sort of magical animal."

"A hind?" Unnoticed in the darkness of the Jaguar's interior, there was something odd in the set of Penny's upper body; she was straight-spined, somehow rigid. "A white hind?"

"Oh my." Ringan, under the lash of discovery, hadn't noticed the strangeness of Penny's posture. "Yes, indeed. *And as he rode himself alone / It's there he spied the milk-white hind.* A white hind. A perfect match for Richard II's white hart."

The car changed direction suddenly, turning hard right. The maneuvre was illegal, and dangerous; had the street borne its normal load of traffic, the Jaguar would have been broadsided. Ringan wrenched his head to stare at her.

"Penny—what are you doing?"

"I need to go to the Bellefield." Her voice was slurred. "I need to go *now.*"

Ringan's heart stammered for a few beats. Backlit by the street lamps as the car raced below them, Penny's profile was masklike. She looked like an ancient statue given breath, a golem. What she didn't look like was Penny.

He couldn't stop her, not without grabbing the wheel and sending them into a tree or another car. He forced panic down and heard his own voice, astonishingly reasonable.

"Why do we need to go to the Bellefield, lamb?"

"Something's wrong." The Jag jumped and accelerated, not enough to be dangerous, enough to be noticeable. Ringan put a hand forward to steady himself. "I can feel it. It's like drums— thump, bang, like jungle drums. Warning, danger, hurry, go—dear God, Ringan, can't you feel it? We have to go there, we have to go now."

"All right, love. We'll go, then." Ringan was sweating, a true fear sweat. Dear heaven, what was happening to her? "Do you have the keys with you?"

"I don't know. I think so." She lifted one hand from the wheel and pressed it to her forehead. "I've got such a headache—it just came on, a few minutes ago."

"Mind that bus, will you? He's taking the corner wide." Ringan, dry-mouthed and thanking the luck for the Jaguar's excellent steering, watched with relief as she put both hands back on the wheel. The rain was pelting down now, an audible counterpart to the thrumming of the Jag's engines. He could hear it, the voice of the season and of his own fear of the situation.

Penny looped off Fleet Street and into Bouverie. The street was empty, no cars at all. She swung left and edged the Jag into the loading area at the back of the Bellefield.

And suddenly, out of the darkness and the driving angry rain, whatever it was that had driven Penny into that hard fast push across London found Ringan as well. A sense of urgency, a level of intuition beyond anything he'd ever experienced, slammed into his awareness and ran through his blood like rampant microbes. Penny had been right; he could feel it all through his body, a thumping urgency close to pain, behind his eyes. It was audible, violent, intolerable.

Ringan made a noise in his throat, pulled off his safety belt, and jumped from the car. His whole body seemed electric with unde-fined need. Penny was already out, hurrying up Bouverie Street to the Bellefield's front entrance on Hawthorne Walk, scrabbling franti-cally in her purse as she went. Ringan caught her up as she reached the front doors.

"Keys?" he asked. He was incapable of unnecessary speech. Penny, silent as well, pulled the heavy familiar ring from her purse. With fingers that seemed stiff and uncooperative, she got the multiple locks undone. As she slammed the dead bolt open, she stopped suddenly.

"Ringan." She was whispering, a grainy sibilance nearly carried off on the wet wind. "There's something. . . . "

He saw it, even as her voice died away. Light had begun to leak and froth around the edges of the heavy black-painted Victorian doors, a cold phosphorescence. It curled and moved like a sick par-ody of London's famous fog, twisting out into the night, spilling over Ringan's boots, beginning to circle and wreathe around him.

He was hot, he was cold. Where the light touched him he could feel the heat of the fire, flame fuelled by the hawthorn used to in-sulate these walls, the walls of John Saxton's little house, but he was cold too, cold at wrist and ankle, cold where the iron manacles he must wear until someone came to rescue him from this inferno touched him, until he could make confession, until he could ease the weight of what he knew, what he had done, from his stained soul, until the headsman brought the great axe down and offered the death stroke and then there could be peace, absolution, a place in eternity away from these visions, these dreams of blood and torment. There were smoke, and flame, and somewhere there was someone screaming. . . .

"*Ringan!*"

The scream was right there, at his side. It brought Ringan back to himself, took his awareness, and forced him into the present day.

"*Ringan!*"

Penny's voice. It was Penny who was screaming.

She was pulling at him now, pointing with her free hand, gesturing, as her mouth formed shapeless unheard incoherencies. Ringan looked down at himself, saw that the icy burning light had reached his waist, and jumped backwards and away. As he moved, pulling Penny with him, he followed her still-pointing finger, and saw what she had seen.

The entire south side of Hawthorne Walk was obscured by that same unnatural glow. It was pouring out of the interstices between the bricks of the Bellefield's dancing arches like sand from a fractured hourglass, spiralling heavenwards, distorting alike the substance and shadow of the night as it went.

Ringan got hold of Penny's elbow, and clamped hard. He dragged her towards Bouverie Street, feeling her resistance.

"Come along." His teeth were chattering, a pulse in his brow slammed like breakers on a rocky cliffside, and his stomach was in an uproar. They were both drenched to the skin. It would be a miracle, he thought grimly, if even one of them came out of this without pneumonia to show for it. "Bloody hell, woman, will you move! I'm wet, I'm cold, and I'm not letting you go back there tonight, so you might as well just come along."

"The front doors." Penny's voice was as unsteady as her legs. "The theatre. Unlocked."

"Sod the front doors." He pulled her across Bouverie and away from Hawthorne Walk entirely. It had eased up, now that they were out of contact with the building. "You really think someone's going to try to break in? Fight their way through the Demon Queen's light show? To do what? Steal an old ladder or some paint cans? Let them. That's Darwinism at work."

"No, you're right. I'm sorry." Penny's face was turned away from him, and her voice was muffled. Ringan saw her shoulders contract, and with helpless horror, understood that she had begun to cry, slow wrenching sobs visible down the length of her spine. In nearly eleven years together, he had never seen Penny cry.

He reached out and gathered her in.

"It's all right." The words were ridiculous, he thought. It was absolutely nothing like all right. In fact, he wasn't certain how it could possibly get worse. At this point, he wasn't sure there was any way to get Agnes Maldown out of Hawthorne Walk and to her eternal rest, even if they brought Jesus, Mary, and all the saints along for backup. And those lost moments at the Dallows' flat, what of those? Had Agnes found a way out of the Walk, hitching a ride like a parasite, travelling in Penny? Oh, God. "You're all right," he repeated.

"Oh, right. I'm simply too ducky for words." Penny hunted around in her pocket, found a tissue, and blew her nose resoundingly. "Ringan. You felt her, this time, didn't you? Did you see anything? Visions?"

"Not here." His voice was flat and cold. "Let's get away from the theatre, across town, get home and warm and dry. We're going to talk about this, by Christ we are, but not just about this. There's something else needs to be said."

He glanced across Bouverie Street to the southwestern edge of Hawthorne Walk. There was nothing but the blackness of the hour, and a fine misty rain falling; as he had stood comforting Penny with inadequacies, the chilly light had dissipated like sewer steam on a busy street. The Bellefield, with its ornamental arches and its newly refurbished brass fittings, sat as though nothing more unusual than a cancelled performance had ever disturbed its patient serenity.

———

Penny, huddled in front of the gas fire with her hands wrapped securely round a mug of hot tea laced with brandy, sat and waited for just the right moment to break a long silence.

The drive back had been accomplished without a word spoken; all Penny's attention was deliberately pointed at a safe, trouble-free drive on the treacherously slick roads, and Ringan had made it quite clear that he would say nothing until they were home. His silence had produced an unfortunate effect; Penny became convinced that he was mad at her for some reason. Since trying to figure out what the source of his annoyance might be was futile, Penny turned her brain off to anything but driving.

Once they were safely indoors, however, it became obvious that whatever might be troubling Ringan, it wasn't anger or annoyance at her. He got them both out of their wet clothes and into warm robes, got her a towel to rub her hair dry, settled her down and turned on the gas fire, and marched off into the kitchen in search of something comforting for her to eat. Penny let herself relax a bit, but kept quiet.

After he'd given her the doctored tea, Ringan did something unusual; he hunted through her kitchen cabinet until he found a bottle of gin, and poured himself a good stiff shot. Since he rarely drank anything other than cider or beer, something unusual and momentous was clearly in the offing.

The silence stretched out. Just as Penny felt she couldn't bear it any longer and was opening her mouth to say something, anything at all, Ringan finally spoke.

"You asked me if I felt her. The answer is no. I *was* her." His tone was perfectly level, and a bit distant. Penny gaped at him, speechless. "I knew what she was. I knew what she wanted. I felt her need, this enormous driving need—something weighing on her, a secret, something no one knew, something she hadn't told anyone. That's what you've been getting, isn't it? Suddenly knowing what Agnes knew, feeling what she felt?"

Penny found her voice. "Sometimes. Not when Ray Haddon died, though. That time was different. I was seeing through her eyes. But you already knew that, Ringan."

"And what about tonight?" He was staring into the fire, turning the gin around in one hand, letting the glow play off the faceting in the glass, off the face of the clear liquid it held. "Did you see through her eyes tonight?"

"At the theatre?" She watched him, puzzled. "No, that was more just a sort of knowledge, a kind of—"

"I'm not talking about the theatre." His head turned partly towards her; the dance of colour from the gas fire cast his bearded profile into sharp relief against the flat's pale walls. "I'm talking about at the Dallows' flat. After dinner. I'm talking about the two times tonight when you went away."

She stared at him. He took another mouthful of gin. It came to her that he was unwilling to meet her eyes.

"What are you talking about?" The question was quiet, but with an urgent backbite. "What in hell's name do you mean, I went away? I didn't go anywhere. Tell me what you mean. And look at me! Why won' t you look at me, Ringan? What's wrong with you? What, are you scared of me, all of a sudden?"

"Not of you, Penny. *For* you." He turned his head then, and she saw the fear in his eyes. Her throat closed.

"You don't remember." It was a statement, not a question. "Twice. It happened twice. First time, it was just a moment, a flicker, really—Chrissie or Lucy or someone was talking about smelling smoke and you said something about smoke and fire, but it wasn't your voice—you went all dreamy and absent, the way you did last summer. It only lasted a moment, I might have been mistaken, but the second time was more distinct—Chrissie wanted to know what happened to Hugh Maldown. Do you remember what you said, Pen?"

"No." Her face seemed locked into place. "I don't remember that. What did I say?"

"You said, he died. It wasn't your voice, and even more to the point, you smiled and it wasn't anything like your smile, love. You had this chilly, sensual, satisfied moment—it wasn't you. It wasn't anything like you."

He gulped the rest of the gin and set the glass down, rather too sharply. "Now you're saying you don't remember. You want to know if I'm frightened for you? I'm bloody terrified. And you need to know why? Sinead McCreary's why, Penny. And in case you hadn't noticed, you're vulnerable to this. I don't know how it happened, or why, but you're open, full throttle; something about the haunting at Lumbe's seems to have left you with no defences against this sort of thing at all. You can't keep these things off— you can't block them out. Last summer, you nearly faded out right before our eyes—it was as if you wanted to be drawn into the world those ghosts were stuck in."

"Ringan, for heaven's sake! If you think I want any part of this psychotic that's making all our lives so damned miserable, you must be psychotic yourself. I loathe this woman. How can you even think . . . "

"I don't." He was suddenly in front of her, hands clutching her shoulders. "I think she wants a part of you. I think tonight, she got a part of you, not once but twice."

"Why?" Penny whispered. "Why would she want me?"

"I think she may have found herself a way off Hawthorne Walk." His voice dropped and broke. "And I don't know, not for the life of me, what we can do to stop her."

# Eight

*And how she wept as she changed her name*
*From Fair Eleanor to Sweet William*
*Went to court to serve her King*
*As the Famous Flower of Serving Men*

"Excuse me. Are you—you're Madeline Holt, aren't you?"

Maddy, sitting at her desk and reading an official memorandum about purchase orders for new revolving storage facilities, glanced up at this unexpected voice. She was at a disadvantage, since she had a mouthful of half-chewed Cadbury's caramel chocolate to contend with. Moreover, she recognised her visitor at once. Her best friend Candida's famous sister Penny was hard to miss.

She swallowed the chocolate as quickly as she could, narrowly avoiding choking, and got to her feet.

"Yes, I am—I'm Maddy Holt. And you're Penny—the last time I saw you, I think it was Richard and Candida's wedding. My name was still Valroy in those days. I'm not sure if you remember, but we met then?"

"Yes. Yes, I do remember. You look rather different."

Maddy looked up at Penny, wondering. While she knew Penny was merely stating the obvious, the fact was that Penny herself looked different enough to be startling. It was certainly Penelope Wintercraft-Hawkes, there was no mistake about that, but something was wrong, or perhaps just different about her. She was the same physically, if a few years further down the time line, but what Maddy remembered of Penny from their last meeting was not what Maddy was seeing now. The woman she had met had been the enviable possessor of a self-assurance so tangible it was intimidating. Something had gone awry; it was subtle and hard to define, but something seemed missing, or watered-down, somehow.

At a loss, that was it. Penny looked uncertain, tentative, unsure of herself. While an uncertain Penny was obviously possible, it was also unnerving.

"I'm sorry," Penny said. "Is this a bad time?"

"No, no, of course not. Please, have a seat, do. Can I get you a cup of espresso? Is there something I can help you with?"

"Coffee—yes, please, that would be lovely. Help me—yes, I expect so. I hope so." Good heavens, Maddy thought, was that diffidence she was hearing in Penny's voice? "I need to go somewhere to go find out something and I think you may be the only person who can tell me where I ought to be going. And what I ought to be finding out. Or the best person, anyway."

"I see." Maddy rummaged in the cupboard beneath the window, pulling out two cups, and a small tin of butter cookies. "This is about Agnes Maldown. Isn't it?"

"Yes." Penny watched her as she prepped the little espresso machine. The world outside the window was a uniform grey wall of fog. Even the outlines of the tower housing the King's Collection were blurred and amorphous. The building seemed oddly muted, as if all sounds were being filtered through a mesh of wet air.

"Here—this will only take a minute." Maddy waited until the machine ceased its hissing. She poured two cups, and passed one to Penny. "Can we be really frank here, about what you need? Ringan told me about your aunt and the Bellefield—he also told me a bit about what's going on."

"Our haunting, you mean? Or the fact that she seems to be getting stronger? That she would like to leave Hawthorne Walk? That perhaps she has found herself a way?"

Maddy stared at her, the base of her spine taut. Something had gone wrong with Penny's voice, a kind of deepening, a dip in the pitch, a sudden soft curving change in the emphases of her vocal formations. She was speaking English, yet the vocal mannerisms all sounded French.

Penny's face was changing as well. It was happening before Maddy's eyes, hardening around the jaw, lines that had no place on Penny's bone structure forming along the length of her cheeks, something that was not a right thing, that didn't belong, melting and reshaping the musculature as if it were putty, running like a disease through the very essence of what made Penny herself.

Maddy sat very still. Something was looking at her, some evil homunculus behind Penny's eyes. It was not Penny.

*"Vous ne me brûlerez plus,"* Penny said coldly. Her eyes had become long, chilly slits. *"Je ne resterai pas ici. Je ne brûlerai pas. . . . "*

Maddy opened her mouth. She was frightened beyond anything she had ever felt; what had invaded her pleasant office, riding the January wind and Penny's inability to shut this thing out? Maddy had no idea what she was going to say, no idea what in the world she could do. What came out of her mouth surprised her as nothing in her life had ever done.

*"Il n'est pas temps pour vous de partir, Agnes."* She heard her own voice as if it came from a mountaintop, a thousand light-years beyond that encompassing wall of winter fog outside the Library. *"Revenez à votre endroit."*

She was quiet a moment, hearing as if through another's ears the cold, calm implacability of her own voice. *"Ecoutez, Agnes, écoutez. Quand votre moment de paix viendra, vous saurez. Ecoutez."*

For a moment, an eternity, time itself seemed to listen to Maddy's command to wait, and to obey.

Penny's face softened. The predatory, raptorlike edges eased and went. Her eyes opened wide, fixed on Maddy, blinked. The pupils, which had been pinpoints in a sea of icy grey, widened to normalcy.

She began to sob. There was no warning, no buildup; she simply broke. In the passage of ten seconds or less, she was convulsed into a gale of weeping, shuddering, knowing perhaps that she couldn't control it and certainly making no attempt to stop. She let it come because she had no choice.

Maddy got to her feet and went to stand behind Penny's chair. She was trembling, tiny darts of reaction to her own part in what had, most unbelievably, just happened to them both. Without thinking, she draped her arms over Penny's shoulders and laid her cheek against the curly dark hair, and began to rock and croon as though to soothe a child waking from a bad dream.

"It's all right." Maddy heard herself, her light clipped tones with their usual cadence of higher education and good upbringing now a shapeless singsong of comfort. "Hush. It's all right. She's gone away. You're all right. Hush now. . . . "

Penny whimpered. Her hands came up and clutched those soft, encompassing arms. The shudders lightened, lessened, became a spasmodic jerk of flesh and spirit, and faded out altogether.

They stayed as they were for a few seconds, breathing deeply, testing the air in the pleasant office and finding that it was, for now, clear of anything wrong, of any unwanted intruder. Then, in a clear signal, Penny gently patted Maddy's arms and dropped her own hands to rest lightly on her knees. Maddy straightened up, blowing hard to release pent-up air from her lungs. She hadn't even realised she'd been holding her breath.

"Jesus." Penny stood, trying to balance herself; her knees were trembling and uncooperative. "Thank you. I don't know what just happened, I don't remember, but I heard you talking, talking in French. Thank you. What—what did I say?"

Maddy picked up her cooling cup of espresso and tipped the contents down her throat. Her hands were unsteady.

"You didn't say anything." She shivered; the coffee had a kick like a horse. "Whatever was using your mouth said that I, or whoever she was talking to, wasn't going to burn her anymore. That you, she, whoever, wasn't going to stay here." The power and rage of that remembered presence were sickening. "And then she said, 'I will not burn.' That's all."

"It was her." Penny had wrapped her arms around herself. She looked sick. "I heard you call her Agnes. It was. She was here. She was in me. Wasn't she? It's true?"

"I think so. No, I'm sure of it. I don't know how I knew it was her, though; I just sort of felt her, saw her, understood her." Maddy's face puckered, her high brow glistening and clammy. "She went, anyway. I told her it wasn't her time to achieve peace, I told her to wait, that she'd know when it was her time, and she went. It had to have been Agnes. I knew what to say to a dead woman, and I talked to a dead woman, and she responded." She turned suddenly and reached for the wastebasket on the floor beside her desk. "Oh, God," she managed, and was violently sick.

"This has to stop."

Something in Penny's tone took Maddy's attention. She swallowed the bitter taste of bile laced with coffee and chocolate, fought back another spasm of nausea, and looked up at Penny. The wide grey eyes were intense and angry, and Penny's generous mouth was compressed with might have been rage, or concentration. "I can't do this. I can't let this happen. Someone's already died because of this woman, at least one person, and I suspect more have and more will. She's getting stronger. She's using me to get stronger, and I won't have it. I won't allow it. It has to stop." She met Maddy's eyes. "And you have to help me. I can't do this alone. Ringan can't help, not on this. I need you. Will you help?"

"Yes." Maddy rubbed the back of her hand across her lips. There was something heartening, nourishing, about Penny's firmness and sense of purpose. It jumped between them, a spark of determined power, impossible to disregard. "You're damned right I will. But I don't know how. Do you?"

"I think there's something we don't know, something about Agnes." Penny looked around for her chair, and sat back down. "I've been thinking about it, and measuring it against what I felt when she was close, or touching me, or trying to use me. I couldn't pin it down, not until last night. But last night—we had this enormous feeling, a pull, that we had to go to the Bellefield, that something was wrong. Ringan felt it, too. And we went, and this time, Ringan felt her as well. He said that for just a minute or two, he thought he was her. Not that she was using him, just that her presence there, her need, was so strong that he put it on like a coat, or a second skin."

"Then you're right. She really is getting stronger."

"Yes." Penny's mouth was grim. "But you see, we both felt the same thing last night—a sense of secrecy. She's keeping a secret. It's something enormous, something huge. I think that, whatever it was, it may be the thing that's keeping her tied to Hawthorne Walk."

"All right. Let me process this—sorry, I want to think out loud. I find it helps." Maddy perched on the edge of her desk, drumming her fingers on the polished surface. "What do we know, in simple straight terms? A woman, a French royal bastard, from a family of questionable sanity. Presumably a bit loopy herself. Sent off to marry a complete pig in England. Has a child, Eleanor. Husband wastes the estate, terrorises her, probably brutalises Eleanor as well. Husband dies unexpectedly, Agnes brings the estate back to a bit of fiscal health. Suddenly decides her daughter is taking the vows. Her daughter disagrees, runs off, gets married, gets pregnant. Agnes apparently goes thoroughly off her nut, hires some masked men to murder Eleanor. Husband and child killed instead; Eleanor escapes, cuts her hair and borrows her late husband's clothes, calls herself William Caulfield, and becomes a valet to the King of England. King finds out, has Agnes arrested, tried, convicted, and sentenced to beheading. Peasants' Rebellion breaks out, Wat Tyler's boys set the north bank of the Thames on fire, and instead of having her head taken off at Smithfield, Agnes cooks in the wardour's house on Hawthorne Walk, apparently being left to die and unable to run because she's got leg irons on. Now she seems to be infesting the entire street where she died and would like to spread her sphere of influence, and we want to stop her. Have I missed anything? You look—I don't know—puzzled."

"Go back a bit," Penny said slowly. "What you said about her family being of questionable sanity, and about her probably being a bit mad as well. Is there anything to support that?"

Maddy tilted her head. "What's in your mind, Penny?"

"Why are we assuming she was mad? I can't see it. She brought the Maldown estate back from ruin. You yourself gave Ringan the notes, all those purchases of good cattle and changing crops to make more money. She doesn't sound mad to me, Maddy. She sounds like a fighter, like a woman who was determined to salvage the estate for herself and her child. She sounds tough, smart, and eminently sane. So why does everyone think she was mad?"

Maddy turned it over in her mind. Penny was right. Nothing in

Agnes's history before 1381 showed any signs of madness. It was that final cataclysmic action, that irrevocable moment in which she paid three men to kill her only child, that had led them to think she was insane. That, and one other thing . . .

"When Ringan came up here that day, he spoke about the haunting—he said you all felt she was insane." Maddy's trained historian's mind had clicked into high gear; it was working, sorting, arranging and making sense of random facts. "So if we take what you believe—and I agree, it makes sense—and assume that she was sane right up to the point where she hired those killers, then what happened? What drove her out of her mind? What could that breaking point have been?"

"I'm not convinced it happened when she hired the killers."

Maddy blinked. "What are you thinking? Come on, Penny, talk to me! I can't help unless I know what you know."

"I don't know anything. I want to know. I just don't think the murder was her breaking point, that's all. I think that whatever happened, it was connected to Eleanor's refusal to take the veil. And I want to know why Agnes wanted her there in the first place, badly enough to lose her mind when Eleanor refused. There had to be a reason, surely? And I don't know where to look. I don't know where to begin."

"I do." Maddy's eyes were alight with realisation. "My God, I'm a twit. We've been looking at the wrong set of facts."

"Meaning?"

"We've been concentrating on Agnes. But nothing in any of the recorded history dealing with her is going to tell us why she lost her mind. Believe me, I've got the facts damned well memorised. There's nothing there."

Penny's face was drawn. "Then what are we supposed to do?"

"Don't you see? This isn't about the mother, it's about the daughter. We need to find out about Eleanor. And she supposedly went back to France after Richard found out she was a woman. That was on the information card at a display of de Valois artifacts I saw at Cluny. God, I'm an idiot! If I'd made this connection in my head sooner . . ."

"What are you talking about?"

"A woman called Angela Duperres, curator of the de Valois exhibit—she's the one who filled me in on a lot of things I never knew about Agnes. Thing is, she said—crikey, I'm a fool. She said that the mother was interesting but the daughter wasn't exactly boring, and to use all the tools, and find tools if the ones I had weren't enough." Maddy's eyes were blazing. "I never had any real interest in Eleanor. Because, well, it was her mother who fascinated me, and her mother apparently died in 1381, so I never saw any reason to go hunting after that. But if that card had it right, the one at the Cluny exhibit, Eleanor went back to France. She had a pension from Richard, for her service to the Crown. That probably stopped after he was killed, or when he was imprisoned at Pontefract, when his cousin Henry Bolingbroke came back from France and claimed the throne. But there should be a trail—there must be. This is all about Eleanor. If there's anything left to discover, it's all about her. We have to track down Eleanor."

"Then that's what we're going to do." Penny was up, her own eyes gleaming. "Wherever Eleanor went, that's where we have to go. Do you know where?"

"No, but there's a very good chance I will by tomorrow. I've got a better handle on my tools than I used to. I know precisely where to start looking, at the de Valois family records. I've got a colleague in Paris who shares my speciality, medieval France." She grinned suddenly. "That's to say, he's another de Valois maniac, except he likes the ones that actually got crowned. I'll call him and set him on it. Logically, Eleanor would have gone to one of two places: either to her great-uncle the king, that was Charles VI, or to her maternal grandmother's family. There was no one else for her to turn to, not in France—her father's family was English. I know where the king was, but if she went back to Agnes's mother's family, a bit of hunting may be needed. Still, as I say, I've got my sources these days."

Penny slid into her coat. "So, what do I do?"

"Just pack a bag, and be ready to spend a few days in France. I'll call you in the morning, and let you know what's going on."

At just past three the following afternoon, Penny and Maddy got off a commuter flight from London to Paris, and picked up a rental car at Charles de Gaulle Airport.

The trip from England had been made in a peculiar silence. Penny had taken Maddy's phone call at ten that morning, a simple "I've got what was wanted. We're going to a town called Bernay, in Normandy. Make sure you've got a brolly—it's raining in France. See you at the airport." She'd given Penny the flight number, told her what time to be there, and rung off.

This suited Penny, who found herself disinclined towards unnecessary conversation. She was in a strange frame of mind; sometime between her breakdown in Maddy's office and the end of the nearly sleepless night that followed, she had come to terms with a few simple truths, and asked herself several difficult questions to which, as yet, she had no answers.

The truths, stated baldly to herself, were unnerving. A woman who had been dead for more than six hundred years was trying to use her as transport away from the place in which she had burned to death, and to which she seemed tied. This, in itself, was unsettling enough; the addition of the dead woman's probable murderous tendencies and extreme violent madness should have caused Penny nightmares.

But the truth was, Penny had spent those hours lying beside a lightly snoring Ringan, staring into the darkness of her comfortable bedroom and wondering about Agnes Maldown. Somehow, the live woman and the dead woman could not be made to cohere as the same person in Penny's mind. The factual gulf between the seeming history and the events of the past weeks was too great. What could have happened, to push a tough, sane, financially savvy woman into enough of a mental meltdown that she would send those killers after her only child? What was the secret that both Penny herself and now Ringan, as well, had felt as such a crushing weight on Agnes's spirit? And was it even going to be possible to send her on her way? How could you exorcise a ghost who was fire, and smoke, and cold angry light? How did you banish a scream in the shadows?

Sometime before Penny finally closed her eyes for a scant three hours of restless sleep, a phrase popped into her mind and lodged itself there. It followed her into the realm of dream and REM sleep, moving sinuously through the detachment of her slumbering consciousness. It was there when she woke, far back behind her red-rimmed eyes. She was too tired to track it down to its source. But it was there, nonetheless.

*We buy what we loathe with what we love.*

Maddy, unlike Penny, had slept long and dreamlessly. She was in a far more satisfactory state of mind; just before bed, she'd got the phone call she was hoping for, from her colleague at the Bibliothèque Nationale. Her hand was steady enough as she jotted down the gist of the information she believed would tell them what they needed to make sense of Agnes Maldown's behaviour. As she listened to directions, dates, roads to be taken, all the tension, the fear, the dizzying sickness that had troubled her since her own unexpected reaction to Penny's moments of unnatural tenancy faded out like ground fog. This was the peace attained by the scholar who was also the hunter, passionate and hungry to know, finding and absorbing the power of information.

Maddy had reserved a rental car. Penny, detached and placid in the rarefied fashion that attends complete exhaustion, settled down in the passenger seat. Maddy got in behind the wheel, consulted a map, made a mental note, and slid the map over to Penny. Penny let one hand rest lightly on the carefully folded paper, but truth to tell, she barely noticed. She was out of her body, half-stupefied with tiredness.

Maddy eased the car through the curving interchanges leading away from the airport. She nosed into the dense stream of traffic headed into Paris proper.

"Penny?"

"Yes, what is it, all right, I'm awake." She wasn't awake; she'd dozed off momentarily. *What we loathe,* she thought dreamily, *what we love,* and then pushed the line away. It was beginning to annoy her; where in sweet hell had that phrase originated? She'd heard it, she'd spoken it, it was almost tactile in her mind's eye, and yet, she couldn't place it. Surely it wasn't Shakespearean. . . ? She opened both eyes and noted the ugly Parisian outskirts. "Hmmm. We're going into the city, then?"

"Yes, for the night. What we need is actually at the Abbey of Bernay, in the Haute-Normandie. It's about three hours from Paris and it's awfully late in the day to start. The abbot is expecting us tomorrow, early afternoon. He says he'll give us lunch." Maddy accelerated, swung the car around a lumbering lorry whose driver didn't seem to believe in or understand the concept of lanes, and picked up speed. "We've got rooms in a nice little hotel I know, near the Ecole Militaire."

"In the seventh? Good. There's a brasserie I know over there, and they do an outstanding *belle Hélène* for dessert. I adore pears with ice cream." Penny rubbed her stinging eyes. "I must have a quick shower once we've checked in," she remarked. "So, we're likely to be gone—what? Two nights?"

"At least two." They'd reached the Péripherique, the road that rings the City of Light, and Maddy was watching for their exit. "Philippe—that's my friend at the Bibliothèque—didn't tell me what the information was, not in detail. He simply chased down the name, Eleanor Caulfield, and says that according to his database, there's rather a lot about her in the records at the Abbey in Bernay. But for all I know, whatever they've got could send us racketing halfway across France. Is that a problem? Do you need to clear your schedule, tell people?"

"No, that's fine—I called David Harkins, the senior actor in my troupe, and asked him to explain to the rest of the cast. And I left Ringan a note." Penny was waking up, now that they'd actually entered the city. Paris is, at one and the same time, geographically pleasing and visually invigorating, and Penny, who adored the place, was not immune to its spell. "Silly man, he shot out the door at a hellish hour this morning. He had to drive down to Lumbe's—that's his cottage in Somerset, near Glastonbury. He's got an ancient tithe barn, and apparently a bit of the thatch fell off one corner of the roof. So the master restorer bloke, not trusting the locals to do what they've been doing to complete perfection for a thousand years, has gone down to oversee repairs. If we have to stay longer, I'll phone him." It occurred to her that Maddy might well be in the same position. "What about yourself? Does the Library allow open-ended jaunts to the Continent?"

"Jaunt?" Maddy grinned. "This is a busman's holiday for me, I'll have you know. I did my thesis on the de Belleville family and everyone at work knows I've been trying to track down more about Agnes for a good eight years now. They wouldn't dream of trying to stop me. I even get paid for it."

"Can't beat that, can you?" Penny's mind was elsewhere. The fabulous Parisian skyline was beginning to declare itself against the evening sky. Monuments popped into and out of the frame of her vision: the stately dome of Invalides, Tour Montparnasse, unapologetically ugly and modern, and there, with its lights just sparking to exquisite life, the stolidly massive bulk of the Eiffel Tower. Penny closed her eyes and felt herself relax into a kind of calmly energised pleasure.

"We buy what we loathe with what we love," she said aloud, not realising, and jumped as Maddy, easing the car into a space that had just opened up, replied.

"*Iphigenia*. Nice, if weird. I adore that play."

Of course, Penny thought. That was the source: the distraught mother Clytemnestra, learning of her husband's plan to sacrifice their beloved daughter, confronting him, listening to him lie, going face to face with evil and exigence to protect her daughter, willing to go to her knees to beg help from Achilles, a perfect stranger, the man who would never have been Iphigenia's husband and who had been used by Agamemnon. Somehow, somewhere, a deeper meaning. We buy what we loathe . . .

"Penny? Hello?"

Jerked back to reality, Penny realised that the car was parked and the engine turned off, that Maddy was standing on the dark windy pavement with her suitcase in hand, and that she was patiently waiting for Penny to extract herself and her overnight bag as well. Moving slowly, Penny eased her longer legs out of the small car, got hold of her suitcase, and followed Maddy up the street to the hotel.

Maddy greeted the concierge, presented papers, signed in, offered credit cards. Penny smiled when addressed, murmured, but her mind was moving and moving fast. The one line, stuck in her memory— it came from the very play she would not have considered producing for a moment, had she not been overwhelmed by a need to look at it since walking through the Bellefield's doors. Surely it meant some- thing? Surely there was a meeting place, a moment in time or space within the haunted realms of life and death and history, where Agnes Maldown's reality and the reality of that much-maligned, famously embittered, passionate would-be murderess Clytemnestra touched and melded? And why, knowing as she did how strange was her need to present this very play, and how linked was that need to Agnes and the haunted galleries of the Bellefield, had she not looked at that need before now?

She followed Maddy into the minuscule ornate lift. It stopped on the second floor, and she pushed the folding wrought iron gate back and held it while Maddy got out and led the way down the hall to Room 202. Penny was scarcely aware of any of this. Her mind was churning.

Once through the doors and into the room, she allowed her at- tention to be diverted. It was a charming, old-fashioned hotel room; traditional high ceilings, painted plaster cornices, two twin-sized beds with carved iron headboards and soft thick duvets on the mat- tresses. There was a large dresser for their clothes, and a free-standing wardrobe for things that needed hanging; there was a smallish bath- room with a wonderful tub and not enough light. Penny sighed with pleasure, and kicked her shoes off. The room was unremit- tingly French; if she'd had any doubts about where she was, this room and all it embodied would have dispelled them. She was in Paris, and glad to be there.

She pushed the fret of questions away. The shower she had prom- ised herself kicked her back to full consciousness; the water was hot and the pressure powerful, a balm to tired muscles. She dried her hair while Maddy took her turn under the hot water, and pulled on fleece and her down coat and soft flat boots. Rosy-cheeked, restored, and hungry, they went out into the night in search of dinner and a *belle Hélène* for dessert.

The following day, they left Paris behind them early in the morning and headed east towards Bernay and the Haute-Normandie.

They had cleared Paris, and were travelling east under a steely sky and through light traffic, when it occurred to Penny that she had no idea whom they were going to see.

"Oh," Maddy said, "he's called the abbé Arnaud. He's the man in charge. Philippe said he was an older bloke, rather nice. I got the impression that he was a bit on the chatty side. Which," she added thoughtfully, "might be all to the good for us, depending on what he wants to chat about. If he wants to rabbit on about architecture, or church history, though . . . "

"Oh, I think we can likely steer the conversation our way." Penny, one eye on the road, saw a sign that matched her instructions. "Here, our turn-off's coming up—we want E402, the Route Nationale. It's the direction marked 'Bouille.' "

They continued on for awhile in companionable silence. Each had reached the same point in their thought processes. There was no point in worrying, because whatever knowledge they might take away from this day's work, that result was no longer up to them. It lay in the hands of the unknown abbé Arnaud.

They reached Bernay shortly before midday. The town itself was beautiful, set into a green valley created as two rivers, the Charentonne and Cosnier, intersected. They drove slowly past charmingly angular houses with odd little architectural bits; here a dormer like a wink, there an ancient door like a dimple.

The Abbey was easy enough to find, hardly surprising, since it was at the town's centre. Maddy found a parking space on the Place de la République. As churchbells around Bernay began to toll the noon hour, the women walked into the Abbey and were escorted through an exquisite welter of ancient stone columns and wondrous Gothic architecture, directly to the abbé Arnaud's private sanctum.

The man himself was a surprise. For the two women, raised in the genteelly unemphatic bosom of the Anglican Church, the mental picture of a powerful Catholic prelate was wildly different from the reality. Where they had subconsciously been expecting a small, elderly man in dusty black robes and full tonsure, the abbé Arnaud proved to be a sleek, sixtyish man with a beautiful mane of ordered silver hair. His cassock was certainly not dusty. He wore the abbot's badge of office, a pectoral cross of heavy chased silver depending from a thick chain, with an air of confidence bordering on elegance.

"Dr. Holt? And Mademoiselle—I'm so sorry, I don't have your name. Welcome to you both." He stood to greet them, shaking hands in a courtly fashion. His voice was smooth, well educated; he spoke in charmingly accented but fluent English. "*Bonjour.* I hope the traffic from Paris was not too difficult?"

"No, no, not at all." Maddy, mentally adjusting as quickly as she could, stole a sideways glance and saw that Penny, looking slightly dazed, was in the same predicament. She saw, too, that Penny was peering surreptitiously at the abbé's hair, presumably in search of a tonsure. She hurried into speech. "Oh—I'm so sorry. This is my friend, Penelope Wintercraft-Hawkes. She has a very personal stake in the information we're looking for."

"A pleasure, mademoiselle. The gentleman at the Bibliothèque Nationale was very specific—he asked about our records concerning an Englishwoman, Eleanor Caulfield by name. I confess to some surprise—I would not have thought anyone beyond the walls of our own Abbey or perhaps the Charter House would have known of this woman's existence. She has a specific connection to our Abbey, but I think she is not famous otherwise. And she has been dead for six hundred years." He smiled suddenly. "I forget my manners. Please, will you not be seated?"

They sat. Penny's heartbeat was erratic, and her breath wanted to catch. There was something here, something they needed, something they could use. She could feel it.

"I asked our archivist to select the volumes you would most likely need. He should be here any moment—ah." The door behind the women opened quietly, and a robed and cowled monk, a much younger version of what they had expected from the abbé, came in, pushing a tiered library cart on rubber wheels. "Thank you,

Brother Clovis. If you would bring that here? Yes, leave it, please. We don't yet know which of these will be needed."

Maddy's eyes were glistening. "My goodness, four registers? How lovely! Surely—Father, do these actually go back to the fourteenth century? They look far more modern than that."

"The fifteenth century, but only just; the earliest of those is from November 1400, and the last is an astonishing confession from 1407. These are copies, you understand; the original documents are, of course, much too fragile and valuable to be handled. During the nineteenth century, we began hand-copying every document within the Abbey. When I tell you that we have kept records here since the Abbey was consecrated in the twelfth century, you will see that this was no small undertaking." He caught the rapt look on Maddy's face, and tilted his head. "Ah. I take it that you are a historian, Dr. Holt? Or an archivist, perhaps? You have that look."

"She's a librarian and a historian. I run a theatre troupe that specialises in Jacobean and Elizabethan drama. I study a good deal of history as well." Penny was staring at the abbé, her eyebrows drawn together. "Father, did you say—a confession? I thought those were always completely private? Wouldn't it be a breach of something, to write that down?"

"Indeed, they are private. This was not a confession in search of absolution—it is more of an account. The Lady Eleanor—she was Madame Eleanor Lésurier at the time of her death—tells of a crime, in some detail." He sounded suddenly austere and the planes of his face, while not unfriendly, had subtly shifted, in a way that somehow set his visitors at a distance. "Her deathbed confession, most likely made to whoever held this office in 1407, would not have been shared, I assure you. That is between the penitent and the priest, the intermediary for God."

"That's what I'd understood. I'm sorry, Father. I meant no offence. Please do remember, I was raised Church of England. We're terribly ignorant of the rituals of the Catholic Church, mostly, but I did remember that one." Penny smiled at him, genuine and warm, and the remote chilly look that had settled over his carved features relaxed.

"It's I who should apologise. Forgive my bad manners, please. Of course, I took no offence." The abbé touched the cross around his neck, a light caressing gesture that spoke eloquently of an action done so often that he was no longer even aware of its performance. "Madame Lésurier died in January 1408. Her account of the crime in question was given to the abbé shortly before Christmas of the previous year. She knew she had only a short time left in this world, and I suspect she wanted a record for her children."

"My word, what a phenomenal memory." Penny was genuinely impressed, and the abbé chuckled suddenly, a warm rich laugh that was somehow completely Gallic.

"I wish I could lay claim to such," he told them. "But lying is a sin. In truth, I looked through these last night, after your colleague called from Paris. May I offer you lunch in our refectory? The brother whose duty lies in the kitchen this week is proficient, and we have a catch fresh from the coast this morning. After lunch, you can begin."

As Penny would later tell Ringan, it was fortunate that Maddy had shown enough sense to bring along a digital camera. Without that tool to hand, they might have spent days at the task of isolating and copying what they needed.

Even with the camera handy, both women groaned audibly as each carefully lifted a leather-bound register to the huge refectory table, and took their first looks at the Abbey's record keeping. The penmanship, executed by some unknown monks more than a century earlier, was for the most part careful and clean. It was also tiny and, in a few unexpected places, wildly ornate, madly fancy curlicues and whorls adorning upper case letters in a block of otherwise flat script. It was, Maddy remarked, as if the monk assigned to this job simply hadn't been able to resist this little gesture of idiosyncrasy. After all, the task of hand-copying hundreds of pages of history in as plain a hand as possible must have been mind-numbingly dull.

"I don't blame him," Penny agreed, and changed her mind as she looked in dismay at what appeared, at first glance, to be a solid page of undistinguished script, so small that it might have been written by elves. "All right, I lied. I do blame him. Wretched little man, whoever he was. This is going to be tricky."

"Let's get down to it." Maddy sighed, and dropped a stack of small spiral-bound notebooks and pencils on the ancient table. "I've got the one for—hello, what's this?"

"Oh, my lord." Penny had found what Maddy had seen. She blew her breath out forcibly in relief. "Someone, presumably Monsieur L'Abbé, was kind enough to slip markers into the appropriate pages. I'd offer to kiss him but I doubt he'd take me up on it. What does one give a monk as a thank-you gift?"

"I have no idea." Maddy looked happier than she had a scant two minutes earlier. "But we owe him, absolutely. Which one have you got? I've got one from 1403."

"First one over here, I think. He said 1400 was the earliest, didn't he?" Penny pulled over a notebook and pencil, and began to read. "Right, tally-ho, excelsior, away we go. First marker in the book. This is a record of a baptism: goodness, it seems to be twin boys, François and Charles, born to Eleanor Marie Lésurier and Henri Lésurier. May 1400. She'd have been, what, nearly forty? And twins, no less. I wonder how uncommon it was for both twins to survive in those days?"

"I don't know. Rare enough, I should think." Maddy's eyes were narrowed. "Penny—there's something odd about this entry."

Penny got to her feet and went quickly around the enormous table. "What is it? What have you got?"

"Listen. Tell me what you think—I'll translate from the French. Bear with me. Damn, if I had half a brain, I'd have brought a good magnifying glass." Maddy cleared her throat, bent her head closer to the page, and read slowly. "To be disbursed by the Order of St. Benôit . . . oh, right, that's the Order of St. Benedict in English, of course. Anyway—for the benefit, I think this word means benefit, of those daughters of the town—no, township. Area, perhaps? Damn! Anyway, of Bernay, those daughters left without the protection of any mother but the breasts—what in sweet hell? That can't be right—oh, whoops, sorry, the bosom, I think, I can't believe my

French is slipping—of Our Most Sacred Mother and Holy Church, Madame Lésurier gives the sum received this day from England."

There was a long silence. Penny broke it. "That's peculiar, all right. A sum received from England? What's the date?"

"No specific date given." Maddy picked up the digital camera, adjusted the focus and light, and took several pictures of the entry. "It's June, if that helps—this register is kept in chronological order. So, June 1403. I don't know about you, but I find this incredibly suggestive. What are you doing?"

"Seeing if Eleanor made a habit of it." Penny was hunting for markers in the register for 1400, turning the thick vellum pages carefully. "Seeing if a mysterious someone in England made a habit of sending these sums. A regular receipt would sound very much like a pension to me."

"Could it be Richard?" Maddy was thinking furiously. "No, what am I talking about—Richard died in 1400. He was murdered at Pontefract Castle—starved to death, poor bastard. So if someone sent Eleanor a pension in 1403, it wasn't he." She added, irritably, "And why is this table so huge, anyway? Takes forever to get around it."

"Here, shove over a bit. I'll move my pile." Penny pushed her register and notebook across the vast expanse of wood, sat down, and began to hunt for the chronology. "April, May—aha. And here it is, and our wonderful host has slipped a marker into the page. I adore the abbé Arnaud. Yes indeed, three years earlier—would you do the honours? This medieval French reads like more of a patois. . . ." Her voice died off, and her colour faded. "Damn. I just remembered that first time at the Bellefield, when I heard whispering. I told Ringan it sounded like Cajun or perhaps some form of Acadian French or Québécois I didn't know. A patois. But it wasn't. It was this I heard. Medieval French. Damn. And I wonder why, how, it's been modern French since that day?"

"I don't know, unless Agnes was adapting to her listening audience, or we were filtering. But here, let me read it," Maddy said quietly. "For the benefit, et cetera—yes, indeed, essentially identical wording we've got. Any money on an entry like this one every year while she's alive?"

"I never bet against certainties." Penny met Maddy's eyes. "All right. Eleanor came back to her maternal grandmother's connections here in Bernay—at least, I assume that's why she came here. I'm not sure it matters why, really; it's the fact itself that we deal with. Anyway, she returned here, made a connection with the Abbey for some reason, married a chap called Henri Lésurier, had at least two children with him, and all the time she was receiving this money from England, and not keeping it. Mystery source. I wonder who?"

"So do I. We need to see if there's a source listed anywhere among the markers the abbé provided." Maddy shook her head. "Twin boys in 1400. I keep going back to that in my head. Nearly forty years old, at a time when even a routine pregnancy had a better than average chance of ending badly, and twins—if they survived to be baptised, they must have been a reasonable size and healthy. I wonder if that birth contributed to whatever killed her a few years later."

"Well, once we get to that supposedly astonishing confession of hers, 1407, we'll know." Penny met Maddy's eyes. "Right, then, I'll admit it. I'm dying to skip all the rest and go straight to that. I'm itching to know. Aren't you?"

Maddy grinned. "I'd be mental if I wasn't. But I also want to see if there are any unexpected little bits in here. In fact, I have to do that, Penny. I need to check them all. We have different ends at stake here. You want the information for practical purposes, to find a way to get rid of Eleanor's mama. But Eleanor's mama has been the focus of all my study. I need to know as much as there is to know. You understand, don't you?"

"Of course I do." Penny touched the page before her with one fingertip. "But I'm curious—what happens when you know the entire story? When the mystery is solved? When there's no more research left to do on Agnes? Isn't that a sort of exorcism?"

"Oh, God." Maddy's eyes were wide and blank. "Do you know, I never thought about that. Well, hopefully, we'll find out soon enough. Let me go through these. There's no reason for you to—"

"Oh, yes there is," Penny interrupted. "I have a stage to set in my head. I want to see Eleanor. I want to know her."

They worked a while in silence. Maddy, more proficient at deciphering the archaic French, finished first, checking and making notes on the registers for 1403 and 1406. There was nothing of major importance in 1403; charitable donations by Henri Lésurier, the purchase of a manor house and what seemed to be several acres of land, a contribution to the order of money to help repair some unspecified damage to the Abbey's Charter House.

In the register for 1405, however, the abbé Arnaud had marked two points of interest. One was what seemed to be a regular entry in June, for Eleanor's donation to the Abbey of that money from England. The second, later in the year, made Maddy raise her brows.

"Penny," she said, "I think you were right about that late childbirth of hers."

Penny, working more slowly and finding nothing she could use, looked up. "Something?"

"A note, a personal memo. It looks as though the abbot of the day was very fond of the Lésurier family, or at least of Eleanor and Henri. Anyway, this seems to be a personal note that was incorporated into the register. And I don't have to translate; someone already did." She cleared her throat, and read slowly. " 'I am grieved to see Madame Lésurier in such a state. She has never been in full health since the birth of her sons, but the unnatural growth in her belly can be felt now. She is wasting away, with no improvement, despite our prayers and the good care of the nuns. The pain increases daily, and the dose prescribed to enable her to bear this affliction seems to affect her mind and speech, so that at times her memory fails her, and she knows nothing of the life and family which have sustained her. After all she has borne in her life, we hope she will find strength and solace in the glory of God, for she has shown herself to be a true daughter of the Church and a true friend to those in need. We say special prayers for her daily, and for her boys as well.' "

Maddy's voice trailed away into silence. Penny swallowed hard, and shook her head.

"Sounds like one of those horrible slow-moving cancers," she said quietly. "Doesn't it? Ovarian, stomach, intestinal? That poor thing. She held on a good long time, though. A fighter, rather like her mother."

"There's something else." Maddy had moved to the penultimate marker in the 1407 register, and pulled it free. "This is a note. I think it's for us, from abbé Arnaud. In English, written in ballpoint pen, anyway."

"Oh, my." Penny sat down. "Come on, woman, read it!"

"I'm going to. Here, listen." Maddy scanned the single sheet of paper and modulated her voice. " 'Rather than subject you to the labour of searching registers past Mme Lésurier's death, I will tell you that the contributions every June continued to be made in her name, by her husband, until 1412. After that, despite checking the page for June for several years beyond that time, there is no further mention of the family being involved with the Abbey to any significant degree.' "

The two women stared at each other. "Well," Penny remarked, "you're the historian. Did anything memorable happen in 1412? I mean, an invasion or an epidemic or a civil war or something? All I can think of is something about a papal schism, although why that should stick in my mind is anyone's guess. I mean—was there anything political or social to account for those payments stopping when they did?"

"I don't think so. Maybe whoever was sending them in the first place found out Eleanor had died. Or maybe the sender died." Maddy took a long breath. "So. We know there were these pay-- ments being sent, once per year. We can assume Eleanor wanted nothing to do with them, because she gave them to the Abbey, and her husband continued to do so for five years after she died. We know she had twin boys late in life, and we know she developed something fairly gruesome in her forties, and died of it. And I think we've done our homework. Isn't it time to get down to the juicy bit at the end?"

"Curtain," Penny agreed. "Let's see about that confession."

# Nine

*And as he rode himself alone*
*A dreadful oath he there has sworn*
*That he would hunt her mother down*
*As he would hunt the wildwood swine*

Under a cold blue canopy of sky, mantled with crisply defined edges of cloud, Ringan drove from Glastonbury to London. With his attention on the road before him and his background thoughts spiralling in different directions, Ringan was aware of some gratitude for the first significant break in England's run of bad weather since Christmas. He'd been a busy man for the past three days; lining up the thatchers had been easy enough, since Albert Wychsale knew of everyone in the county who performed such work, but the weather had threatened to change moment by moment, and they'd had to work on the tithe barn's roof at high speed to outrun the forecast of possible sleet showers.

There had also been the task of explaining in detail what Penny had only told Wychsale in vague terms: why, precisely, the rehearsals for *Iphigenia* and the projected opening of the Bellefield had been put on indefinite hold. Ringan hadn't relished the task, but he'd done it; Wychsale, as a major investor in the theatre, had a right to know. Luckily, since the Right Hon had experienced both the haunting and exorcism of Lumbe's Cottage firsthand, Ringan hadn't had to worry about the believability quotient of an explanation based on the presence of a dangerous ghost on the premises. Albert Wychsale, Baron Boult, knew all about ghosts.

Ringan, mindful of nervous lorry drivers and standing puddles of icy water in the road, kept his old Alfa Romeo well within the speed limits. He was wondering just what he was going to find when he got back to town. He'd called Penny on arrival in Somerset, only to find a voice mail message awaiting him: the same morning he'd gone south to Lumbe's Cottage to get his roof repaired, she'd gone chasing off to France in search of information about the Famous Flower herself, the Lady Eleanor Caulfield. Penny expected to be back within a day or two, she'd call if she was delayed. *Click. Beep.* End of call.

The message, coming from the usually crisp and decisive Penny, was strangely brief and unadorned. Her voice, too, was a bit odd; she sounded distracted, somehow fuzzy around the edges, in a way Ringan associated with sleep deprivation. And how peculiar, for her to have gone alone, and to have left no contact information at all. Where in France? What had she found?

Ringan reached the southwestern edge of London and headed the car into town, towards Muswell Hill and Penny's flat. Part of him, barely acknowledged and shoved firmly away, wanted to turn east and go to the Bellefield. They hadn't been inside for well over a week, either of them, and they hadn't been near the building itself since the night of the dinner party at the Dallow flat, the night when for the first time, Ringan had felt what Agnes felt and got inside her, understood her, the night when she'd sent something of her rage and madness and secrecy and need leaking out from a thousand tiny un- seen exits in the Bellefield's walls and into Hawthorne Walk.

A small, insistent voice at the back of Ringan's mind posed a short barrage of questions. That light, for example, that cold unnatural light. Suppose it was more than that? Suppose it had burned inside the theatre? Suppose it had damaged the velvet curtains, the newly replaced seats? Suppose there were smoke marks on the walls? Sup- pose the light out of doors had been flame within? Oughtn't he to go take a quick look?

As he was telling the voice in question that his keys to the Bellefield were in a drawer in Penny's kitchen cabinet, and to kindly shut up because he was damned well not going near the theatre alone even in broad daylight, he pulled the Alfa into Penny's street.

As he did so, a taxi turned in right behind him, opened, and disgorged Penny herself, holding an overnight bag in one hand.

He tapped the horn. She glanced up, saw the Alfa, paid the taxi driver, and headed over to Ringan at a fast trot.

"Ringan! My lamb, this is amazing timing, you simply couldn't better it. My flight got in from Paris just about an hour ago." She looked rested, energised. Her eyes were bright; in the cold air, her dark cloudy hair seemed to crackle with electricity. "God, I was hoping you'd be back. I've just dropped Maddy off at the library."

Ringan's jaw slackened. "Maddy? Maddy Holt? You went to France with Maddy Holt?"

"Why not? I mean, who better, for what I needed? She knew where to look and oh my, did we find what we needed. Look, I'll tell you all about what led up to it later, but right now, let's get indoors. I've got all sorts of things to tell you, but I think we need to have a gathering of the tribes, so to speak, so that I only have to tell it once. Well, on second thought, maybe twice." She became aware of her surroundings suddenly. "Oh, dear. Best park the car, yes? I'll meet you inside. Have you eaten? Do you want some tea?"

She was up the stairs and letting herself in before he could form a cogent reply to any of this. He slid the car into a space across the road and followed her indoors.

The first sound to meet his ears as he closed the door behind him was unexpected: he heard the clacking of fingers on the keyboard, followed by the hum of the printer. There was the buzz of a page sliding into the tray, and then Penny's voice, in a wordless whoop.

Ringan made for the bedroom, where Penny kept her computer equipment. She was staring at the printout she held.

"Penny for them?"

She started, saw him, and relaxed. "Gladly. No payment required, though. A picture, after all, is worth . . . how much?"

She held out the single sheet. "Read it," she said. "Out loud, please. It's in English—Maddy translated the French."

There was something in the set of her face, a kind of triumph, dark and a bit unnerving. Aware of an inexplicable reluctance in himself, he took the paper from her.

"What is it?" That look on her face—it was new in his experience. How much of a mark, sooty and dark as anything left by the invisible smoke and thunder of the haunting itself, had dealing with Agnes Maldown left on her?

"It's Eleanor's account of how her father died. As told by Eleanor herself to a monk at the Benedictine abbey in Bernay, in France. She was delirious with pain at the time. It's not a real confession. Just her story. And it's our explanation for quite a lot." Her lips were a thin line. "Come on. Read it."

"In a minute." He searched her face, trying to find where this new thing, this difference, lay hidden. "I'll read it after I know a bit more about how you got it and what sent you off to get it. That way, I'll feel a bit less like I've come in at the end of the play, you know?" He saw her open her mouth, as if to protest, and his own voice hardened. "No. This isn't open to discussion. Talk to me, lamb. How did you hook up with Maddy Holt, and what sent you off to France in search of Eleanor? Why not Agnes? And why didn't you tell me? Talk to me."

She told him. She omitted nothing, downplayed nothing; her sense of dislocation, of helplessness at not knowing where to look next, her sense that Maddy might know what to do, Agnes and her appearance at the Library, Maddy's instinctive response and her offer of help—everything came out, the entire story of the past three days.

Ringan listened in silence, controlling himself, biting back words that were better left unspoken. He felt his skin lift into angry gooseflesh as he looked into Penny's dark eyes and shared her panic at the moment Agnes had come through her. He said nothing until she had finished.

" . . . and just now, I checked my e-mail. Maddy downloaded all the digital photos we took of the registers, the moment she got to her computer. They're all lined up in my e-mail; she's going to send them on to Richard Halligan as well. But that, what you're holding? That's the prize." She looked at him, seeing his reluctance and understanding that it had grown out of his fear for her. "We worked for this, Ringan," she said quietly. "We agreed, didn't we, that the only way to rid the Bellefield of the Demon Queen was to find out what that secret was, that we both felt her hiding? Well—here's the secret, told first person by our Famous Flower of Serving Men. This is where we begin to fight back, with a weapon in hand, some knowledge. They say knowledge is power, don't they? I've told you what happened. Read it."

Ringan's gaze dropped first. He looked at the sheet he held, took a deep breath, and read aloud.

"'I was a child, a small child, I was seven years old.'" Ringan's voice was flat, deliberately devoid of emotion. It was obvious, after the first sentence, that this was going to be impossible to read cleanly if he allowed himself inside the child Eleanor's feelings. But it was going to be an uphill battle, maintaining that flat calm, and Ringan knew it. He could feel himself wanting to shake. "'My father—he would come to me and touch me, in ways God never meant a man to use. He was wicked, he was wicked and accursed of God. I know Jesus died to redeem him but it destroys my heart, my faith, my courage, to feel that such as he might be forgiven, by God or man. He did wrongly and we paid, my mother and I, we paid for his sins. Forgive me, I mean no blasphemy, but how could such as he be redeemed, with nothing paid for his crimes or his sins, either? But my mother—she made him pay. She exacted the forfeit that Our Saviour could not, because Our Saviour is wise and compassionate, but my mother did not bleed from new wounds when murder was done. Yes, she took a price from him, for all his evil done to us. There was a flask in the cowshed—I saw it there. She warned me from touching that—it was poison, my mother said, from the monkshood plant, and she told me I was never to touch those black flowers, they grew in the fields two handspans high and if I touched the flowers, she told me, if I touched the flask, I would sicken and die.'"

Ringan stopped. There was something wrong with the muscles of his throat. His mouth was dry and Eleanor's voice in his head, brought to dreadful febrile life by the words he read, was vivid and scarifying.

"Go on," Penny said, and touched his arm gently. The hard

bright edge, the darkness he had seen in her a few minutes earlier, was gone entirely. "I know. I sat there in the Abbey while Maddy translated it. Go on."

"All right." He cleared his throat. " 'We went to the church of a Sunday, and the priest spoke against my father from the pulpit. He called him by name, he called him the name of wickedness. We were shamed by it, my mother and I, shamed that even the Church should see that he had no righteousness, and speak to it, as if he were in the Devil's bed. And my mother—she brought the flask from the cowshed into our house. She brought it into her bower. She never knew then that I watched, that I saw. And my father died. He died with the bloody flux and his lips blue, with no breath coming into him, only going out of him. And I was never sorry for that, Father, I never thought on it or remembered it, except as it might be some dream I had in fever. But when I did remember, my mother turned against me, for all that she had cared for me above anything in the world. She tried to make a nun of me, to cloister me forever behind a veil of silence, that I might never say what I had seen, how my father died. And when I ran from the nuns, ran to a man who loved me, who would take me with no dowry, ran to my marriage bed, she took a price from me.' "

Ringan faltered and stopped. He was staring at the page he held, at the final line of it, as yet unread. He seemed to have no moisture left in his own body. The fevered words, from the dying memory of a woman gone for six hundred years, were tangible in the air. They hung before him, real and dreadful.

"There's a bit more." Penny's mouth was trembling. "Isn't there? A bit more to read, yet?"

Ringan read it.

" 'She took my babe unbaptised. She took my knight. And she did not bleed from new wounds, when murder was done.' "


The next morning, an hour before it officially opened its doors for the day, The Beldame in Ashes was the scene of a hastily organised and extraordinary meeting.

Gathered around the bar was a curious assortment of the immediately concerned and intellectually curious. At one end of the long bar was the Hawthorne Walk contingent, where Lucy Radleigh and Chrissie Alexander exchanged information with John Roberson, who had missed the dinner party. From the centre to the opposite end, stools had been claimed and hastily occupied by the Tamburlaine Players, and by Penny and Ringan themselves. Penny had a stack of paper close to hand. A bit apart were the two professional historians, Maddy Holt and Richard Halligan; they were deep in conversation about an abstruse point of contention concerning Queen Margot. Behind the bar itself, the Dallows drew pints and poured coffee, pushed bowls of salty snacks at everyone, and made sure the group was kept satisfied.

Mike Dallow glanced at the clock on the wall, pulled a small bell from a shelf beneath the bar, and gave it a single practised shake. Startled, everyone looked up.

"I'm calling time," he announced. "That is, time to get down to business. Why we're here—if everyone will give an ear—we've got some information you all need to know. Penny? You're on."

Penny stood up. Calmly, pitching her voice to make certain everyone could hear her, she ran down the list of what most of those present didn't yet know: the cold light sliding out of the Bellefield and enveloping Hawthorne Walk like a toxic cloud, Ringan's momentary ability to feel what Agnes felt, the overpowering sense that she was keeping a secret. She spoke dispassionately about her own visit to Maddy at the Library, her reasons for assuming that Agnes had not been mad during the years leading up to the attempted murder of her only child, the visitation of Agnes away from the confines of the place where she had died, the trip to France in search of Eleanor's last years, Bernay and what they had found there. She passed out the stack of papers she'd been guarding, one copy to everyone present: the English transcription of Eleanor's story of her father's murder.

"So Agnes murdered her rotter of a husband? And the child Eleanor saw her do it?" There was a crease between Petra's brows. "You know, I'm having a bit of trouble processing the motivation on this one, Penny. Suppose little Nell did see it. That doesn't explain very much, when you come down to it, really. I mean, if Agnes knew she'd been seen, why wait, what, ten years or something, to arrange for the witness to take the veil? And it doesn't really explain why she sent those hired blokes after Eleanor. What happened? What made her go starkers? What turned her from Mum of the Year to what she became?"

"Petra's right," David Harkins said slowly. "This simply doesn't add up, Penny. I'm not speaking so much of the crime itself—I suppose it's possible Agnes didn't realise Eleanor had seen her do it. Maybe Eleanor kept silent about it until she was a teenager, and then did or said something that clued her mother in to the fact that there'd been a witness. But honestly, I don't believe that would have been enough to send Agnes over the edge that hard. And besides, that leaves us with the larger question: Why is she stuck here? Why can't she rest?"

He glanced at the others with a faint smile. "I'm a Catholic," he remarked. "I think about these things. In point of fact, Agnes was condemned to die. She would have made a full confession of her sins, and been granted absolution before her execution. In case you're wondering, she'd have confessed and been absolved long before she was taken to the gallows or the block or whatever. It's not a last-minute thing, not a situation where she would have been deprived of her chance at absolution by being caught in a fire. That's the way it works."

"That's right, isn't it?" Richard Halligan, veteran of decades at St. Paul's Cathedral, was thinking furiously. "But Penny, Ringan, everyone in the Tamburlaine troupe heard her, begging for a priest. Didn't they? If you're right, David, and she'd confessed and been absolved, why would she need one?"

"My God, that's right!" Ringan was off his bar stool and pacing around in a burst of nervous energy. "I didn't hear her—for one thing, that was the day Ray Haddon died and I wasn't in the house, I was out in the lobby. There's also the fact that I don't speak French. But Penny—what did she say that day, lamb? You were in the thick of it, you could feel her and hear her. I know it's a bit tricky, but—can you remember?"

"It wasn't that day." David looked drawn, remembering. "It was the day Penny and I were alone in the Bellefield. We were discussing why Penny was so insistent about doing *Iphigenia*. And I remember precisely what Agnes said—it's burned into my memory. In French—*un prêtre, je veux un prêtre, s'il vous plaît, ne me laissez pas brûler.* A priest, I want a priest, please, don't let me burn. No chance of error, not about those two things: she was begging for a priest, and she was terrified she was going to burn."

"Burn for real?" Maddy asked. "Or burn in Hell?"

Everyone turned to stare at her. She continued, calmly. "Was she ever actually on fire? I mean, physically? Or was her fear of burning purely her terror of the fires of Hell? Sorry, David; I'm not Catholic, and I think about slightly different things. Right now, I'm wondering about spiritual versus physical burning."

"Good question." David was smiling faintly. "But I got the feeling it was real, live, physical fire that had triggered her. This was flesh burning, not spirit. Penny? What do you think?"

"It was both." Penny wrapped her arms around herself, suddenly chilled. She remembered the day Ray Haddon had been pulled from his high ladder and destroyed. She remembered the smell of smoke, the feel of heat flickering against her, hot metal against her ankles, the thud of someone's footsteps as they ran free to escape the inferno, leaving her there to burn alive, leaving her to asphyxiate and roast in madness and agony. "I saw it, remember? I felt it. That was no metaphor. The building was ablaze, there were bits of hawthorn stuffed into the walls and they burned like kindling, and she couldn't run, she had chains or something on her ankles. She was stuck, and her skin was scorching. I could feel it. David said she wanted a priest, but it was well beyond that. She was *desperate* for one. She had a secret, something that hadn't been confessed. I could sense it, sitting on her shoulder like the hand of God."

"I felt it, as well." Ringan came to Penny and put an arm around her shoulders, steadying her. Gratefully, she leaned against him. "And I'm with Petra. Eleanor's story is a big piece in all this, but there's still something we haven't got. Look at it this way. Are we really supposed to believe that Agnes hired people to slaughter her child?

After she'd poisoned her husband to protect that same child, in the first place? And that she did it because she found out the child had witnessed her crime? Because I don't believe it. She was willing to commit murder to protect her daughter. She finds out the daughter saw her doing it, so she tries to push the girl into a nunnery, and when Eleanor won't go, Agnes goes bonkers and tries to kill her? Do me a favour. That's rubbish. I don't buy a word of it."

"Neither do I. But if that's right, if there's still something we aren't seeing, it leaves us with the main problem miles from being solved, doesn't it?" Lily Dallow spoke decisively. "Tell me if I'm wrong here, but basically, it's like this. We've got a dead woman tied to our street. She has a secret that's keeping her from going off and doing whatever it is dead people with secrets do, I don't know, dancing naked in the Elysian Fields, or whatever. We've got no way to find out anything else in the usual fashion, because we've exhausted all the written bits and whatnot, at least we've exhausted all the obvious ones. And time's becoming an issue. So my question is, what do we do now?"

Ringan was looking steadily at Penny. They had discussed this moment, argued it into the small hours of the previous night; they had both known it was coming. Penny spoke to the room, her gaze never breaking from Ringan's.

"Agnes wants a priest," she said calmly. "I say we get her one. And we let her tell the priest just what the big bad secret is that's keeping her earthbound. Does anyone see another option? Because I don't."

For a minute or two, everyone was quiet, as they digested this. Ringan spoke up first.

"I may as well tell you right now, I'm completely against this." His voice was controlled, but something rasped along the edges, wanting out. "In fact, as bad ideas go, I rank this one up there among the worst ideas ever. I can't think of a single way we can control the situation, once we summon Agnes into the Bellefield and confront her with what we know. And what happens when we make it clear there's things we're demanding of her, and try to force her into disgorging those facts? We'd have to stage this at the Bellefield. That puts anyone on the premises for the event in danger, especially

Penny; Penny's already susceptible. There's also the little matter of being marched off to a psychiatrist, because how do we explain this to a perfect stranger, priest or no priest, without sounding like refugees from a mental institution?"

"I see your point, Ringan, but really, Penny summed it up." Richard Halligan sounded thoughtful. "What options do we have now? It's live with her or get rid of her. Living with her is impossible; at least one person has died because of her mere presence, I suspect the number may very well be higher, and you yourself got a nasty gash across the head when you first played her theme song, so to speak. Let's face it: you're not going to have any peace until Agnes finds some peace herself. And that won't happen until she confesses what she apparently never confessed in her lifetime, and gets absolved for it."

"There may be another problem," David said hesitantly. "From what I remember of the church's stand on exorcism, a priest can't simply wander in and exorcise. That needs permission, a special dispensation, from the Pope. And that takes months."

The dismayed silence that followed this information was broken by Donal McCreary. "But we aren't looking to perform an exorcism, are we?"

Robin, who had been silent to this point, nodded at him. "I was thinking the same thing. An exorcism—that's a casting out, a forcible sort of 'begone, never darken our door again' affair. What we're talking about, that's totally different. We're talking about letting a soul in torment get it off her chest, so she can catch a lift heavenwards, if heaven there be." He looked around at the rest of the gathering. "Well, aren't we?"

"Um—I'm a bit curious." Lucy Radleigh had finished her drink. She slid off her stool and glanced at her watch. "I need to go open the shop soon. But, does anyone here actually know a Catholic priest? One we could approach, that is, if Penny decides she wants to do this?"

"I do," Donal said. "And I'd trust him with this, in a heartbeat. I'd trust him with my life, never mind my soul. I trusted him with the truth about what happened to Sinead at Callowen House. So I'd not be afraid to tell him about this. He'd believe us—he'd believe me."

"Donal, that's a godsend, literally." Penny touched him on the arm. "Are you sure you can get hold of him? Can you find him in a hurry, if need be?"

"Seeing as how it's my brother Paddy, I know where to find him, yes." Donal managed a brief smile at the effect he'd produced. "He's the parish priest in a small town in the west of Ireland. If you're sure you want to go this route, I'll call him tonight. No harm, however it goes; the worst he could do is to tell us no."

Father Padraic McCreary, spiritual adviser to the Catholic population of the town of Ailbhinn, County Clare, Ireland, arrived at his brother's London home three days later.

There was a strong physical likeness between the brothers. Both were on the short side, both were stocky and powerfully built, and both moved with a kind of sturdy grace that marked them as children of the same bloodline. The differences—and they were varied and profound—lay in their attitudes and beliefs, in the way each man faced and took his place in the world. Where Donal wore his well-controlled turbulence like a badge of honour, Padraic was calm, quiet, slow to rouse.

"Paddy, this is truly beyond the call of duty. Thanks for coming, and with so little warning." Donal, knowing his brother's fondness for strong sweet tea, had a pot waiting for him. The flat, five airy rooms in South London off the Fulham Road, was warmed against the return of winter. The sky outside, steely and uncompromising as a Dürer woodcut, held the grim promise of unremitting chill yet to come. "I'm sorry to be asking this of you, but there's no one else I'd trust with it. Was the flight across very bumpy?"

"It was, but I've taken worse. It's a cold, unpleasant month of weather you're having here. The ancients would have despaired of the sun ever coming again." Padraic blew the steam from his first cup of tea, took a cautious mouthful, and sighed. "Perfect tea, this is, and needed, too. How are you keeping, Donal? You're looking less worn than the last time I saw you."

"I suppose I am." Donal's lively, earthy features smoothed out for a moment, becoming blank and masklike. "Last time I saw you—things were pretty raw. Losing Sinead, it was still new. An open wound. I'll likely never get over it, so don't tell me how time heals everything, but I've grown a bit more accustomed to an empty bed and too much empty space in my life."

"I wouldn't tell you anything of the kind. How could I, when I don't believe it myself? The truth is, I'm not convinced time does heal. I do think it dulls the edges a bit, and if it makes things bearable, that's a blessing." Padraic set his cup down and looked steadily up at Donal. "Are you still having those dreams? About trying to find her, in Callowen House?"

"Yes." Donal's mouth thinned, then relaxed. "Only rarely, though. Maybe time does dull the edges. But why I asked you to come, Paddy—that's nothing to do with me, or with Sinead, either. I told you it was a haunting, didn't I?"

"You did. And there's things I need to get clear. But can you tell me more about what's happening here?"

"I can. It's about a woman who wants a priest, but she died over six hundred years ago, so it isn't just any priest I could ask to offer her an ear." Donal settled himself into the chair opposite his brother. "She's violent, and confused, and there's a mystery in there somewhere. Stuck where she's been stuck, though, and she's been there six centuries, I expect I'd be violent and confused, as well."

"Six hundred years? A good long time to sit in torment. But who's to say that a moment in time is any different to her than a millennium would be? That's with God." Padraic, his third cup of tea disposed of, sat back, sighed, and folded his hands in his lap. There was a tranquility about him, a genuine calm, that Donal lacked. "Can you tell me what you know about her? And you said, on the phone, that this wasn't an exorcism. I want us to be very clear about that. I can't perform an exorcism for you—you know that, right? Not without special permission."

"No exorcism. All we're after is giving her what she wants, and what she wants is to confess something."

Padraic watched his brother, and stayed quiet. Donal continued, his powerful voice flat and uninflected. There was no point in being dramatic with Padraic; the priest was completely unsusceptible to theatrics. "We're not trying to cast her out. We just want to let her get whatever the sin is off her chest, so she can go get herself a bit of heavenly rest, and let the living get on with it. That's not an exorcism, Paddy, is it? Just an ear lent, and absolution given. You can do that, surely?"

"No, it's not an exorcism. But I'll need to know more. Are you saying she died unshriven? That she was given no chance to confess? That's a peculiar thing, if it's true."

Donal gave him the entire story as he knew it. It took close to an hour.

Padraic, as superb a listener as any good priest must be, offered no interruptions. He slowly and steadily drank his gradually cooling tea. When Donal had finished the tale, the pot was empty, and Padraic went straight for the gist of what his brother had related.

"All right," he said. "From the standpoint of the church, this is what I see. She'd have seen a priest after she was condemned. She'd have made confession. She'd have been granted absolution for what she confessed. But your thinking is that, for some reason, there was one thing she couldn't bring herself to confess? And that at the last minute, in fear and madness from knowing she would burn alive with that one sin still unforgiven, she repented and wanted that final chance? And by the way, I'm curious. Have you seen her, does she take form, walk, the way ghosts are said to do?"

"Saints, Paddy, you should have been an actor." There was a genuine smile of admiration glimmering around Donal's mouth. "Or maybe a producer, with a cast to direct. Summing up like that, that's a skill to be envied. No, we've never seen her; she's all stench and noise and light. As to the rest of it, yes, that's our thinking. I'll be honest with you, and tell you right now, asking you to confront Agnes on any level, that's asking you to put yourself in harm's way. There's no way of knowing how she'll jump; she's not safe to upset. And I'm ashamed to say I've forgotten—do you speak French?"

"French? Yes, reasonably well." Padraic's smile mirrored his brother's. "I took Modern Languages at school, remember? While you were taking Classics?"

"So you did. I remember you took the languages—I just didn't know if French was one of them. It's not an idle question. If you're willing to jump into this lunacy, you'll need it. We've heard her speak nothing else."

Padraic got up and headed for the loo. When he came back, he had obviously been thinking.

"All right," he said. "I'm certainly willing to help if I can—it's my duty, after all. I agree with you, an Anglican clergyman wouldn't fit here. She was certainly a Catholic. And I'm with you, too, in thinking I need no special dispensation for this. As you described it, there's no exorcism. We don't take casting out a soul lightly, but this—she's been suffering a long time, from what you've said, and it's time she was heard and given what she needs. What's the next step?"

"I'll call Penny and Ringan, and tell them you're here. My thinking is, if they agree to this, the four of us should meet at the Bellefield. I'd like you to get the lay of the land, so to speak, and a feel for what you're up against. And who knows, maybe we'll get lucky—I know you're not much for theatrics, and this would have to be at the theatre itself. We might have to call her in some way—play that song I told you about, the one Ringan thinks is all about her girl, the one she tried to kill. Or we might have to do a bit of the play my boss is so wild to have us all put on, a play all about the murdering parent of a daughter. She'd respond to that, Agnes would."

There was a manic edge to Donal's voice. As if suddenly hearing himself, he visibly took hold of his speech and his self-control alike. "Or maybe not. I suppose there's always the chance we'll get lucky. Maybe she'll catch a look at your cassock and collar and just spill her guts and confess, and then we can be done with it, no more damage done to anyone, and the poor soul off the hook."

"I'd not hold my breath too long hoping for that." Padraic had been watching his brother. Now he spoke quietly, almost gently. "What is it, Donny? There's something else, isn't there?"

"Perceptive lad. Yes, of course there is. I'm surprised you haven't guessed it, you of all people."

"Sinead?"

There was no change in the priest's tone, but suddenly Donal's eyes were wet and his face imperfectly controlled.

"Of course it's Sinead. D'ye think I want anything to do with this filthy mess? My soul tries to crawl behind me and hide when I remember that night at Callowen; it's burned into me, memory and spirit and nightmare, like a slaver's brand. And I was there, at the Bellefield, the day that workman died. I heard Agnes. I *smelled* her, smelled her flesh burning. I felt her panic and the extremity of her terror and I thought then, this is what it must be like to be locked inside the skull of a lunatic. Ghosts, madwomen—I'm not equipped to deal with it. I want no part of this, Paddy. But I've got no choice, do I?"

"You could walk away." Padraic kept his eyes on Donal's face. "Just turn your back. No reason for you to get involved in this woman's personal nightmare. You've already been through your own and there's not a soul would blame you, or misunderstand. You could stop caring so much. After all, it isn't your pain and it isn't your job. I have to do it—murderess or no, mad or sane, it's my calling and my duty to give her the peace God promised her. But you don't have to care. Why should you?"

"I suppose I could walk away, couldn't I? On paper, anyway. In theory." Donal was smiling, a genuine smile. "But I won't, and you know it. You knew it when you started that little speech. When will you learn, I know you near as well as you know me, Paddy?" The smile went suddenly. "Or maybe you don't know my reasons as well as you might. Fact is, I don't give a damn for Agnes. But that could easily be Sinead, suffering and striving for some peace out there, in all that darkness. And that, well, I've no choice, but to care about that. So no more silly speeches about me not having to care. All right?"

The priest sighed, a long exhale. When he spoke, there was a certain finality in his voice.

"You go call your friends, then. Set it up; I'm here as needed. But we shouldn't dawdle, any of us. Six hundred years, I'd say it's time we ended this."

# Ten

*And he's brought men up from the corn*
*And he's sent men down to the thorn*
*All for to build the bonfire high*
*All for to set her mother by*

Under a silent canopy of velvet curtains and Victorian caryatids, those people most nearly concerned with the final ending of Agnes de Belleville Maldown gathered on the Bellefield's empty stage.

None of the Hawthorne Walk contingent was present. The Dallows and the other merchants, while notified of what was planned, had not been invited; Ringan had said, rather grimly, that the fewer people they exposed to the probable blast of supernatural unpleasantness they were likely to unleash, the lower Penny's insurance rates on the theatre would remain. The corollary, that the fewer deaths to explain and dream about for the rest of their lives, the better, remained unspoken.

Richard Halligan was there, and Maddy Holt as well. Both historians had announced that they were unwilling to consider staying away, even for a moment. There had been a short row over their presence, but between them, Maddy and Richard had done so much of the work that had brought things to this point that excluding them wasn't really an option. A kind of rivalry had sprung up between them, friendly, but with a definite edge to it. It became clear that, while technically colleagues and obviously mutually respectful of the other's expertise, they were also mildly competitive. If one was going to be here, so was the other.

The Tamburlaine Players were there, all of Penny's troupe except

Donal, carrying their sections of the bound version of *Iphigenia* that was, at the moment, the Tamburlaines' working production copy. The old building vibrated with nerves drawn taut as piano wire, and it was from Penny's contingent that the sense of breathlessness, of high drama in the wings awaiting a moment in which to burst out like a spring tide, chiefly emanated.

Ringan, setting the grand guitar Lord Randall in its stand in anticipation of probable need, caught himself wishing that theatrical people could turn it off completely at will. He considered that, between the presence of an angry tortured spirit and the impending arrival of the priest who had come to draw her forth, there was likely to be enough *sturm und drang* to suit even the most drama-starved among them without any more from them.

And, of course, Penny was there. She was her usual self, bustling around, making adjustments to the stage lighting, conversing with Richard, occasionally putting her head close to Maddy's to whisper something, bringing folding chairs from the storage room and setting them centre stage. Ringan, his own setup work complete and his presence on stage now unnecessary, stepped back and kept an eye on Penny. Somewhere in the pit of his stomach, he was very much afraid for her. But he saw nothing. If there were overtones, if anything sat on her shoulder and cast a shadow that matched nothing of the woman he had loved so long, Ringan couldn't see it. She was, for the moment, the woman she had always been.

"Where's Donal?" Petra's voice fluttered, sliding up and down the scale of her vocal range, and she bit the words off, flushing. Ringan glanced at her, wondering: were the nerves she was obviously battling to control the by-product of fear of what was to come, or nothing more than simple performance jitters?

As if she had caught Ringan's unspoken thought, Petra met his eye, and grinned. "Sorry," she said easily. "First time reading this in front of non-combatants. And it's not my usual style at all, this play."

"Not to worry, love, you'll be fine." Robin touched her shoulder, but his gaze and attention were elsewhere. He kept glancing around the auditorium, up at the shadowy hidden places of the rafters, at the overhead rigging and flies far above their heads, at the house aisles that stretched, dim and dark, towards the doors to the lobby.

Penny, without a word, went down the stairs at stage left and headed for the light switches backstage. Moments later, the rows of soft lighting that lined the underside of the second-level gallery came up to pale life.

"Robin's right, we want some light. It was too dark in here. We don't need it dark," Penny remarked, as she rejoined the others on-stage. She looked around, saw Ringan standing off to one side, and headed over towards him. He was staring at her, every nerve in his body alive with foreboding.

"Penny. What did you mean, Robin was right?"

She blinked at him. He continued, forcing out the words. Something in him was suddenly disinclined to talk at all. "Robin didn't say a word about it being dark in here. How did you . . . ?"

"I don't know." It had hit her, as well. She swallowed, her eyes wide. "I wish I could say he was obviously thinking about how dark it was, but it wouldn't be true. I heard him. Words. Rob's voice, wishing—I don't know, wishing for light."

"I heard him, as well." Maddy, unnoticed, had come to stand beside them. "I'm sort of catching random thoughts, stray bits of voices." Her face was the colour of old parchment, and she kept swallowing, as though her throat was dry. "Fragments. Half-sentences. I don't think it's all coming from us."

"It's not all English, either, at least not English that I can recognise." David Harkins spoke up from his chair. His shoulders were hunched, his elegant hands balled into fists. "Echoes, really—short choppy lines of thought. Penny, my dear, would you mind very much if I said how much I hate this theatre of yours? At least, right this moment?"

"It's Middle English." Halligan had moved up close to David's chair, with Robin and Petra following. "At least, some of it is. That's not all I'm hearing though—the occasional scream. Rustling. Distant noise, as though from very far away."

He shuddered suddenly. Ringan, acutely aware of a purely atavistic need to be as close to live flesh as possible, went quickly towards the knot of people on centre stage. Penny and Maddy, clearly unwilling to be left behind, hurried to catch up. It came to Penny that no one wanted to be alone, to be farther than arm's reach from the nearest person. There was something in the atmosphere, something different from anything they had felt before within the confines of the Bellefield: the very walls of the theatre seemed to be readying for something to happen.

"Where—where's Donal?" Robin had hold of Petra's hand. He was breathing irregularly. "And his brother? They should be here by now. We need them."

"On cue," David said, seemingly out in space, and the entire group turned to stare at him in bewilderment. A moment later, they all heard the front doors opening. Penny, something unpleasant she couldn't quite catch at or identify moving along the edge of her awareness, called out from the stage, pitching her voice to carry.

"Donal? Donal, is that you?"

"It's them." The house door was opening and Donal was coming through, but Petra, her eyes closed and her body swaying, was not seeing him. "I can hear him. He's wondering if he ought to have locked the street doors. My God, this is too damned peculiar."

*My mother did me deadly spite.* . . . Ringan heard the lyric run through his mind, and for a mad second wondered if he had thought it, or if someone else was thinking it. Then he realised that the others had turned to look at him, and he understood he had hummed it aloud.

He clamped his lips down hard against the song that wanted out. His skin was prickling, his entire nervous system on alert as it had not been since his first encounter with the shade of Elizabeth Roper, now gone to her rest, many months ago.

Padraic McCreary, in cassock and collar and with his alb draped over his shoulders, came to the foot of the stage, mounted the stairs, and stopped abruptly.

"This place—it feels odd. Noisy." No introductions had been made; Padraic, his head canted tensely forward like a hound on the hunt, let his right hand come up and close around the cross he wore. In his left hand was a small black bag. "I can hear things. I can—I can feel things."

He crossed himself suddenly. *"Benedictus, domine,"* he said softly. Donal, moving his head like a swimmer shaking water from his ears, muttered, "My brother Paddy, he's the priest, come from Ireland. He's come to help."

"And not an instant too soon, I'm thinking." Paddy craned his neck at an impossible angle, staring up into the Bellefield's invisible upper corners. "She's here. You know that, don't you? All of you? She's everywhere in here. I'd be hearing her breathe, if a woman gone so long had any breath in her." His face contorted momentarily, echoing something, a kind of grief, that was creasing Maddy Holt's face, and making Petra's face screw up in what might have been sorrow. "The poor woman," Paddy said quietly. "Her name— it was Agnes?"

"Agnes de Belleville Maldown. A tainted child of the de Valois, sent too young to marry a man who loved nothing."

Ringan jerked his head around, so fast that a twinge of pain travelled down his back. Dreamy, slow, elsewhere, cold and completely detached—Penny's voice was all wrong. So was her face; her eyes, which had been pupils open to catch the scant light, were now narrowed to slits.

Beside him, barely audible, Petra whimpered. Ringan heard Maddy whisper to herself, a wordless susurration of recognition.

Father Padraic McCreary, watching Penny's face, barely seemed to blink.

"Agnes de Belleville," he said evenly, "come out."

A long silence, silence that was the unheard echo of six centuries, settled on the shoulders of the living like the dust of the grave. While the silence held, nothing in the building seemed to move. Breath was taken and let go again, jaws tightened and relaxed, eyelids performed their allotted function, blinking in obedience to the body's unspoken command. None of this was visible, or audible. The universe had contracted to an enclosed space within the walls of a Victorian playhouse. Within that universe, the rules no longer seemed to apply.

A rustling, a whispering. They came from everywhere and nowhere, those small fragmented sounds; around those who had come to play their parts in the happenings of the day, where they stood beneath the proscenium arch, tiny noises washed the ancient boards and eddied, only to die off again into that same unnatural stillness. The whispering came again, noise that moved like mist, slipping between ankles and chair legs. A word came out, forming itself into sexless intonation: *Eleanor*.

Paddy stood immobile, his brother at his side. Something in Donal's stance was warlike, dangerous. His brother looked like a medieval painting, one hand on his cross, one finger lifted towards the Bellefield's unseen heights.

"Agnes? Agnes de Belleville?"

So intent was Ringan on watching Paddy, so absolute was his concentration, that he nearly missed what was happening to his left. Penny, her slitted eyes now black light-starved pools, had begun to speak, to form words, mouthing them, savouring them. When at last language was given volume, everyone turned to stare.

"We buy what we loathe with what we love."

Maddy Holt felt her heart trip, its rhythms faltering and catching. For a split second, she was on the road to Paris again, easing the rental into a tight space, hearing those same words come from Penny, recognising the source . . . words spilled out into the house, beautiful full-bodied language, powerful and hot.

"What a wondrous thing is motherhood—it carries with it a potent spell, whereof all share, so that for their children's sake they will endure affliction."

Ringan was breathing hard. Who had spoken? He couldn't place the voice—it was as passionless as river-water, without gender, without weight. The air in the Bellefield was thickening, muddying, carrying the taste of something unspeakable.

*Eleanor, ma fille, que s'est-il passé ici? Comment pouvez-vous croire que je vous laisserai de cette maison! Mon Dieu, mon Dieu, qu'avez-vous fait?*

It came from the luxury boxes, the curtains, the empty chairs in the auditorium. They all heard it. And Ringan, who spoke and understood no more French than the most uneducated tourist, understood what had just been said. It came to him clear and clean, the voice of the woman long dead, never resting, in the language he knew: *Eleanor, oh God, what happened here? How can you believe I'd let you leave this house? My God, my God—what have you done?*

They all heard the response, as well, another language, another heart, the same high uninflected tone. This time, Ringan turned to look.

It was Maddy Holt, standing apart from the rest, eyes wide and unseeing.

"Where now does the face of modesty, or virtue, avail you anything? Now, that godlessness holds sway, that virtue is neglected by men and thrust behind them, now that lawlessness over law prevails?"

A torrent of French, louder now, growing in strength, anguish at its core.

*Eleanor, comment avez-vous pu faire ça? Pensiez-vous pouvoir vous sauver? C'est mon défaut, mon crime, mon péché. Eleanor, Eleanor . . .*

Penny spoke. She sounded fully conscious, fully herself. Ringan thought, dreamily and from a great distance, that he'd never heard her sound so urgent.

"Ringan. Play the song. Hurry!"

Through a thick red mist, Ringan moved towards the guitar in its stand. The building was full of shapes, forms, people, and things he couldn't properly see or put names to; everyone seemed wreathed in dense smoke, pungent and red-edged. A man in the centre of the stage, still as the rocks at Stonehenge and apparently unable to move at all, that was Donal's brother, surely—he was dressed as a priest, so he must be Donal's brother, because Donal's brother was a priest. And the slender girl off to one side, with the mass of red hair, that was Petra. It had to be Petra, because she alone had red hair, red hair, and a sweet, plangent voice. . . .

"Destroy me not before my time," Petra said softly. "For it's a sweet thing, to look upon the light. Force me not to visit scenes below."

Paddy's lips were moving. Ringan couldn't hear a word. He had

*193*

his left hand on Lord Randall's neck, his right on the shoulder strap. He hoisted the instrument out of its stand, and got the strap somehow over his head.

"Look upon me." Something was happening to Petra's voice now, something was cascading down from heaven, smothering all sound, obscuring it, a wild stamping, the shouting of many voices, something Ringan couldn't make out but it was wrong, it was obscene, a dark rampant chittering. . . .

"Give me only one glance," Petra said, and her voice began to spiral out of control. ". . . one kiss bestow, that this, at least, I may carry to my death as a memorial of thee, though thou heed not my pleading oh God oh no no no no, this isn't happening, it isn't, it isn't. . . ."

A tapping, distant at first, faint and faraway. It grew quickly in volume, tiny feet, the clatter of needle-edged paws on hard stone, pouring from the walls, driven into the modern age from the flames set by men themselves long turned to dust, the plague carriers, the dark hordes of Europe's medieval cities, red-eyed and flea-infested with *Yersinia pestis,* their bald tails flicking as they came. The sharp edgy sound of a thousand rats filled the building, a million, their teeth brilliant and ominous under the stage lights. Rats. Rats . . .

"*Ringan!*" Penny screamed, and he swept his hand down across the Martin's strings, flooding the universe with music.

All around them, throughout the Bellefield, the unseen whirlwind of sound paused, the needle of ghostly history lifted from the turntable by what might have been nothing more than surprise. Lord Randall was a loud guitar, with strength and purpose in its full range, from bass to treble. The powerful first chords of the song took on a recognisable and compelling beat as Ringan settled into its familiar structure.

He sang the first verse, his voice ringing out with ease, needing no more amplification than what the acoustics of the Bellefield provided.

*My mother did me deadly spite / For she sent thieves in the dark of the night.*

Something brushed the tops of Robin's feet, stopped, then slid across Richard Halligan's shoes. Richard, frozen in place, stared at the empty stage where something moved, invisible and sly, sniffing at him, investigating him, acknowledging his presence, perhaps pausing to gather itself for a vicious bite. Beside him, Richard heard Robin, breathing raggedly.

*They couldn't do to me no harm / So they slew my baby in my arms.*

"No." Penny heard herself whispering and bit the word back, unwilling to draw even that much attention to herself. She could hear the rats, smell them, present in legions like bacteria, waiting to catch and bite and glare, as the water rat had done to Candida so many years before, while the child Penny stared in terrified paralysis, unable to help. Rats. The fire had driven them here. She could smell them. She could smell the smoke from the burning city. Rats. And there was more, there were screams, full-throated cries that might have been fear or pain or might have been the living reality of the mob as it rampaged through London on a June day, searching for the king's uncle, burning everything in its path, buildings and people and . . .

*I cut my locks and I changed my name from Fair Eleanor to Sweet William went to court to serve my King as the Famous Flower of Serving Men.*

Maddy heard the rats, caught the glint of fangs in the uncertain light from the Bellefield's mains. She ignored them, as she ignored the ever-thickening smell of smoke, and the song coming from Ringan. Her awareness was attuned to something else entirely; behind the cacophany of violence and noise from the dead world, she could feel the presence of a single heartbeat. It shone like a beacon above the rest, now steady, now scudding high and panicked. *Agnes,* she thought, *is that you? Ten years, I've been trying to find you. Is that you? Show yourself. . . .*

*So well I served my lord the King / That he made me his chamberlain.*

Petra heard none of this, no rats, no screams, no smashing of burning timbers from roofs set ablaze. She stood, a bit apart from the others, her eyes fixed on something none of the others could see. A bedchamber, once comfortable, now threadbare with lack of money to maintain it. Hangings riddled with moth, and the winter sunlight leaving vagrant touches on the stone walls of the manor house. Her father's house, his bedchamber and her mother's as well, a room she hated and feared, where she was not supposed to be. A flask, hidden in the ragged folds of the bed hangings.

She had watched her mother bring that flask into the house. She had watched *maman* make up its contents, distilled from the black blooms of the monkshood, black flowers that were death, even the root was death to man or beast. Her mother had told her so, when she realised Eleanor had been watching. You are not to touch this, Eleanor, *maman* had said. This is death to swallow, and this is mine, for me, you are not to touch this, or even the flowers in the fields, do you understand . . . ?

*But all alone in my bed at e'en oh there I dreamed a dreadful dream I saw my bed swim with blood and I saw the thieves all around my head.*

Donal heard everything, saw everything. He heard the screams, he saw the rats; he saw the visions that danced through Petra's eyes and he saw Penny's paralysis and the cause of it. He didn't give a damn for any of it. He was having a vision of his own, over and over, a nightmare memory of Sinead, healthy and brilliant and beautiful and vital, one half of his life, more than half, lying down beside him in Callowen House, and waking with most of her soul gone. He stood in place, ignoring his surroundings both real and spectral. His shoulders were massively hunched with a remembered rage, an incurable grief.

*Our King has to the hunting gone / He's ta'en no lords or gentlemen / And as he rode himself alone / It's there he saw the milk white hind.*

The priest stood calmly, centre stage. He was waiting, knowing what was to come. The time was not yet; Agnes was still hidden, still not listening.

*And all around the grass was green / And all around there a grave was seen / He sat himself all on the stone / Great weariness it seized him on.*

Ringan played, and Ringan sang. Penny was behind him, and he dared neither stop playing, nor turn to assure himself of her safety. The first time he had played this song under this roof, Agnes had laid the side of his face open and thrown him to the ground. Today, it seemed, she was leaving him entirely alone. He sensed nothing of the rats, not after he had begun to play. He smelled no smoke, he heard no screams from the past. Where the first time of playing had been an invitation to Agnes's violence and retribution, the second seemed to be talismanic.

*Eleanor—le flacon, celui que je vous ai dit de ne pas toucher—où est-il, Eleanor?*

A voice most of them had heard before cut through the dense air and the noise. It was calm, cold, as implacable as the voice of God; refusing to answer was unthinkable.

*Great silence hung from tree to sky / The woods grew still, the sun on fire / As through the wood the dove he came / As through the wood he made his moan.*

Just out of Ringan's line of sight, Petra whimpered, the stifled cry of a frightened child.

*Our King cried out, and he wept full sore / So loud unto the dove he did call / "Oh pretty bird, come sing it plain."*

Father Paddy began to mouth a prayer below his breath. There was something coming, the confession he had been told to expect, but something wasn't right. It seemed to be coming from the wrong person.

*Oh it was her mother's deadly spite, for she sent thieves in the dark of the night. They come to rob, they come to slay, they made their sport, they went their way.*

"My father did great harm to me." There was defiance in Petra's voice now, all fear gone, and with it the childish sense of duty. "Why should I not do great harm to him?"

*And don't you think that her heart was sore as she laid the mould on his yellow hair, and don't you think her heart was woe, as she turned her back, away to go?*

Soothing, soft, so very gentle, Agnes's voice came. Could this be the same voice, the same woman? *Oubliez ceci, mon chéri. Vous n'avez fait rien de mal. Il n'y a aucune raison pour que vous rappeliez.*

"Oh, lord," Penny whispered. The words from *Iphigenia* came flooding in, one line hard upon the next, their context making sense as it had not before: We buy what we loathe with what we love. What a wondrous thing is motherhood—it carries with it a potent spell, whereof all share, so that for their children's sake they will endure affliction. "Oh, Agnes. You told her there was no sin. And you told her to forget. Did she? Did that poor murdering child obey her mother?"

*And how she wept as she changed her name from Fair Eleanor to Sweet William, went to court to serve her King as the Famous Flower of Serving Men.*

From the roof of the Bellefield, smoke began to pour. A shower of charred blackened flakes, bits of the burning city, showered the watchers on the stage below, only to fade to insubstantiality, leaving no touch of themselves behind.

*Oh the bloody tears they lay all around / He's mounted up and away he's gone / And one thought come to his mind / The thought of her that was a man.*

David Harkins, like Father Paddy, was praying. He spoke French fluently, and he had heard and understood all of it: the mother's accusation, the child's fear and defiance, the mother taking the child's sin upon herself. With understanding and compassion for both women in his heart, David Harkins prayed for their souls.

*For there's four and twenty ladies all / And they're all playing at the ball / But fairer than all of them / Is the Famous Flower of Serving Men.*

Penny understood. She saw the scene in her mind's eye, just as Petra had lived it in the child Eleanor's shoes: Agnes, distilling the poison, the child hidden and watching, the mother bringing it indoors—why? Had she meant to use it as a weapon against Hugh Maldown, the wastrel and violator? Had she meant it for herself, a quick means to the peace life had denied her?

*Oh he's rode him into his hall / And he's rode in among them all / He's lifted her to his saddle brim / And there he's kissed her cheek and chin.*

"Petra?" Robin Sayles had spent many hours onstage with Petra Morrison. She was his favourite leading lady; he had played Romeo to her Juliet, instigated the smothering of her fragile Desdemona as a particularly chilling Iago, done read-throughs during the small hours with her, held her hand through nerves and dress rehearsals and opening nights. She was as close to him as a twin might be.

But she stood bare inches away from him now, not seeing him, wearing a sense memory that left her unrecognisable. "Petra? Come back, please," he said urgently. "Petra?"

Eleanor's voice came, pulsing now. Or was it her voice pulsing? Something was taking the very reality of the space in which they all stood and softening its lines and edges. Was it sound, or was it light? *J'ai fait le nécessaire les nonnes. Vous serez l'une d'elles, ma fille. Vous trouverez la paix au couvent. Le diable rit de ceux qui n'admettront pas leurs péchés.*

"God, the Father of mercies," Father Paddy said calmly, and his brother turned to stare at him, "through the death and resurrection of his Son has reconciled the world to himself . . ."

"French," Donal said urgently. "In French, Paddy, and hurry, for the love of Christ, the walls are melting."

Ringan heard them. Donal was right; the velvet curtains and wooden doors were becoming cold light, weaving like the robes of dancing priestesses under ancient firelight. Only a few verses left, now . . .

*And he has sent his nobles on / Unto her mother they have gone / They've ta'en her that's did such wrong / They've laid her down in prison strong.*

"I will not go to the Holy Sisters." Petra's voice, contorted with rage, slammed out across the stage. "I have a man who loves me, a true knight, who would marry me, with no dowry to hand. Why would you send me to the nuns? "Because I saw what you did to your husband, your intent? So that I would say nothing of it to anyone, never speak of it? Rest easy, I will not speak of it. But neither will I go to the sisters. Do not bring this up to me again, Mother. I mean to be whole again. I mean to marry. Do not offer me peace, when what you intend is to immure me in expiation of your own crime."

"Ringan." Penny was behind him, beside him, breathing hard. "Ringan, hurry. We don't have much time."

*"Dieu, le père de la pitié, par la mort et la résurrection de son fils a réconcilié le monde à lui-même a envoyé l'Esprit Saint parmi nous pour la rémission de nos péchés"*—Father Paddy's voice was picking up

strength and smoothness now, the French flowing more evenly—
*"par le ministère de l'église peut l'élasticité de Dieu . . ."*

*Mon péché?* There was a rasp in Agnes's voice, a tinge of darkness, a
darkness that had not been there before. Something moved blackly
down Ringan's nerves; here it was, the first stab of the insanity that had
outlasted her. *Ne vous rappelez-vous pas qui a donné à votre père sa dernière
boisson, ma fille? Pensez-vous pouvoir trouver la paix dans ce monde de la
chair quand bien-même le Saint Esprit n'a pas donné l'absolution?*

"You lie." Petra was white with rage and loathing. "I did nothing. Who was it who distilled the monkshood? Who was it who
brought the flask indoors? Who was it who hid it against her need?
Who did this killing? Not I, Mother. Say no word to me of wishing to protect my soul. Better that you look to your own."

The theatre was flickering in and out, hard and fast, light writhing
from the floor beneath their feet. Here it was, full madness, snaking
like a newly set flame into conflagration. Was it her insanity they
could smell, or was something burning? . . .

Ringan's teeth had begun to chatter. He pushed his voice back
into a semblance of clarity.

*And he's brought men up from the corn / And he's sent men down to
the thorn / All for to build the bonfire high / All for to set her mother by.*

" . . . *par le ministère—*" The priest's voice was wavering as well.
London was seeping in through the flames and the smoke, a London
of burning rickety thatch, of filth in the Thames, of a vast castle to
the west, burning against the skyline. They could all see it, they
could smell it now: death on the wind. Father Paddy faltered, and
began again: *". . . par le ministère de l'église, Dieu peut vous donner le
pardon et la paix, et je vous absou au nom du Père, du Fils, et du Saint
Esprit. . . ."*

*Vite, je vous en prie, enlevez-moi les dispositifs d'accrochage, s'il vous
plait.*

For Penny and David, the words were familiar. Penny, inches
from Ringan's side and desperately trying to understand what was
real and what was not, felt a nightmare sense of *déjà vu*. This is what
they had heard Agnes screaming, she and David, alone that day in
the Bellefield. These were her very words, begging for a priest,

begging for the shackles to be taken from her, begging not to be left to burn. . . .

"Agnes!" Penny cried out suddenly. "Agnes de Belleville! There's a priest here—*voici un prêtre, pour écouter votre confession!*"

Silence, breathless and tortured. For a heartbeat only, suspended between moving indistinguishable rivers of time, the mayhem stopped.

"Speak, *ma fille.*" Paddy spoke clearly. "Speak."

The Bellefield dissolved around them. A marching parade of scenes, vignettes from a life lost, moved like cinema before them all:

The child Eleanor, carrying a bowl to her father, watching him drink with expressionless eyes.

Agnes, finding the flask with the monkshood gone.

Hugh Maldown, dying in his own blood and vomit.

Years passing, no more than the beat of blood in a living pulse. The young knight, Sir James Caulfield, buying cattle from the Maldown holding, seeing Eleanor, falling in love. Agnes, with the knowledge of Hugh Maldown's murder, refusing to allow it, consecrating her daughter to the nuns. Eleanor refusing to go.

And then the same scene, over and over and over: the child, watched through her mother's eyes, taking the flask, pouring the poison, again and again, never stopping as her mother remained silent, a nightmare loop of death and complicity.

Eleanor's voice, soft now, resigned. *Pardonnée mes péchés, mon père.*

Petra's eyes were blind with tears, as she hovered between worlds, realities, times. Maddy and Richard, silent in the face of impossible truth, moved quietly closer to her. Robin was already there. And Father Paddy's voice rang out.

"May God give you pardon and peace. I absolve you from your sins, *in nomine Patris, et Filii, et Spiritus Sancti.* Go in peace, my child. Go, and find the rest you were promised. *Vous êtes pardonné.* Amen."

"Do you know," Albert Wychsale said mildly, "I'm still not certain I really understand what happened. Was the mother always a nutter?

Or was it the daughter who was a bit off? And who killed who, precisely?"

Three days had passed since the cataclysm at the Bellefield. That Agnes was gone, that she had accepted the absolution Father Paddy had offered, was past doubting. They had felt the change within moments of Paddy's final amen. As Robin said wryly, a Hollywood director with a billion-dollar special-effects budget couldn't have produced a change more immediate, or more convincing. The very air of the theatre had suddenly tasted sweeter, and felt lighter.

Albert Wychsale had come up from Somerset, hours after hearing the news from Penny that the theatre was their own again and that the rehearsals for *Iphigenia* were pushing ahead at full speed. He had come up to town ostensibly on completely coincidental business. If both Penny and Ringan privately felt that the long arm of coincidence was beyond belief in this instance, they were polite enough not to say so. After all, he was a partner.

Now, relaxed and curious, Albert sat in a patch of watery winter sunlight in Penny's Muswell Hill kitchen. The season's death grip had eased a bit. While it was still cold, still the heart of the long dark months, there was just enough lightening to convince those who were silently superstitious about such things that the spring would eventually come again.

"Neither. Or both. It's not quite that simple." Ringan had Lord Randall on the kitchen table, face-up on a pile of soft towels. The D-45, looking oddly naked and defenceless, was minus its strings; Ringan was rubbing the mellow wood with guitar polish and a chamois cloth, cleaning and buffing out an inch at a time. He set the cloth down on the table and flexed his tired wrists.

"I'd say it was a case of repressed memory, running into too strong a conscience, like two lorries colliding head-on. You know? Irresistible force, immovable object." Penny had pushed her chair away from the table to allow Ringan maneuvering room, and was straddling it. "You have to understand a few basic things about Agnes de Belleville Maldown. First, she was a devout Catholic, with all the baggage that entails, and she was devout in a time when devotion really counted for something."

"All right. Faith accepted." Wychsale pursed his lips. "Most people were, back then, of course. What's the next fact?"

"She was a fanatically devoted parent." Ringan's eyes were fixed on what he had seen, what he'd heard and felt, as he stood and sang. "Think about her for a moment, and you'll see why she'd almost have to be. Bastard child herself, shipped off young to another country, no sign of love from her own father, likely a source of shame for her mother—and then look what she's married off to. If Agnes was capable of love, then she'd likely be damned near starved for it. And Eleanor, the brutalised little girl for whom Agnes was ready to kill her horrible husband—well, who else would be the focus of all that feeling?"

"So the husband was no prize? I see." Wychsale crossed his ankles, and stretched a bit. "He abused the child? Is there any documentary proof of that?"

"You could ask Petra Morrison," Penny said drily. "She was the one speaking for Eleanor that day. She said, 'My father did great harm to me, why shouldn't I do great harm to him?' I think that's fairly self-evident, don't you, Ringan?"

"Oh yes. And besides, Hugh Maldown was enough of a swine that the local priest stood up and preached against him in the county church, as a defiler of children. There's your documentary evidence, Albert. I'd say that's a given." Ringan met Wychsale's eye, and Albert was startled at the cold dislike he saw there. "He sexually molested his own daughter. And she'd have been no more than six. I hope he's burning."

"Ugh. Yes. If there's a Hell, let's assume all his relevant bits are very unpleasantly toasty indeed, and move on. So who poisoned Maldown? The mother, or the daughter?"

"Eleanor poisoned him. The daughter." Penny got up and plugged in the electric kettle. "I want coffee. Anyone else? Eleanor gave her father the poison, but Agnes distilled it in the first place. She went out, she cut the monkshood—it's a thumping nasty poisonous plant, monkshood—and she distilled the stuff. I wondered, back at the theatre, if she could have meant it for suicide, in case things got to be too much to take, but of course that was incredibly stupid of me.

She was a devout Catholic, as we said, and suicide is a mortal sin. Besides, she'd never have abandoned Eleanor to Maldown's tender mercies."

"So, Agnes brewed the poison. And yes, given what you're saying, she meant murder—that would have been a sin in its own right, of course, the bare intent." Albert's eyes, behind their small glasses, were interested and intelligent. "And Eleanor gave it to her father. Did Agnes egg her on to do it? I mean, was this a joint venture—the women getting rid of the horror-show husband and abusive father?"

"It doesn't seem likely, not from what we heard. I mean, I certainly don't think she told Eleanor, here, this stuff's poison, go slap some into Daddy's soup. But subconsciously, she may have encouraged the girl." The kettle whistled, and Penny set cups out. "From what we got from the conversation, Agnes warned Eleanor about the flask with the potion. Told her not to touch it, said it was death to go near it, explained in great detail what it would do. She emphasised it. This was after she caught Eleanor watching her making up the raw poison. Eleanor promptly liberated the stuff from where Agnes had hidden it, and poured it into Hugh's ale or whatever, and Bob's your uncle, a tragedy worthy of Shakespeare or Marlowe, right there in the making."

"Or Euripides. Don't forget him." Ringan's voice was grim. "Agnes let her small child commit murder. Her conscience, her piety, whatever you want to call it—it failed her there, just long enough for her to let her daughter know how to do it, to know what her daughter was doing, and for her to not stop the girl. She could have, you know. Agnes could have prevented it. All she had to do was move that flask. Maybe she convinced herself she wasn't certain of what Eleanor intended. Maybe she told herself someone so young, so wronged, so innocent, wouldn't pay the heavenly price for the most mortal of sins. Who knows? We never will. But the fact, that she let her do it and then told her to forget, that she was innocent, that she'd done nothing wrong—that, we do know. It was there, in the exchange between the women, three days ago."

"You said repressed memory. And conscience. I see the conscience, but did Eleanor actually manage to convince herself she hadn't killed her father?" Wychsale was clearly staggered by the idea. "Good heavens, is that even possible?"

"She went one better than that. Ringan, can you put your nice clean guitar back in its stand, please? Ta." Penny slid a cup of coffee to Wychsale and waited until Ringan had moved Lord Randall off the table before setting a cup down in front of him. "Eleanor not only convinced herself she'd done nothing wrong, she managed to come up with an amazing psychospiritual syllogism: I didn't kill my father. My mother told me I didn't kill my father. Someone killed my father. Therefore . . ."

". . . my mother killed my father. Oh, dear God." There was pity on Wychsale's face. "Those poor women. Yes, I see; not only possible, essentially inevitable. So Eleanor decided to go off and marry a young man of good family who'd fallen in love with her, and her mother went mental?"

"Again, not so simple." Ringan took a mouthful of coffee, and sighed. "This is where the immovable object makes itself felt. You see, Agnes had a conscience, a rather formidable one. She'd pushed it away once in her life, just the once. But now, it came charging back. She honestly felt she couldn't let Eleanor go out and live in the world, as someone's wife and mother, without the girl acknowledging her sin. Such a thing was beyond her. By Agnes's creed, Eleanor would burn in Hell for that; she'd planned on confessing her own intent on her own deathbed, I'd imagine. So she confronted her daughter with it, told Eleanor she'd made arrangements for her to go into a nunnery, for her to remember, to expiate, to come to terms with what she'd done."

"And?" Wychsale, his coffee forgotten, was intent on the tale. "What happened then?"

"What happened was that Agnes's entire world came crashing down around her ears. Not only did the beloved daughter believe the lie her mother had told her to believe all those years ago, the beloved daughter believed Mum was guilty of the crime herself, and despised her for it."

"And Eleanor was pregnant." Penny looked drawn and tired suddenly, as if the memory of what she had sensed was taking a fresh toll. "She was pregnant and furious and frightened, and here was her mother, wanting to separate her from young Caulfield and stuff her into a convent for no reason at all, since after all, her mother had done the deed, not her, right? So she ran away with James Caulfield, married him—he really seems to have been very much in love with her. We know she bore a child, a boy, to Caulfield. When the child was three days old, three men broke into the Caulfield house and killed James and the infant."

"And now, I am officially sceptical. I just thought I'd mention it." Albert sounded mildly indignant. "Listen to what you're telling me here, will you? First, the mother adores the daughter. She even plots to kill the husband to protect the daughter. The daughter kills the husband instead. All right, fine, I have no trouble with that. A few years down the line, the daughter fetches up pregnant and wants to get married. Mum won't hear of it, tries to arrange for the daughter to go spend a long weekend with the Holy Sisters or whomever, and the pregnant daughter bolts. And this is where you lose me entirely. You're asking me to believe that this doting mum hired a bunch of men to kill the daughter she supposedly adored? Rubbish. Sorry. But, well, really. That sounds like the most complete rot."

"I don't know for certain," Penny said slowly. "I'm not sure we can ever know for certain. But from everything we learned of Agnes, I don't believe that the men she hired to find Eleanor were supposed to kill her. I don't think they were supposed to kill any-one. From what I sensed of her, from the pictures she was letting run through the theatre, I think it was a kidnapping gone wrong. She would never have tried to kill Eleanor. Eleanor was her world."

"So you believe Agnes hired those men to do no more than find her daughter and bring her back to her mother? Or to the con-vent? No damage was intended?"

"One or the other, yes. That's right. It's the only thing that makes sense—she wanted Eleanor to face her sin, and ask forgive-ness from God. And Agnes didn't know there was a child, that she had a grandson. How could she? Eleanor was hiding."

They were all quiet for a few moments, as Albert turned this idea over in his mind. "Well," he said finally, "you're right. It does make some sense. So—what happened, do you suppose?"

"I expect Sir James tried to defend his wife and things got out of hand." Ringan, his cup empty, had laid Lord Randall across his lap and was carefully installing a new set of strings. He wound the bass E in place, stretched it, adjusted it. "I mean, wouldn't you fight back if three strange men broke into your bedroom and tried to drag your screaming wife off into the night? With, most likely, your infant son in her arms?"

"My word, yes. So you think, what, they made straight for the Lady Eleanor's bower, not expecting to find anyone there but her, and instead they found the husband and the newborn as well? Wouldn't the family normally—no, never mind, how stupid of me. Only an extraordinary circumstance would have had Sir James in his wife's bower. Men didn't sleep in bowers; it was the lady's place of refuge. And unluckily for everyone concerned, those extraordinary circs were there, all right. A newborn son."

"There's a bit more of an indication of how things were at the time of the catastrophe. There's no mention in the song, or the trial transcripts, of anyone else being there." Penny answered the unspoken question in Wychsale's eyes. "No wetnurse. Highborn ladies had wetnurses. If Eleanor was nursing that infant herself, then the baby was delicate and she wasn't risking leaving it for an instant. And the adoring husband would be even less likely to leave his wife."

"Do you know," Wychsale said quietly, "these people have been dead for six centuries. I'm astonished at how sorry I am, for all of them. Sir James—do you suppose he managed to injure one or more of them? I can't think of anything else that would have provoked the hired kidnappers to such extremity. After all, murder— and of a nobleman, no less—wasn't something to be taken lightly. Prisoners were tortured in those days."

"I don't know, Albert. It's likely he did do some damage to them. They may have injured the newborn, if Eleanor wouldn't let go of him. Sir James would have fought like a mad thing." Penny shook her head. "I don't know whether I'm glad or sorry. He'd have lost his wife, but maybe kept his life and child. And he could have got his wife back. But of course, he had no way of knowing that, did he? They'd hardly have strolled in and said, hello, we're here for the Lady Eleanor, her mum's asked us to escort her to a convent at swordpoint."

"Well, all right then. I'm officially not sceptical anymore. It's disgustingly logical, all of it." Wychsale had relaxed. "So Eleanor buried her dead—I'm going by the song—and decided her mother was completely mental and she, Eleanor that is, had best go into hiding. So she went into drag and hied herself off to, where, Sheen Castle? Wasn't that Richard's favourite digs?"

"Until his first wife died there and he torched the place, yes, I believe it was," Penny replied. "Call it Sheen. The boy-king—he wasn't even a teenager, barely thirteen—he'd not have recognised her as a woman. And the starved maternal thing she'd have had going, losing her own child so soon after birth, well, she'd have been madly dancing with post-partum hormones. She'd have been the most nurturing valet in history. Richard likely adored her, his Famous Flower. He had no mother, and suddenly, here was this protective, nourishing servant in his life."

"I'd love to know what actually tipped everyone off to Sweet William really being Lady Eleanor." Ringan was regretful. "Because obviously, Richard wasn't off hunting by himself and no magical animals showed him anyone's graves. But something did, and of course, he had to get the story from Eleanor. End of the line for Agnes."

Penny shuddered. "She was mad by then, of course. For months, she'd have known that the men she hired had done the unthinkable. For all she knew, her daughter was dead. After all, why would she have believed them, when they told her they'd killed the father and the infant but run off and left the daughter alive? All she had was their version. Her conscience, oh God, I don't even want to think about what she must have gone through for those months. Sitting alone in the Maldown manor, going progressively crazier every day, not knowing."

"She knew eventually." Ringan touched Penny consolingly. "When Gaunt's men showed up and said, oi, your daughter's been outed as the king's valet and she told us about the hired men and we tracked them down and they're all rather longer than they were when we started, having been introduced to Mister Rack, and by the way, lady, you're under arrest, so come along to the Savoy, the king wants a few words with you."

"So they got the story, at least in part, out of the would-be kidnappers." Penny took up the tale. "They named Agnes as the villain and that must have put Richard in a major bind. After all, like it or not, she was a de Valois. You didn't just tie French royals up and tickle their feet with hot coals, or something. And you certainly didn't dump them in the dungeons with the lowborn prostitutes and whatnots. So they consigned her to Martin Saxton's care and she was kept under house arrest at his home. Except for the actual trial, I don't know that she ever left Hawthorne Walk again."

"She was taken into custody in May, I remember that from the arrest warrant that Richard Halligan found. She would have been tried very quickly indeed. And she was found guilty, and sentenced to beheading at Smithfield. Unusual, that. Wouldn't they have taken her to Tower Green?"

"Not if Richard wanted to keep it quiet." Wychsale spoke authoritatively. "And he would have. There was a lot going on, Wat Tyler and tensions with his uncle and the Appellants and whatnot, and the last thing he wanted was to tick off the French by making a big do out of beheading one of the family." He grinned suddenly. "Don't look so surprised, you two. I'm a nob, remember? I know a bit about this stuff. No crowd at Smithfield, no announcement. He wanted it done quickly and quietly. Pity he picked the day Tyler's men invaded London and set fire to both banks of the Thames."

"So she died at Martin Saxton's house. The peasants torched Hawthorne Walk because they figured it belonged to Gaunt. And Saxton ran, and left her there to burn alive." Ringan forced his tight mouth to relax. "She never got the chance to confess her own part in allowing the murder. Agnes, mad as a hatter, protected that girl to the very end. And Eleanor apparently went to her grave believing in her own innocence. No confession. Everything Agnes did was wasted. You know, I can't help wondering whether Agnes was the only person to die on Hawthorne Walk that day. Because the entire street has a history of supernatural events associated with the smell of smoke."

"True. I remember Mike Dallow, at the Beldame, talking about that," Wychsale said. "The structures would have been thatch, wood, straw, and hawthorn, all incredibly combustible. They'd have gone up like kindling, and if there were people caught inside . . . it's been haunted ground for a good long time, now. I wonder if the whole street is clear, or just the theatre?"

They were all silent, thinking, digesting. Finally Ringan spoke up.

"Penny," he said curiously, "there are still a few things I'm curious about. Petra, for one thing—that wasn't possession, was it? I thought, when she first started doing her Eleanor thing, that we'd got two ghosts in there, but now I don't believe that. I got the sense it was more of her simply acting out what Agnes remembered of those conversations with her daughter."

"Remembered, rightly or wrongly. That's what I thought, as well; she wasn't possessed, she was basically allowing heself to be a sort of shadow-puppet, to show us what Agnes wanted us to see. And Petra doesn't think she was possessed. She should know."

"True." Ringan's eyes darkened. "What's really worrying me was that Agnes had such a violent reaction to poor Ray Haddon. She was violent towards me, as well, but I think mine was mostly the song. But Ray . . ." His voice died away.

"I've wondered about that myself, just because it seemed personal. Her reactions seemed stronger whenever she was confronted by men: you, Ray Haddon, David. He was so hard-hit that first time, I thought he was having a heart attack. Of course, Agnes had no reason to cherish men. Still, her reaction to Ray, the way you described it, was really over the top." She thought back, remembering. "It may lie in what she was screaming that day: get out, get out, the devil is laughing at you, you belong in Hell. I wish we had some sort of visual reference for Hugh Maldown; maybe Ray reminded Agnes of the husband." Penny shook her head. "Another unanswered question. You're still looking puzzled, Ringan."

"I am. There's something I can't quite pin down, trying to

connect in my head. Come on, prove me wrong, or right. Have you got that letter? Your aunt's letter, the one she left you?"

A light had come on in Penny's face. "Oh lord. Ringan—yes, I do. Half a tick."

She hurried away and was back a moment later. She scanned the letter, as Ringan looked expectant and Wychsale puzzled. As Penny reached the final paragraph, she let out a long sigh, and read the last bit of the letter aloud.

" ' . . . I ask only that you perform to the top of your considerable bent, and that you will perhaps find a little season for the work of the greats, and dedicate that season to my memory's honour, if only in your mind. Yours etc, Marie-Thérèse Ysabel Lésurier Heatherington, wife of Stephen.' "

There was deep satisfaction on Ringan's face, but Wychsale was merely bewildered. "I don't understand," he said plaintively. "Why is that important?"

"Because the Lady Eleanor Maldown Caulfield died as Madame Eleanor Lésurier, wife of Henri, and mother of at least two healthy twin boys." Penny sighed. "My aunt by marriage was apparently a descendant of Eleanor. Of Agnes."

"I wonder how much of the story she knew?" Ringan was fascinated. "I wonder if she knew the place was haunted, and by whom? I want to believe she did know, Penny—I want to believe she thought you could get Agnes the absolution she craved."

"We'll never know for certain," Penny said, and tucked the letter back into its envelope. She sounded resigned. "There are a lot of things we'll never know. I still want to know where that money came from, the sum that came every summer for Eleanor from London. She wanted nothing to do with it—she gave it to the church. Who sent it? What was it for? Just one of those little things that are going to drive me out of my mind trying to puzzle out at three in the morning."

# Epilogue

*For the fire took first all on her cheek*
*And then it took all on her chin*
*It spat and rang in her yellow hair*
*And soon there was no life left in*

On a soft May morning in the year 1412, Martin Saxton sat down at a table in a small sunny house in Southwark, to perform an annual act of contrition.

He was an old man, only sixty years old but aged beyond his time, tired and ill and unable to cope with having seen too much. The times in which he lived, from first breath until today, had been turbulent and extraordinary. He had taken it in stride, all of it, until the day he had lost his courage for the first and last time, and left a madwoman to burn in chains.

The world had changed around him, spinning out of control, righting itself, moving inexorably onward. Richard, the boy-king he had first served, had been starved to death at Pontefract Castle. The Angevin line was dead and gone, and with the bastard seed Henry Bolingbroke on the throne as King Henry IV, Saxton had asked leave to retire to his widowed daughter's home, after years of service to the crown. He had been granted that leave; Henry wanted no remnants of the murdered Richard in his service.

There are plenty to call June England's loveliest month, but for Martin Saxton, it was a month of remembered horror. He had tried to push the memory away, during the first years following the rebellion and the nightmare at No. 1, Hawthorne Walk. He had failed, and he no longer tried. It was just, that the Lady Agnes's screams should haunt his dreams. June was Martin Saxton's personal month of atonement. And the dreams began in May, every year, as regular as a harvest. They began every May when he sat down and filled a purse with coins, thirty pieces of silver as befits a man who had betrayed a trust. Those coins went to France with a servant he trusted. It was good, he thought, that the manservant, who had risked life and limb in Saxton's own employ, was trustworthy. Trust was a needful thing.

He wrote slowly, his hands crippled and deformed with the arthritis that had got into his bones. It would kill him soon, that and whatever had taken hold of his lungs. He didn't mind, not really; death was not something he feared. The blessed Jesus only knew, he had surely seen enough of it.

"To the Lady Eleanor Lésurier," he wrote. The pen scratched the words out. "The sum of thirty pieces of silver, in sorrow and regret, that it may ease the weight of grief."

Martin Saxton laid the pen down, and blew gently, hastening the drying process. His tired mind, detached from the everyday, moved down odd alleyways in his memory. He thought about the day William Caulfield, young Richard's pet manservant, had been found winding bandages around her breasts, disguising herself. He thought of the story coming out, of Richard's white rage at Eleanor's mother, of the imperious summons to his uncle Gaunt. The arrest of the three men, the screams of their torture, the confessions, the naming of Eleanor's mother as the driving force. Agnes's arrest, the quick trial, the rambling confession in French. The verdict: a quick, quiet beheading. She had been consigned to Saxton's care, to be lodged at his house.

And then the day of execution, in June. She had been shackled, leg irons in place, as the law commanded. His servant, that same servant who now carried a bag of silver every year to a woman in Bernay, had gone to fetch the cart that would take them to Smithfield.

He had never come back with the cart, not because he had betrayed his trust, but because London was ablaze. The key to those leg irons was in the servant's pocket. And the house at Hawthorne

Walk had burned like a pyre, as the woman inside screamed and the swarms of men, inflamed by a heady mix of past injustices, present bloodlust, and the rhetoric of the preachers John Ball and Jack Straw, shouted and moved to the next house, flaming pitch-soaked rags at the ready, setting thatch afire, repeating again and again the chant that had rung through the streets of the Surrey Bank for days past: When Adam delved and Eva span, Who was then the gentleman?

He could have dragged her free of the building. The fact haunted Martin Saxton as nothing in his life had ever done. Yes, the leg irons were heavy, and it was true, he could not have freed her—the key was not to his hand. But he had run away, in terror of the fire and the shouting angry peasants and the chant of rage and freedom, and he had left his prisoner, his charge, there to die.

Neither Richard nor Gaunt had asked him any questions. Agnes was dead, that was all that mattered; if the young King of France should happen to ask Richard for news of his relative, Richard could say with all truth that Agnes had died in the revolt. Nothing else mattered to the king.

It mattered to Saxton, a man with a conscience, a man who had taken his trust seriously. If a part of him was a coward who had let that trust down, he would and did try to make amends.

So, every May, the servant had crossed the Channel to the Haute-Normandie, to deliver thirty silver coins and a note of re-pentance to Agnes's daughter. What she did with it was her affair. This was likely to be the last year. His time was coming to an end, and Saxton knew it.

He sealed the letter within the bag, and handed it to the servant. The servant, who had done this for many summers past, bowed, and left.

*Another year gone,* Saxton thought, and got up to stretch painfully. One more year, in so many, to make eternity.